John,
Best wishes,
Enjoy Enough!
Tony

Enough

C. D. "Tony" Hylton, III

Publisher Page
an imprint of Headline Books
Terra Alta, WV

Enough

by C. D. "Tony" Hylton, III

copyright ©2020 C. D. "Tony" Hylton. III

To order additional copies of this book or for book publishing information, or to contact the author:

Headline Books, Inc.
P.O. Box 52
Terra Alta, WV 26764
www.HeadlineBooks.com

Tel: 304-789-3001
Email: mybook@headlinebooks.com

Publisher Page is an imprint of Headline Books

ISBN 13: 9781946664891

Library of Congress Control Number: 2019949907

PRINTED IN THE UNITED STATES OF AMERICA

Dedication

To the memories of

Harriet Lee and Charlie Hylton

Professor Paul Atkins

Charles Martin Whited

Characters

Al Dill – Rick's right man at the *Crier*

Annabelle Lawrence – Principal of school

Aubrey Wyatt – Lawnsville Police Chief

Basil Hammer – Patriarch of one the county's largest families.

Baxter Edwards, Jr. -Leader of Jordan County's reform political faction

Benjamin "Ben" Howland – Closest ally of Mayor on city council

Bill Joe Hamrick – Old-line member of the county commission

Charles W. Beauregard, Jr. – Party leader of one of the old-line factions

Edward "Big Ed" Marcum, Sr. - Patriarch of one the county's largest families

Edward "Little Ed" Marcum, Jr. – Oldest son of Ed, Sr.

Edward Whitmore –Board President

Elmer Abernathy – Chairman of the Jordan County Republican Executive Committee.

Eva Newland – respected retired school principal

Jim Dowling – Lawnsville's first black police officer

Joe Ed Green– Reform candidate opposing Bill Joe Hamrick.

Joseph "Red" Bell, Jr. one of two leaders of the corrupt political faction

Joseph Ballengee – former publisher/owner of the *Crier*

Lester Brown – Lawnsville town drunk

Marvin Wood – Chairman of hospital board of trustees.

Oliver Browne is insurance agent

Rick Hill – publisher of the *Lawnsville Crier*

Sam Brownly is President of Jordan County Council of PTA Presidents.

Sam Greenside – President of Jordan County Commission

Sammy Monroe – Candidate for Governor backed by Red and Charles.

Samuel Johnson – Lawnsville street commissioner a

Sheriff Eddy Bill Graves – recognized old-line office holder

Wayne Adkins – Mayor of Lawnsville

Will LeMasters – County hospital administrator

Chapter 1
The Dream Up in Smoke

Lawnsville Crier publisher Rick Hill was exhausted when his head hit the pillow about 11:00 last night after covering the 'anything but boring' county hospital board meeting. His presence at the meeting was part of a major change he was bringing to the *Crier*'s coverage of Jordan County government bodies.

This new policy was different than anything seen in the county for decades and very disturbing to many. The *Crier*'s former publisher used the paper to protect his friends in the corrupt old-line political machine from any public scrutiny.

"I'll be damned if I'm going to run the *Crier* like Joseph Ballengee - the people deserve better," he said to his wife, Anne, who scoffed at the idea the people of Jordan County would accept the new *Crier*.

Rick believed holding public officials accountable was the principle that brought freedom of the press to the U.S. Constitution's First Amendment. That's the way he intended to run the *Lawnsville Crier*. His decision would bring him face-to-face with an armed gang ready to stop the *Crier* at all costs.

When he left the *Crier* office after finishing the hospital board story, Rick left all the lights on so his guardian angel could check things during the night. He thought the warning after his story on the City Council was a bit far-fetched, but he accepted the offer of protection after his wife's tirade about the "scum that don't want the truth."

It was 2:30 a.m. when the phone's ring jerked the young publisher from his sleep. Thinking about other late-night calls he'd received since taking over the *Crier*, Rick was certain it was from someone who'd caught 'the biggest catfish ever,' or trying to win a bar bet on the score of a Wildcat football game ten years ago. Rick rolled over and, smiling, picked up the phone.

"Rick, come down. There's a fire at the paper, hurry," Steve Perkins, the city's fire chief said quickly over sirens in the background, hanging up before Rick could respond.

"There's a fire at the paper. Steve said I should come right down," a stunned Rick whispered to his wife, who was now sitting straight up in bed.

"Bastards," she snarled. "Bastards," Anne sputtered reflecting her disdain for those in Jordan County who bitterly criticized Rick for bringing them the truth.

"I'll wake Charlie and Harriet," she mumbled.

"Let 'em sleep a while longer. This is going to be a long day," Rick replied, still dazed.

Pulling out of the driveway, Rick saw the glow in the sky, the lump in his throat grew as he sped along the narrow streets toward Lawnsville's small downtown. Careening around the last curve, he could see the flames shooting above the houses surrounding the old building that held his dream of running a newspaper based on the solid principles of journalism centered on holding public officials accountable.

As he got closer to the flames, lights came on in houses facing the Civil War-era courthouse and people in robes over their clothes were walking toward the burning 70+-year-old building.

When he got out of the car, the *Crier*'s front window cracked and crashed to the sidewalk.

Fire trucks and volunteers from departments from out in the county arrived to help the small group of Lawnsville volunteers, fight what was clearly a futile battle. Flames raged in all parts of the building, from the front office and composing room to the rear wall and up from the basement.

Etched on native limestone embedded within the façade of the weathered red bricks were the words *Lawnsville Crier*, now blackened by smoke rolling up through the hole that moments before was the *Crier*'s front window.

This squat one-story building was built like a fort—solid brick, steel beams under a reinforced-concrete floor—to hold the weight of the heavy hot-metal equipment used to create the *Crier* every weekday.

In front of the first floor was the bullpen of an office into which the managing editor, community news editor, sports editor, classified-ads person, ad manager and bookkeeper were shoe-horned.

The publisher's office was walled off, with an old couch, a desk with a typewriter perched on top and a bookcase, lit by a large single light bulb hanging from the ceiling.

In the rear, taking up more than half of the first floor, was the composing room crammed with the linotypes, headline machine, and layout turtles so the heavy pages could be wheeled about as that day's edition, moved each day, toward the seventy-five-year-old, but dependable press in the basement. Off to the side was a restroom (the nice one, for female staff). The men had to go down to the one squeezed into the corner of the dark and dank basement. In that dungeon-like space, the press reigned supreme, surrounded by heavy rolls of newsprint.

And most surprising: it all worked. The old press cranked to life every weekday about noon for its forty-five-minute run creating a product that sent the good people of Jordan County to discussing, cussing, yelling and, at times, particularly near an election, fighting.

The firemen didn't even try to get at the fire in the basement. The heat was intense as the flames attacked huge rolls of newsprint sending smoke and ash roaring up the stairway.

As the fire crackled, Rick, almost in a trance, slowly walked down the alley next to the building, carefully stepping over the hoses manned by the city's fire department's volunteer members, aiming water at the flames devouring his dream. *Knew I should have had an electrician check the wiring,* he thought.

An invisible force pulled him down the alley lit up by the fire. The smell of gasoline was everywhere. He stopped cold. The back door was in splinters, barely hanging from its hinges.

Then he noticed a sledgehammer at the alley's edge and he snapped a picture of it, having a feeling it might be needed as evidence.

Then an explosion rocked the building. He could hear parts of the old press careening off the basement's thick concrete walls.

In a few weeks, the young publisher would learn from the state fire marshal's report the huge roll of newsprint on the press had been soaked with gasoline and a small stick of dynamite placed under the press. Another placed under the plate-maker failed to explode – and was another key piece of evidence.

Rick's reporter's instinct took over as he continued down the alley. The fire, set early in the morning, was burning throughout the building, indicating probably more than one arsonist. The eight-foot-tall windows facing the alley were shattered about midway up. His best guess was they spread gasoline throughout the building and tossed bottles of gasoline through the windows to get the fire going simultaneously upstairs and down.

While the flames made it easy to see the alley, the flickering light did not penetrate the darkness far enough to illuminate underneath the back porch of the old Brown family home just across from the *Crier*'s backdoor. As Rick's searching eyes slowly swept the alley, he couldn't see the makeshift nest—a filthy, worn blanket and pillow made from a torn shopping bag stuffed with leaves—where Lester Brown, recognized as Lawnsville's town drunk, was jarred from his stupor by steel smashing the wood door barely thirty feet away.

There were other drunks in the small town, but Lester Brown was out front about it, on the street, rather than hidden behind the doors of some of Lawnsville's stately old homes where many of the pillars of local churches deceptively sent their yard men to the state liquor store.

Continuing down the alley, the heartbroken publisher wondered what had gone wrong with his late-night protection.

Where was he? Something had gone very wrong, Rick thought, remembering the warning. When he'd left the paper late last night, Rick, as instructed, left all the lights on so the guardian angel could check the paper on his multiple after dark rounds.

Rick was continuing to walk farther down the alley when the city fire chief called out from his weather-beaten 1950 Ford pickup. "What's wrong, Steve?" Rick asked, seeing the chief was trembling.

"Deputy Sheriff Tom Meadows just called. He found Jim Dowling's city patrol car out on River Road with Jim in the back seat. He's been shot in the head. They don't think he'll make it."

Indeed, something is very wrong, Rick thought as he sagged against the old pickup.

After absorbing Steve's disturbing news, Rick was again drawn down the alley. *I'm missing something.* Walking slowly past the *Crier*'s back door, a reflection of the flames flashed in a pothole. He bent down picked up the shiny city police badge hanging from a piece of ripped cloth, clear evidence tying the fire to Jim Dowling's shooting. Rick carefully put the discovery into his pocket.

Emerging from the alley still in a reporters' mode, Rick looked for two faces in the growing crowd, Joseph "Red" Bell, Jr, one of the two old-line political powers, who lived just two blocks away, and Lester Brown, Lawnsville's after-dark mayor who was always in the late-night shadows and would never miss a chance to be on the front row for something like this. Neither face was there.

As Rick walked toward the crowd, he was greeted by grim faces. His pastor, Preacher Erwin Edward Hathaway stepped out of the crowd and asked Rick to join him in a short, private prayer asking the Good Lord's blessing during this time of trial for the publisher. After the "amen," Rick noticed Al Dill, his right hand at the *Crier*, and several other members of his staff huddled together across the street. He walked over and hugged each one through the tears.

"What happened?" Al asked in a tone reeking of suspicion.

"Not sure," the publisher replied carefully not to divulge what he'd just discovered in the alley.

"They set it," came the distinct, gravelly no-nonsense voice of Belinda "Billy" Amherst, the *Crier*'s community news editor with a hard edge of certainty that invited no challenge. Other staff members were stunned as they watched the flames consume an important source of income for their cash-strapped families.

As he watched his dedicated staff, Rick recalled his mother's story about his first experience with newspapering. On her first venture out of the small apartment after giving birth to her only child, his mother took her infant son to the *Logan Banner* where Rick Sr. was sports editor. While Rick Sr. was showing off his pride and joy, Franklin Benjamin, the *Banner's* grizzled back-shop foreman, brought out a piece of newsprint and a small can of ink and a roller. The smiling father held the squirming infant as Franklin rolled the ink on little Rick's foot and made a foot-print on the newsprint. Ink was in Rick's blood from that day forth.

The trip down memory lane was interrupted by the crash of the *Crier's* roof. *Is this nightmare the end of my dream?*

Chapter 2
Peeling the Onion

When Rick first drove with wife, Anne, and two kids—Harriet, 6, and Charlie, 4—into Lawnsville, it reminded him of a picturesque town from a bygone era. It was nestled along an ancient river—said to be the second oldest in the world—winding gently through the majestic green hills, where life seemed to flow, rather than driven.

Rick loved the mountains—their lushness in spring and summer, the blaze of autumn colors and even the strange beauty in the barrenness of winter that was spectacular when heavy snow clung to sagging limbs.

As long as Rick could remember, he and his dad had talked about owning a small-town newspaper. No small daily they could afford came on the market in the state. Over time the thought had faded. Rick had a public relations position with a steel company in the northern part of the state in a family-friendly community.

Rick Sr. had worked at the paper in Rick's hometown for nearly thirty years, but there was no chance the family in control would sell it. Then Rick Sr. learned the *Lawnsville Crier* was for sale. The two couples get together to discuss the possibilities. Despite some initial misgivings, Anne supported the decision knowing how much it met to Rick.

To make the buy, Rick Sr. and his wife, Esther, placed a mortgage on their paid-off small comfortable home. Rick Jr. and Anne sold the stock he had received from his former employer and used most of their meager savings to make the down payment. Their only reserve was a small inheritance from Rick's grandmother.

Two weeks after their signatures made the deal final, Rick Sr. died of a massive heart attack. After the initial shock, Rick Jr. knew he had but one choice—to move forward and quickly.

Then the second shock hit. Rick Jr. realized his dad's life-long desire to own a paper with his son had prevented a prudent, businesslike evaluation of the *Crier*'s financial records. Rick Sr. had taken as gospel the former publisher's assurances of a viable money-making enterprise. He never asked the key question, "If the figures are true, why is Joseph Ballengee willing to sell it?"

One look at the advertising billing records showed Rick the disturbing reality behind why the *Crier* was full of advertising. The rates billed to advertisers were far below those on the rate card Rick Sr. had been shown.

That wasn't the only serious problem being faced by the new publisher. The paper was a political mouthpiece. A major cog in the rural county's corrupt political structure was former publisher, Joseph Ballengee. For decades, he had used the *Crier* to support and protect the old-line political faction. Joseph had benefited from that alliance, being appointed to a coveted board seat at a local bank.

After the initial talks with Rick Sr., Joseph Ballengee felt he would be able to reap the financial benefits of selling the paper while being able to make sure the old-line would be favorably portrayed in the news columns. Addressing his cronies' concerns, Ballengee explained he'd been asked to continue a daily column that had been a *Crier* staple for the past thirty years.

When he gave his assurances, Joseph wasn't aware the new owners had agreed that Rick Jr. would be in charge of the *Crier*'s day-to-day operations. That was key in Rick's decision to make the move. Another rude awaking awaited Joseph. The new young publisher wasn't interested in being on the bank board or using the paper for anything but serving its readers.

At the top of Jordan County's political power structure were Joseph "Red" Bell, Jr. and Charles W. Beauregard, Jr. Control was maintained through multi-layers of influence. They exercised political power through the Board of Education, county govern-ment (including the county hospital) and to a lesser extent

Lawnsville city government. Another layer was local business owners who benefitted from business and favors from these various local governments. Rounding out the unholy alliance were the local officeholders who owed their offices to the two. Using county jobs as patronage, Red and Charles controlled thousands of votes when the employees and their families went to the polls on Election Day.

An essential cog in this corrupt alliance was Joseph Ballengee, publisher of the *Lawnsville Crier,* that served all of Jordan County and bordering areas of four adjacent counties. Ballengee made sure almost nothing critical of the old-line made it into the *Crier*. And he used his popular daily column to extol the virtues of old-line officeholders. Businesses close to the old-line supported the *Crier* with advertising. Then there was a local bank that made sure the businesses supporting the old-line got preferential treatment when they needed a loan and was rewarded with getting county money in non-interest-bearing accounts.

Before the fact, Rick had thought running a small-town newspaper would be an adventure and provide an outlet for his strong independent streak. He signed on. *Signed on? Hell, he'd jumped in with both feet.*

Little did he imagine this leap of faith literally would put his life on the line on one of his favorite country roads in the county. The former publisher not only mislead *Crier* readers on the nature of the old-line political faction, he misled Rick about the nature of politics in Jordan County. Based on his conversations with Joseph Ballengee, Rick was under the impression there was only one political faction in the county.

His right-hand man, Al Dill, informed him about the other faction that bitterly fought the old-line every Election Day. Presently, the reformer group's supporters held seats on the board of education and county commission. Baxter Edwards was the recognized leader. Baxter's late father was a railroader and once part of the old-line. A split occurred because Baxter's father wouldn't go along with a scheme to steer the construction contract for a new Lawnsville water plant to a company operated by a close friend of a prominent Lawnsville attorney close to the old-line faction.

It was a no-holds-barred fight. Baxter and his mother felt the stress brought on by the old-line faction attempting to get Baxter, Sr. fired from his railroad job brought on the fatal heart attack.

Baxter was a fighter for what he felt was right. He had a keen insight into how folks felt, and why. The big difference between Baxter and the old line was that he did not want power for himself. Baxter felt government should serve the people, not line the pockets of individual political bosses.

When Rick had asked Joseph Ballengee about the Baxter-led fraction, he was warned, "Watch yourself when dealing with Baxter Edwards. That bunch can't be trusted and will say anything to win an election."

Rick was finding out that learning about Jordan County was like peeling an onion, every layer revealed more surprises.

To Rick, small-town newspapers were meant to be like Colonial pamphleteers whose in-your-face style of journalism had brought about the founding of the Nation. Due to the danger faced when criticizing the British, it was essential those rebelling firebrands hide behind colorful pseudonyms. This was a shield the new *Crier* publisher didn't have and never thought he would need.

The young publisher understood an important principle behind the First Amendment was the right to criticize government actions and keep *We the People* informed about what their elected officials were up to. Rick had been taught by Paul Adkins at West Virginia University's P.I. Reed School of Journalism the press looking over the shoulder of government was a sacred responsibility and a cornerstone of the Nation's democracy.

This is what he thought he had explained in the front-page editorial on his first day as publisher. "We will build on that strong foundation established by the previous owners," the then naive young publisher wrote.

Although the two political factions bitterly disagreed about nearly every issue, they came to the same conclusion about that one passage, the *Crier* would still be under the influence of publisher Joseph Ballengee.

Both political camps had a different take on yet another key phase in the editorial, "We might own the newspaper, but it belongs to the community."

Those aligned with the old line knowingly smiled with self-assured satisfaction. But the reformers wondered if Joseph Ballengee would continue to actually run the *Crier*. Baxter saw a ray of hope in that second sentence, not a bright ray but at least a dim one.

While the words of the editorial disturbed many of the reformers, what they saw was even more troubling. All three of the former owners and one of their sons remained ensconced on the *Crier*'s small staff.

Joseph Ballengee would continue to write a daily column. Sam Ballengee Sr., the advertising manager, brother of the former publisher, remained in his position. Sam Ballengee Jr., the son of the ad manager and the nephew of the former publisher, was still managing editor.

And Al Dill, a jack-of-all-trades, who had come from the state's largest paper remained.

"We just have to wait, watch, and see," Baxter Edwards uneasily told his band of reformers, almost certain there would be no meaningful change.

While Rick's initial decision to leave staff members in place was made to give them a fair chance to prove themselves, he would soon find that key staff members would leave him cold at a critical time.

As Rick scrambled to straighten out the mess, matters got worse. Rick had been on the job just two weeks when the IRS notice arrived. Agents were coming to examine the *Crier*'s books for the last three years. He nearly fainted and the roar of "shit!" echoed through the office as he reread the notice. In near panic, Rick mentioned the pending IRS audit to the former publisher and was greeted with a crafty smile and smug reminder the new owners had bought not only the assets but also assumed all liabilities. In other words, if there was a corporate tax mistake on the Ballengee's watch, it was the new owners' responsibility to pay up if required.

Great, Rick thought, *in business just a few weeks and already an IRS tax audit. Another layer of the onion.*

Rick was as nervous—the expression went in the mountains—as a woman of ill repute in the house of the Lord. The two IRS agents—Thomas Guthrie and William Pennyworth—showed up right on time to the minute and ceremoniously flashed their badges. Rick handed over records for the years in question and showed them to a small table in the corner of the cramped front office. Rick quickly retreated into his office. At the end of the first day, Guthrie, the lead agent, frowned and shook his head, "We'll be back in the morning, be finished by noon and expect you here to receive the preliminary findings."

At the office an hour before his normal 7:30 arrival, Rick wanted to complete his story on the previous night's contentious board of education meeting, then be available for any agent questions. He was a basket case waiting for the federal agents' findings. As the press rumbled to life in the basement, Agent Pennyworth knocked on the door, "We're finished. We need to meet with you privately."

The agents seemed to relish their power by drawing things out with phrases and words of 'officialese' that conveyed ominous connotations. Shifting in his chair, Rick felt sweat forming under his shirt. His mouth open, he was not sure he heard the agent correctly. "What'd you say?" he stammered.

"The government owes you about $1,200," Thomas announced, a stern frown still in place. Rick was sure he didn't hear correctly. Recovering quickly, he chuckled and asked, "Would you like to check a few more years?" Finally, the peel of a sweet onion.

Guthrie failed to find any humor in Rick's inquiry. Without cracking a smile, he responded with a curt, "No, thank you," and swiftly departed after explaining the check would be along in a couple of months.

Joseph, coming in earlier than usual with his column, sheepishly asked how IRS visit went. Using the tactics of the just-departed federal agents, Rick milked it for all it was worth, shaking his head gravely and motioning the Joseph to his private office.

"They took so damned long, these IRS agents went over every-thing twice, very carefully. They even asked for your home address." That put the former publisher on the edge of his chair. Rick continued, enjoying the worried look on Joseph Ballengee's face, "You know, Joseph, we did buy the assets and liabilities, but you signed the tax returns." His serious face still in place, Rick laughing on the inside watching a frown cover the former publisher's face.

"But as I told you yesterday, you all bought all the liabilities," Joseph said meekly.

Rick couldn't hold it in any longer. "Hell, Joseph, they said we'd get a refund." Joseph, dead serious, responded, "The *Crier* was ours when those taxes were paid," suggesting he should get the refund. "Joseph, you're such a kidder. Thanks for bringing the column in early."

Rick shook his head as he sat down in his chair, thinking, *who would have thought an IRS audit would turn out to the single bright spot in a dismal financial situation?*

One aspect of the news side had gotten Rick's attention, the former publisher's column. He told Joseph in no uncertain terms the *Crier* was not going to endorse candidates. "I don't want anything in your column that might appear to be an endorsement." Taken aback by the bluntness, Joseph readily agreed, not wanting to lose the column he had written for three decades.

Now, the top priority was addressing the *Crier*'s advertising debacle. No matter how good the news coverage was, if the bottom line wasn't positive, nothing else mattered. Rick knew he had to take action after a conversation with the owner of the local men's clothing store revealed Sam Ballengee's advertising sales pitch was, "You don't want to buy any ads, do you?" Rick asked Joseph for suggestions about getting, his brother, the ad manager, motivated.

The response "He's just set in his ways." In an effort to solve the problem, that afternoon Rick had a "prayer meeting" with the *Crier*'s advertising manager. It didn't go well. "They just don't want to advertise," was still ringing in Rick's ears. The next day—a Tuesday—the ad manager walked into Rick's office without knocking and said he was leaving his job on Friday, three days away.

Rick knew immediately the news side of the operation had to wait a little longer for his full attention as he had to make ad calls himself until he found, hired, and trained a new manager.

The following day, as Rick was in the middle of piecing together a plan to handle the advertising side, problems came to a head in news.

With a knock on Rick's door, Sam Jr., *Crier* managing editor, walked into his cubbyhole of an office with a smirk on his face. He said he was leaving at the end of the week. In fewer than twenty-four hours, the *Crier* publisher lost his ad manager and his managing editor.

His twelve-hour workday just got longer. Rick thought, *hell, some of these onion layers are not only bitter but are guaranteed to bring tears.* There was only one option, he'd handle the news side in the morning and once the paper was out, make ad calls in the afternoon.

"You staying?" Rick groused as he related his dilemma to Al.

"Oh, shit," was followed quickly with "dammit to hell."

Regaining his composure, Al said he knew a young kid working at the local grocery store who might be able to handle the ad job. "Get his ass in here as soon as you can," Rick said, louder than he meant.

"It gets this way sometimes," Al said as he went for the phone.

Another layer of sweet onion was about to come Rick's way. The following morning, in a hastily scheduled interview, he found the young man to be enthusiastic and seemingly a fast learner. Larry Loom would start in no later than two weeks.

Rick checked one problem off of the growing list. There was another frustration for the *Crier* staff, late press runs that Rick saw as a valuable learning experience.

When the *Crier* didn't arrive on time to its subscribers, the phones would ring off the hook. People from all over the county were damned mad and not bashful about saying so. The beleaguered staff trying to answer phones while writing stories for the next day could never understand why Rick was so cheerful when calls jammed the phones. It was simple. Rick was beginning to realize the calls indicated the *Crier* was important to people all over the county, even with what he felt was puny local news coverage.

He remembered his father's saying about small-town newspapers, "In a small town, everybody knows what everybody else is doing. They read the paper to see who got caught."

Chapter 3
Black Ink Can Cover Up or Enlighten

The *Lawnsville Crier* didn't reach every house in the county, so there was room for growth in circulation. Rick felt his idea for a new approach to local news coverage could attract more readers. The price of five cents a day for the *Crier* was certainly reasonable. He sold the paper to route drivers and carriers for three cents, leaving them with a profit of two cents a day per each subscriber.

Folks will want to know who got caught, Rick thought. He was sure with incentives – like a free tank of gas for every ten new subscribers - his dedicated band of route drivers would fan out across the county to sign up more subscribers. In fact, when the price of gas recently went up to 22 cents a gallon, they were complaining about how the high gas price hurt their profit.

In town, the *Crier*'s young door-to-door carriers were all eager-beaver junior high students. They'd enjoy a little more spending money earned by signing new *Crier* subscribers. They too had complaints – the price of movie tickets had gone up to fifty cents recently and a chocolate bar at the concession stand was five cents. By promising a prize of one movie ticket for every ten new customers, Rick was sure the youth carriers would be knocking on every door in Lawnsville.

The publisher knew the key to attracting new *Crier* subscribers was to improve local news coverage - give people a reason to sign-up.

And now that the shiny, new ad manager was aboard, Rick turned to that task, strengthening the news coverage. First, Rick wanted to see if his suspicions were correct about the *Crier's* coverage of local government under Joseph Ballengee. Working a couple of late evenings, he dug through the dusty bound files of back issues stored in a musty cabinet in a dark corner of the basement. He dragged them up to his cramped office and reviewed the six months of back issues right before he took over.

"What am I missing here?" the young publisher pondered. Carefully turning the pages of the back issues, Rick discovered the interlocking relationships between the old-line political faction, some leading Lawnsville businesses and Jordan County governmental bodies.

"This just doesn't stop." Next, he turned to analyzing the news coverage of the various governing bodies.

The board of education was the county's largest employer and had schools in every area of the county, but its meetings were rarely covered. Rick found that when a board of education meeting was covered—and that was rare—it was done by the former publisher. Those stories raised more questions than they answered. "So Ballengee didn't want to step on anyone's toes. Some of the *Crier's* advertisers were on the school board."

Continuing to peel the onion, Rick observed the county commission rarely got any coverage, and when it did, some big project or federal or state grant was being announced. As with the school board, there was a leading Lawnsville business owner on the county commission.

Rick's interest in coverage of the county's hospital board meetings was not as a high a priority as the others. "How could a hospital's operation be involved in politics?" Rick naively asked himself. That onion would be bitter.

In another layer of the onion, he would soon learn even death in the little town was a political event since both funeral homes were associated with one or another political persuasion.

Turning back to the living, his next research project uncovered another layer of deception.

Rick spent several hours at the Jordan County courthouse examining the county's financial records including bank statements. The figures leaped off the statement and slapped him full in the face. Hundreds of thousands of dollars of hospital cash flow was a cash cow for the bank since the money was in non-interest-bearing accounts. The largest account kept a standing balance of nearly $100,000 and three others had standing balances of $25,000 to $50,000. The bank could invest money in hospital accounts and keep as its own, the interest earned each year on hospital funds.

After his laborious research, questions cascaded through his brain. An exception to the overall lack of coverage was the city council. It got more attention than any other local governmental body. But that was at best every other meeting. *Why was city council covered at all?* It was the city and a concentration of *Crier* readers were tightly grouped within it. And, the former publisher made no secret of the fact he didn't like the mayor. Rick would discover this was one of the few things on which they agreed.

After his careful examination of the *Crier*'s coverage—Rick decided it was time for major changes. "This shit's going to stop," he said to himself.

Later, other members of the staff once trained, would cover these meetings, but initially, Rick would cover them all at first to get a feel for how the bodies did the public's business.

Rick realized finding people to cover the meetings properly would not be an easy task. Covering the news can be a challenge anywhere, but in a small town, it can be particularly difficult. There is not an abundance of people who understand or who can be taught to understand the intricacies of news gathering—listening carefully, asking the right questions, and developing a bullshit alarm knowing when someone is shoveling crap rather than giving straight answers.

And it's essential reporters understand the importance of accuracy. There will be mistakes, but reporters must be dedicated to getting the facts straight, and ensure both sides of an issue get a fair shot at having their points included.

There was another important aspect of this job, particularly in a small town. Reporters must be ready for the criticism that comes with the job. A reporter can get an earful at the grocery store or church for a story written.

Rick's uncompromising requirements made finding folks a real challenge. He needed only two solid reporters to help him.

At city council and board of education meetings, he had noticed an older lady in attendance taking notes. Rick introduced himself. She was a stringer for the larger daily in the neighboring county. Her stories were decent and her paper was playing up her stories in an attempt to make advertising inroads into the *Crier*'s market. He offered her a job as reporter/community news editor. She started the following week. Next, he found a young local sports enthusiast and hired him on as sports editor.

The final hire was for the managing editor's slot. Al came through again. The son of a friend just returned from a cross-country trip of self-discovery. He had two years of journalism school. Rick was under the gun, so he hired the young traveler who at the time was living with bluegrass-playing friends on a farm out in the county. As with the ad manager's hiring, Rick would find these hires also to be excellent – another sweet onion.

With staffing in place, the new approach to the *Crier*'s local news coverage was launched.

A front-page announcement heralded the first major change in the paper's coverage of local government. All candidates for mayor, city council, major county offices, and the state legislature would get a free 200-word front-page story with photo. The former publisher had previously provided such access almost exclusively to old-line candidates.

The reform bunch found this interesting, but remained firmly in a wait-and-see mode.

To the discomfort of local officeholders, Rick announced these changes under the headline, "Letting the sunshine in."

There would be no announcement of the expanded coverage of local government bodies. Rick would just show up. He wasn't sure about how *Crier* readers would react. *Could it change how folks view their local governments, or would they see it as butting in?*

Despite the uncertainty about the outcome, Rick Hill was certain it was the right thing to do.

He was not prepared for their one-word reaction that would come on the coming Election Day.

Chapter 4
Can't Hide from the Sunshine

The first meeting covered under the *Crier*'s expanded coverage was the city council. Lawnsville's city government wasn't totally unknown to Rick. When he first arrived in town, he made a point to make an appointment to introduce himself to Mayor Wayne Adkins. Nearly all of the meeting was taken up by the mayor talking about how much he'd done for the city and his plans for the future. When Rick mentioned he hoped to begin to cover council meetings. The mayor only said, "If you need anything, just let me know."

Wayne Adkins was a lifelong Lawnsville resident, a star high school football player, had an easy way with people and worked for the railroad. But as Rick would find out below that calm façade was a hair-trigger temper.

The *Crier* publisher expected the City Council meetings would be routine and low-key. Like most of his other expectations, a big surprise would come with the next layer of the onion.

Preparing for the meeting, Rick was curious about an item – "discussion of the position of police chief" – added to the council's agenda just that morning.

About a month ago, there were rumors about the mayor and chief having disagreements about law enforcement. Specifically, talk said the two differences were about enforcement of closing times for beer joints on the edge of Lawnsville and traffic tickets given to several of the mayor's close friends. Both those rumors had quickly died down. Aubrey Wyatt had been a police chief in a small town in an adjacent county before he was appointed Lawnsville's chief about a year ago.

As he walked around the corner and faced City Hall, Rick saw this wasn't going to be a routine meeting. People were milling around. Signs indicated two groups - one supporting the police chief and the other for throwing him out of office.

The council hearing on the City Police Civil Service Commission's report was the first item on an otherwise routine agenda. There was no doubt the chamber would be full.

As Rick entered the council chamber, Elizabeth Fisher, the city clerk, motioned for him to sit on the front row. The police chief, dressed in civilian clothes, was there and everyone knew he always carried a gun. One member of the commission, Henry Sullivan, was a railroad detective who was never unarmed. When the chairman of the commission, Tom Browning, opened his briefcase on the front bench, Rick saw he had a gun among his papers. Albert Farmer, the third member of the commission, didn't have a clue. He didn't have a gun and wouldn't have known which end to point if he had.

Rick took a deep breath, three guns, a standing-room-only crowd of hotheads and only one way in and out of the packed council chamber. *What could possibly go wrong?* he thought as he envisioned being caught in a cross-fire.

It took several bangs of the gavel for the mayor to quiet the rambunctious crowd. The room became pin-drop quiet as the mayor announced, "The first item on the agenda is a report by the city police civil service commission, Chairman Browning."

Seated beside Rick, the chairman rose, went the council table and carefully placed his briefcase within arm's length. He unlatched it but didn't open it.

"Your honor, the commission has been meeting on an important matter over the last two weeks and is ready to report," he said.

"Mr. Chairman, I have something to say," the police chief said, rising without being formally recognized. The tension in the room shot up.

"Yes, Chief Wyatt," the chairman said calmly, his hand moving to the now open briefcase. "I think this damned commission is a joke, nothing but a political move to get rid of me, and it's all illegal," the red-faced Wyatt nearly shouted. Mummers went through the crowd. One side let loose with a barrage of boos while the others cheered. Sensing potential eruption, the chairman glanced at the mayor, who made a barely perceptive nod.

"Well, Chief sounds like there something else we need to hear, so I'll ask the council's permission to delay our report. How about we meet with you tomorrow afternoon at 2:00?" Tom Browning offered, keeping his hand on the briefcase.

"That's fine," the chief said triumphantly.

"Hearing adjourned," the commission chairman said, visibly relieved.

The council quickly dispensed with its normal business items—what streets to pave, complaints about garbage collection, approved the Little League baseball opening-day parade route and problems in the water billing office—with little discussion.

Next was the approval to pay Lawnville's monthly bills. Mayor Adkins asked if anyone in the audience wanted a copy of the list of bills and several people held up their hands.

The publisher got the first copy. He noticed his was folded back to a particular page, unlike the others and Elizabeth Fisher had her finger by one of the line items. The item was a bill for $1,200 from the private construction business owned by City Street Commissioner Samuel Johnson's brother, Jonathon. The charge was labeled 'dump-truck rental.'

Rick and Anne met Elizabeth Fisher at a long time Lawnsville tradition – her family's making apple butter the old fashion-way – cooking in a huge cast-iron kettle over a roaring fire as a horse circled pulling a pole which moved a stirrer through the delightful smelling mixture.

Rick and Elizabeth had a pleasant conversation about her family apple butter tradition that went back nearly 100 years. He had taken a picture for the *Crier* and made sure she got a copy.

The item on the list of city bills got Rick's full attention. About two weeks ago, the *Crier* had a page one picture of the city's shiny new dump truck in front of City Hall. Now it appeared the city was renting another dump truck.

In a hurry to end the meeting because of the mumbling crowd, Wayne Adkins pressed for a motion to approve the bills. It was amazing to Rick that council members, without looking at the list of bills, in robotic fashion obediently moved, seconded and unanimously approved payment of the bills in less than ten seconds.

Approaching the mayor after the meeting adjourned, Rick said quietly, "Good job on the hearing." The unexpected compliment brought a look of amazement.

Rick quickly followed up with, "What's this about the $1,200 for the dump truck rental?" He asked as if this question was an after-thought. If looks could kill, Rick would have been on his way to Memorial Gardens.

"Oh, it was just that the city's truck transmission went bad and Jonathon Johnson offered to rent the city one of his company's trucks. Summer's coming and we've got a lot of work going on and can't delay it, so we took him up on the offer," the mayor replied failing to mention Samuel's role in the agreement.

"Thanks," Rick said as if he considered the subject insignificant.

Samuel Johnson had come to the front of the council chamber and overheard the exchange. Unfortunately for him, he added, "The city truck might be broke for a couple of months since they're having trouble getting parts."

Before the mayor could hush the street commissioner, Rick asked, "Is that the new truck, Samuel?"

"Yes," he said.

The mayor grabbed him by the arm and said, "Let's go downstairs, Samuel."

Rick exchanged a knowing glance with the city clerk as he headed for the door. They both took great care not to let on they were acquainted. They both felt certain the mayor would probably fire her if he knew.

Suppressing the temptation to make the dump truck the lead in the council story, Rick put the complaints on garbage collection as his lead. Those appearing before council had been hopping mad about it and put the council members on notice the problem had to be fixed.

The story noted the Mayor had promised he would talk to the company the following day and get it straightened out. Postponement of the hearing on the complaints against the city police chief was next. It didn't mention weapons in the room or anything other than the commission had agreed to hear more from the chief and would report to council at a later meeting.

Finally came the item for $1,200 for the dump-truck rental. Quotes from both the mayor and the city street commissioner were included, along with the fact the city's brand new $10,000 dump truck, bought just last month, needed repairs and it might be several months before it could be fixed.

Almost as soon as the paper hit the streets, the mayor was on the phone, extremely upset about the dump-truck part of Rick's story. "What the hell are you trying to do to me," he shouted.

"Mayor, first of all, the headline and the first part of the story dealt with you all working to fixing the garbage collection problem. Secondly, I asked you about the dump truck last night and put in what you and Samuel said to explain it, and that seems fair," he explained.

"You're just trying to stir things up," Wayne Adkins grumbled in a softer tone, recognizing the importance of his being seen as taking action on the garbage situation.

"Didn't mean to upset you, Mayor," Rick said, smiling that the mayor didn't realize council wouldn't have to look into the garbage situation if the city had been providing good service in the first place.

On his walk to the post office the day after the story appeared, Rick was stopped three times by people having an opinion about the city council. Not one mentioned the police chief situation. But in the two-block walk, three people remarked on the dump-truck rental using words like "kickback," "crooks," and "stealing."

There was one mention of the garbage situation as another indication of the poor job being done by the city.

He retreated into his office and was going through the mail when the phone rang.

"They've got Jonathon's truck out to the city garage getting new brakes," the eighty-five-year-old lady's high-pitched voice told him. It was only two weeks after Rick had become the *Crier*'s publisher when this anonymous source first called. That first tip was on a minor matter, but Rick found it was right in every detail. Since then, there had been several more calls with the same results. *How the hell does she do it?* he thought, knowing she was bedridden and seldom left her home on in Lawnville's west end. "Thanks for the call," Rick said as he headed for the camera shelf hoping to get the photo in time for the press run in an hour.

"Save me space for a picture on top of page one," Rick shouted to Al as he hurried out the door. "It doesn't get any better than this." Jonathon's truck was there up on jacks with all four wheels removed. It couldn't be hidden or moved. The perfect picture - he had the rear end of the truck showing the Johnson Brothers' company license plate, the company's name on the truck's front door, the Lawnsville City Garage sign in the background and a city mechanic with "City of Lawnsville" written on the back of his coveralls.

As soon as Rick walked into the office, Wayne Adkins was on the phone explaining why the truck was being repaired at the city garage. "Since the city is using it, we just felt we should repair it. You aren't going to use that picture, are you?" the mayor asked.

Rick responded he was not sure whether the photo would be in that afternoon's *Crier*. "What was wrong with the truck, Mayor?" Rick asked as innocently as possible, taking great effort not to burst out laughing.

"Needed a completely new brake job," the mayor offered.

It was clear to Rick the mayor had come up with a scheme to declare the city's dump truck inoperative so the street commissioner's brother could graciously agree to lease his private truck to the city for $1,200 per month, a good portion of which Jonathon would kick back to the Mayor to split (of course not equally) with the street commissioner.

Rick's perfect picture was at the top of the *Crier*'s front page. The caption featured the mayor's word-for-word explanation about why it was being repaired at the city garage along with details about the truck rental from the previous day's council story.

Rick wondered what readers would think about the city in addition to paying $1,200 to rent Samuel's brother's truck providing full maintenance. He wondered if anyone would pick up on the fact the city had been renting the truck for only a month and was already doing a brake job. The buzz was all over town. The carrier who sold the *Crier* in the stores along Church Street and up at the courthouse had to come back twice for additional papers.

This is what a newspaper should be doing, Rick thought, smiling, after receiving a couple of calls complimenting him on the page one picture.

As Rick was contemplating the nobler aspects of newspapering, threats about him and the newspaper were being screamed through City Hall by the nearly unhinged street commissioner. "I'll burn down that son-of-a-bitching paper," Samuel Johnson yelled as he walked back and forth before Wayne Adkins ushered him into his office and shut the door. Only the mayor and a couple of city policemen heard the tirade.

Rereading the city council story - the first story under the *Crier*'s expanded coverage of local government, Rick thought, *not sure the others can match this one.*

Chapter 5
Surprised by Fair News

One of the least understood governmental bodies in West Virginia is the county commission. The three-member body has broad powers—they levy taxes, hire, fire, set the budgets for all other elected county offices, set the overall budget for the board of education, oversee the county 4-H camp, and oversight of the county hospital.

Joesph Ballengee rarely covered the Commission's meetings. Therefore, Rick was not surprised by the astonished look on the faces of the members when he sat down and took out his notebook. None of the three could remember a reporter dropping in unannounced. They had to delay the meeting while the clerk got Rick a copy of the agenda.

Everything was routine, except for discussion of the condition of the city-owned fire station building that was on land owned by the county. Rick was aware of varying opinions around town - from the notion nothing was really wrong to the two-story concrete-block building was ready to collapse. Mayor Wayne Adkins and Fire Chief Steve Perkins were there.

When Sam Greenside, president of the commission said he'd entertain a motion to go into executive session to discuss the matter, it got a quick second and the vote was unanimous. "Rick, you have to leave," Commissioner Greenside said with trepidation, not sure what reaction the banishment would bring.

Rick's hand went up and he was recognized. "This is an open meeting to discuss an important public matter and the public should not be shut out," Rick explained.

Commissioner Bill Joe Ratliff, normally low key but known to have a temper, said, "You either get the hell outta here or I'm calling the sheriff to arrest your ass." The sheriff—coming down the hall outside the meeting room—heard the comment, as did everyone else in the building. He winked at Rick, turned and quickly disappeared. Rick would learn later, the sheriff immediately fled the courthouse to his camp on the river for a day of fishing out of the range of telephones.

The publisher recalled how his relationship with the sheriff, a member of the old-line faction, evolved. When Rick instituted his new coverage policy for local government bodies, Eddy Bill took his cue from the old-liners who were unhappy. The sheriff wouldn't even return phone calls from the *Crier's* staff and refused requests for copies of bank statements for county bank accounts.

All that changed when Eddy Bill found a *Crier* story on a sensitive subject to be fair to his department. About two months after Rick had taken over as publisher, a sheriff's deputy was involved in a high-speed chase through the western end of Jordan County chasing a man who had robbed a gas station and pistol-whipped the owner. During the chase, a man stepped out in front of the deputy's car and was killed.

The dead man's family was upset and said the deputy's reckless driving was responsible for their relative being killed. The deputy said the man, a recognized teetotaler, had staggered onto the highway. The next day, three relatives of the victim invaded the *Crier's* office demanding Rick report their version of the facts and support their call for Eddy Bill's resignation. The family also questioned why the body had to be sent to the state medical examiner, not understanding the procedure was required when a law enforcement officer was involved in a death. After listening to their accusations, Rick called the route driver who lived in that section of the county.

After Rick agreed the route driver's comments would be off the record, he learned the man killed was indeed drunk that day after hearing the news his wife had been diagnosed with terminal cancer. Rick called Eddy Bill and suggested he request the medical examiner to check for alcohol in the dead man's system. Eddy Bill was puzzled by the suggestion but took it. The results showed the man's blood-alcohol level would have made him nearly incapacitated.

The *Crier* story included the family's accusations, the deputy's statement, and the autopsy results absolved the deputy. Given what he'd heard from his old-line supports, Eddy Bill Graves was surprised by the fairness of the story and Rick's important suggestion. From that point, the relationship between Rick and the sheriff had been cordial. Both understood the sheriff was identified with the old-line. That didn't stop them from doing their jobs and maintain mutual respect and trust.

The banging of Sam Greenside's gavel returned Rick attention to the meeting at hand.

Greenside was trying to bring order back to the current commission meeting. Frustrated, the commission president called for order and addressed the publisher, "Rick, this is important and we have to discuss it now."

Not to be outdone by Commissioner Ratliff, Wayne Adkins said, "Hell, we're not staying if he's here," nodding toward the publisher. The fire chief remained silent, as he stood to follow the mayor out.

Looking directly at the commissioners, Rick said, "I've heard rumors about the soundness of the building. Don't you think it's better for the people to get the facts from this meeting rather than let the rumors continue?" Rick suggested.

Rick's mouth fell open when Greenside responded, "I think it'll be okay." The two other commissioners were dumbfounded but went along. This stopped the mayor in his tracks. He and the fire chief sheepishly returned to their seats.

Make no mistake, the commission president didn't care for the *Crier* publisher, but Sam Greenside had a reputation for a commonsense approach to things and what Rick said fit that criteria.

The discussion got to the crux of the matter quickly. There were stability problems that had to be addressed. Next came the matter of costs. The agreement was made that the city and county would share them. In most things, the city and county commission didn't trust each other and didn't do many joint projects. The fire station—was a major exception. One that served both well.

When the meeting adjourned, Rick went over to Greenside and expressed his appreciation, and shook hands with the other two commissioners. George Mullen, one of Baxter's closest allies, readily accepted the proffered hand. Commissioner Ratliff who had threatened the young publisher with jail a few minutes before reluctantly followed the lead of the commission president.

Rick's straightforward story included the fire station's condition (it wasn't about collapse), the scope of the agreement, financial arrangements, and when work would start. Mention was also made about how well the partnership had worked over the years.

The morning after the story appeared, Rick was on his ritual visit to the post office when Commissioner Bill Joe Ratliff came out of Susie's and called Rick over, "I want to apologize for what I said at the commission meeting. We appreciate your story. It was fair."

"I appreciate the apology," Rick replied. "Things can stress us at times. I think the commission and city are doing a good job on this." His cordial manner brought a look of stunned disbelief to Ratliff's face.

They both knew there would times when Rick's stories would not be so well received. But the commissioner now knew the publisher wasn't as bad as he had told - at least, not this time.

Chapter 6
The Job

Politics, particularly local politics, can be rough and tumble at times just about anywhere in the country. Historically, West Virginia is recognized as being a bit rougher than most.

People trying to understand local politics in West Virginia, often find the root of the bitterest episodes involves jobs - particularly after an election - who keeps them, who gets fired and who gets them.

Such a situation would be pivotal in Jordan County's May, 1960 primary election that would fill three seats—a majority—on the Board of Education.

Ed Marcum Jr., eldest son in one of the largest and most respected of Jordan County clans, had always been a hard worker, having grown up on the family farm out on Horse Run. He brought that same work ethic to the railroad when he moved into town twenty-five years ago from the land that had been in his family for over a century. His hard work brought him with a comfortable life for him his wife, Anna, and their only child, Jane Ellen. All had gone well until four years before when Anna was diagnosed with breast cancer. Everything with Anna's recovery had gone fine until recently. Just that morning, she had visited Dr. Brown to learn the results of a recent series of tests. Anna had been a wreck waiting for Ed to get home.

Jane Ellen was set to graduate from college with a teacher's degree and had talked about moving to Charleston to find a job. Anna was in a state of despair at the thought of facing what could be her final battle and her beloved daughter more than a hundred miles away.

Anna came into the living room after dinner and asked Ed to turn off the Reds' game. Ed knew immediately it was important and had an idea it was about his dear Anna's visit to the doctor. "Ed, I've been praying on this all day. Doctor Brown says the cancer is back. He suggested chemo. Other than that, there's nothing left to do."

Anna continued haltingly, not looking at Ed, "I have never gotten into your politics, never. But I just can't go through this without Jane Ellen here. You got to go see Bill Joe about getting her on at the high school."

"Anna, I just don't know," Ed said, gazing softly into her tortured face as tears flowed down his dear wife's cheeks. Sobs followed quickly.

"Ed, I'm dying. I might have only a year or two. That's all. I just can't go through it without her. Please, you have to do this, I …" She was overcome, and slid off the chair, her head coming to rest on his knee. "Oh, dear Jesus," Anna cried out, looking up.

Her devoted husband of thirty years choked up, and now tears streaked his weather-beaten face. She'd stuck with him during his drinking and carousing days - prayed him through it. They both knew he wouldn't have made it without her. She was his rock. Ed stroked her hair and whispered, "I'll talk to Bill Joe tomorrow after work." As he pulled her up, wiped away her tears and held her close. He knew the next day he would do his very best for his dear Anna.

After his shift, Ed hung around the time clock until he saw Bill Joe coming down the hall. "Could we talk a bit?" Ed asked in a neutral tone.

Bill Joe couldn't hide his surprise. "How 'bout I come by your house after dinner?"

"No, I'd rather come to your place," Ed replied, "say about 6:30, just you and me. More private," he added to suggest others had been after the family's support for the upcoming Election Day.

"I'll ask Red to come up, too," Bill Joe said, knowing his own limitations in face-to-face political matters.

"No, it'll be just you and me," Ed said in the no-nonsense tone that was a well-known Marcum family trait.

While Bill Joe was out front in the public eye as a member of the three-member county commission, he didn't make decisions or commitments without checking with "them."

"Sure, see you then," he said.

After the conversation, Bill Joe stopped at the cleaners to tell Red the news. At Red's insistence, Bill Joe called Ed and asked again if Red could sit in. "I said it was 'tween you and me. If I'd wanted Red in on it, I'd gone and talked to him," Ed said with clear warning in his tone. That evening at 6:30 sharp, Ed pulled up to Bill Joe's house on a small farm about five miles west of Lawnsville.

It was Wednesday night. Bill Joe's wife, Polly Ann, was off to prayer meeting and choir practice. They'd have the house to themselves. Bill Joe got nervous when he heard Ed's car in the gravel driveway.

"Can't stay too long," Ed said, looking directly at Bill Joe. "Anna'll be back from church in an hour or so and she doesn't like to go into the house with me not there."

"Glad you're gonna help us in the election," Bill Joe blurted out, wanting to show confidence.

"Now, Bill Joe, I didn't say that I only wanted to talk," Ed corrected.

"Some have been out to see Big Ed," Ed related, bringing his father and head of the clan into the conversation. Bill Joe's stomach was churning. "How can we work it for you all to come with us? Especiaiiy for the board?" he stammered.

"I don't know about that, Bill Joe, the family's still talking," Ed said in a deliberate tone.

Ed knew it was time to get to it dispensing with the normal Jordan County approach to a serious conversation. "You know Jane Ellen will be graduating from over at Bluecord College in May and she'll be looking for a job," he explained, looking directly into his old friend's shifting eyes. "It would be really nice for her to have her first job here in the county. You can appreciate that, can't you, Bill Joe?"

"Well, yes, I think that would be really nice," the county commissioner heartily agreed. "You know there aren't a lot of jobs right now at the high school, what with consolidation and all," Bill Joe said, backtracking, his voice racing like one of the big engines roaring out of the Lawnsville rail yard pulling a long line of filled coal cars. Bill Joe noticed the skepticism on Ed's face.

"I know there will be an opening since Virginia Lou Jarvis is retiring," Ed pressed, his eyes locked in a withering stare.

"I think we—I mean I—might be able to work something out," Bill Joe said, not wanting to seem powerless in the ways of county politics.

Ed sensed it was time to put on more pressure. "Bill Joe, you and I go way back, ever since we played football out the high school," Ed recalled.

Bill Joe smiled, squirming a bit remembering how Ed had taken the fall when he got caught speeding and drunk driving along Three Mile Curve when the two were high school seniors. If Ed had not slid under the wheel, Bill Joe would have been charged, suspended for the state championship game and wouldn't have received that football scholarship to Bluecord.

"Those were good times," Ed said patting Bill Joe on the back, "Glad I was able to help you back then. Well, I'd better be going. Anna'll be home from church in a bit. Sorry you can't give me an answer, Bill Joe. I don't have much time on this. Family'll be getting together next Sunday, and what we're going to do in the election will surely come up."

Heading for the door, Ed added, "Give my best to Polly Ann, and tell her the cookies were really good."

As Ed got to his truck, Bill Joe flew off the porch, nearly falling over Archibald, his faithful hunting dog. "Now don't go and do anything until you hear from us—I mean me. I think something can be worked out," Bill Joe said, shedding his follow-orders status in the chain of command of the county political hierarchy.

As Ed pulled up in front of the small, but well-kept, one-story house in Lawnsville's East End, he could see Anna was already home and pacing back and forth and looking out the window. She was out on the porch before he could get out of the pickup. "What'd he say, Ed? They gonna give Jane Ellen that job?" she asked, trembling.

"Now, Anna, let's go in and have some iced tea and I'll tell you what went on," Ed said, using the big old smile he knew she loved and putting his tree-limb size arms around her shoulders.

"I already got it poured," she said, knowing that, as always, important things were discussed at the kitchen table over a glass of her special brew. "What did he say?" Anna repeated, her hand shaking as she passed the sugar and lemon.

"Bill Joe was positive, but he's got to talk with some others, I think Charles and Red. As I told you before, he ain't the one that'll decide," Ed said, looking into her anxious eyes.

"Ed, they just got to give Jane Ellen a job. They got to," Anna replied as the tears began to flow.

He got up and put his hand on Anna's back. "I'll be talking to the family about it on Sunday."

She looked up and held out her arms, "I know you'll do all you can. I'm sorry to upset you. But I'm so scared the cancer is going take me."

"It'll be okay. The good Lord won't take you yet," Ed said, thinking to himself, *I got to make this happen.*

On Sunday, after church, they stopped by the house to get Anna's special potato salad and a container of her iced tea and headed out to Horse Run. Every month, the Marcum clan from all over the county gathered for Sunday dinner out at the old family farm.

Around election time, the talk always had a political edge. The family's reputation for independence insured they were courted carefully by both sides come election time. It had been three days since Ed's visit to the county commissioner's house. Ed was surprised all he got from Bill Joe since his visit was a follow-up call saying he was still working on it. The County Commissioner repeated it was looking fine and he should know something early in the coming week.

That was all Ed had to report as they turned off Route 20 on to the mile-long driveway up to the old home place.

The spread was under the big oaks in the backyard. All the kids were down in the meadow, skipping rocks across Horse Run before Aunt Jane pulled the rope to ring the dinner bell on the post in the front yard. After a hearty meal featuring legendary family recipes, the women adjourned to the kitchen while the men gathered around the tables under the towering oaks.

Ed's father—Big Ed—usually started the conversation. "I can't wait to find out what's going on. What are you all hearing about the election?" the patriarch asked, chuckling with the others. They all knew he was plugged in all over the county and was counting on this discussion to confirm or challenge what he'd picked up.

"Lots of talk," cousin Jim Bob offered, "more than usual. Folks I talked to are getting more upset about Edward being so power-hungry. Seems it's spilling over to the other campaigns, too."

Big Ed noticed Ed, Jr. staring out toward the creek, not really listening to the conversation. "Ed, what's on your mind? You look like something's eating at you. Out with it."

Little Ed turned and looked at the group. "We've got some problems with Anna. Seems her cancer might have come back. She's worried something terrible.

"Jane Ellen's graduating and is thinking about applying for a teaching job down in Charleston. Anna wants her home for this. They're so close. She's asked me to go to Bill Joe and ask that he get Jane Ellen a job out at the high school. I talked to him the other night. At first, he crawfished just like normal. I hinted other folks were asking us to go their way on the elections.

"I don't think he's the one that'll decide, but he said he didn't see a problem. I hope you all can hold with me on the school board elections. Three of 'em are up, seven's running and Red and them want to keep control real bad.

"What do you all think?" he asked, looking around the group.

"We need to talk more, but I just know Edward has gotten too big for his breeches," Big Ed's younger brother Bob said matter-of-factly. "But as we all know, family comes first and we'll stand together, whichever way we go in this."

"Lance, have you seen Angus lately?" Big Ed asked, knowing his brother stopped by the store up on the mountain nearly every day to visit with the old-line's chief supporter in that part of the county.

"I'll stop by tomorrow and let him know we talked and how important the job is to us," Lance said spitting from the chaw lodged in his cheek.

"We can talk again next month. That's two days before Election Day."

Ed and Anna had no more than walked in the door than the phone rang.

It was Bill Joe, talking so fast it was hard for Ed to understand him. "Did you all decide to come with us?" Bill Joe asked in his zeal to get a favorable report for Red.

"We're still talking and the election is still more than a month off, so we don't think we have to be in a hurry," Ed replied smugly, thinking of Bill Joe with sweat pouring down his face. "I did tell them we'd talked and I hadn't heard anything final back from you," he said evenly, but sending a clear message before he abruptly ended the call.

Bill Joe's hurried call to Red conveyed a serious situation. Red realized this required immediate attention or the old line stood to lose a key family that had influence over several hundred votes. "Just talked to Little Ed. He'd just come from the family's Sunday dinner and seemed none too happy we didn't get back about that job for Jane Ellen. I told him it seemed it was going to work out for her," Bill Joe pointing out how he had headed off a key family leaving the old-line on Election Day. Red, keeping to himself thoughts of killing the thick-headed member of the county commission, curtly said the esteemed officeholder should come down to the cleaners immediately.

Assuring himself his politically astute maneuver with Little Ed Marcum would lead to the old-line machine's support for higher office—maybe even sheriff or a state legislative seat— Bill Joe assured Red he was on his way and should be there in fifteen minutes. Coming off the mountain, Bill Joe pushed his pickup around the curves of the road leading into town and the certain praise from Red.

After Red closed the door, his face turned blood red. Red snared, "Why did you tell him it was going to work out? Damn it, Bill Joe, I told you before, don't go around big-shottin'. You got us in a fix." Red had told all of his people they were to bring anything like this to him immediately, and not, under any circumstances, make a promise until he and Charles had a chance to discuss it. Bill Joe's wasn't a total commitment, but it was close enough.

What made it worse, Red knew Charles had already worked with board members and made a firm commitment for the job to Basil Hammer, the patriarch of another large family in the other end of the county. He had to get to Charles to let him know what happened.

"Don't say anything to anybody about this, understand?" Red instructed as Bill Joe left.

Red's call to Charles, who was in Charleston, got right to the point, "We got trouble," he explained, telling about Bill Joe's fumbling. "We have to talk soon."

Chapter 7
Stepping Carefully Both Ways at Once

Big Ed Marcum didn't go to Lawnsville very often, so after Red's report, Charles knew it was up to him to make the drive to Horse Run.

Charles, the man driving the shiny Cadillac, and Big Ed driving the big green tractor, had known each other for more than thirty years. Big Ed had a reputation for independence and a low tolerance for bullshit.

It was known Big Ed might go with the old-line on most Election Days. Not all, but enough to keep the family on the old-line's priority list. It was Gospel that the whole family stuck together, which meant solid majorities in several voting precincts in that end of Jordon County.

Charles realized he had to be the emissary. Big Ed would take umbrage if an underling was sent. He was certain it was not going to be an easy meeting.

Charles knew Big Ed and his family had careful discussions before making Election Day commitments. But this one was different, very different. Charles hadn't ever known the Marcum family to ask for a political favor. Charles was well aware that failing on this visit could very well bring defeat in the all-important board of education races.

Big Ed saw the Cadillac out of the corner of his eye but kept on plowing across the field that would later in the summer turn into a sea of golden corn. He ignored the hand waving and horn-honking. Big Ed smiled to himself, knowing the mission was important for the Cadillac to travel all the way out to Horse Run.

The Marcum patriarch, ignoring the honking horn, kept guiding the green machine back and forth, picking the corner of the field farthest from the road and the Cadillac's parking spot.

Finally, the visitor got out of his air-conditioned comfort. Charles began his trek across the hazard-laden field, ripping his new suit's pants climbing through the barbed-wire fence and managing to get his shiny black shoes ankle-deep in mud while concentrating on dodging the cow patties dotting the field.

Out of breath, Charles finally arrived at the tractor and then was nearly run over since Big Ed "hadn't noticed" him. Charles waved his hand in greeting. The weak gesture was answered with a slight nod and a broad, almost mocking smile as Big Ed silenced the tractor.

"Charles, don't see you out this way much," Ed said.

"I thought it was important we talk," Charles said, then abruptly turning from the trek's real purpose. "Field looks real good, crops should come in really well."

"Yep," Big Ed nodded, "Lord's been good to us. I'll be planting corn in this field next week or so."

"How's Esther?" Charles inquired, kindly referring to Big Ed's wife of fifty-five years.

"Thanks for asking. Esther is getting along fine, but we're worried about our grandson away overseas with the Marines," Big Ed replied, towering over Charles W. Beauregard Jr. from his green perch.

"How are things with you?" Big Ed asked.

"Things going pretty well. Charlie III. will be finishing college next year and Mona will be having her first baby in September," Charles said, keeping with the county's tradition of visiting a bit before one started talking about the real reason for a conversation.

"That's nice," Big Ed said. "Always good to see 'em move on."

In a 180-degree change of direction, Charles moved the conversation to what they both knew the visit was about. Charles said it looked like Eddy Bill would have a tough time in the sheriff's contest.

Big Ed cocked his eyebrow as if to say, "And the farmer hauled another load away." Through his contacts, Big Ed knew that Eddy Bill, one of twelve candidates in the sheriff's race, was running ahead in every corner of Jordan County.

"Don't believe you all will need our help with Eddy Bill.," Big Ed said, in subtle reminder he was plugged into every part of the county.

"I hope so," Charles said, knowing his attempt at political chitchat had fallen as flat as the cornfield where he was standing.

It was time for Charles to get to the real reason he'd come to Horse Creek. "Ed, we really hope you and the family can come with us in the board races," Charles asked.

Big Ed smiled down and spat some fresh tobacco juice on the ground in Charles' general direction, some of it running down his chin. In as cold a tone as Charles had ever heard, he said, "The family is still talking things over."

"Well, a lot of folks would like to see you go with Edward, Kermit, and Orville," Charles pressed on.

Knowing what the Marcum clan might have to do what Charles suggested, but not wanting to make Charles' first trip successful, Big Ed said, "We'll just have to see. Little Ed was talking about that at Sunday dinner. We're still talking."

He was letting Charles know that Little Ed, who stood a little over six feet, four inches, was the family's leader on the school board decision. Ed Jr. got tagged with the moniker because he was born premature weighing just over five pounds. Big Ed added the "we" just to remind Charles the family would be sticking together.

"I think Jane Ellen would make a fine teacher in the county. We hope we can help her."

Looking down, Big Ed continued in the frigid tone, "A lot of people have been saying that. She's a fine girl and really smart. Bill Joe told Ed he thought there would no problem, but I guess there is a problem." The farmer atop the tractor just had stuck it to Mr. Cadillac.

"Some things take time, you know?" Charles said remembering Basil Hammer at the other end of the county who had been promised the same job for his granddaughter.

"Seems simple to me," the farmer said softly again. Big Ed's eyes flashed behind his sunglasses. "Thanks for coming by, Charles. Don't mean to rush off, but have to get this field done by dinnertime," he added, dismissing the political power with a nod, flipping the switch that returned the roar of the engine.

Both knew this wasn't the last meeting on the subject if Charles wanted to get the family's support. With a face even redder than the blazing sun, Charles replied, "It's nice to see you again," and turned and nearly stepped in the middle of an extra-large bovine gift.

The old farmer smiled at the thought of Cadillac-man making another tiptoeing trip through the field before Election Day. "I'll have to get a few more cows in this field before the Cadillac comes back," Big Ed said to himself, smiling as he watched Charles carefully step across the field.

Charles pulled into his garage. He stripped to his underwear and headed straight to the bathroom to wash the stench that hung heavily on every inch of his body.

Once showered, he called Red and told him the results of his visit with Big Ed. Red's long silence was deafening. "That's not a good sign," he finally responded. "I can't remember when Big Ed or the family ever asked for anything special.

"We have only one choice, tell him she'll get the job," Red concluded.

Charles responded quickly, "Red, there's only one job in the county that'll fit what they want and Edward, Orville, and Kermit have all personally assured Basil Hammer his granddaughter will get it."

"Tell Big Ed, right before Election Day. He and Basil don't talk, and as far as I know, haven't spoken to each other for years," Red said, knowing there was no other choice.

Both knew the two families' support was essential to the old-line maintaining control of the Board of Education, since board members were elected by district and each family could sway two different districts. Red observed, "With Basil and his family going for us in Pipewell, and the Marcums out in Pine Hills, we'll have three strong precincts in each of the two districts that could well assure Edward and Yancy win. Wayne and the city workers will take care of Orville in the city."

"There'll be hell to pay after the election when only one of those girls is hired," Charles said.

"After the election, we can blame the mix-up on Edward," Red said chuckling. "Given his screw-ups, it won't be hard to convince people."

"I'll go back out there Saturday afternoon before the election," Charles said, confident the ruse would get them through Election Day.

Chapter 8
Growing Faster Than Your Britches

Edward Whitmore had an easy time getting on the county school board six years ago when Benny Ogden, a dependable old-line veteran decided to call it quits in the middle of a four-year term after his wife's cancer came back.

Edward was well known. He had four brothers and four sisters who all lived in the county and together, they could influence a large number of voters.

Edward had done all the right things in the community, president of his kid's school PTA, a deacon in the church, and youth baseball coach. With two kids and a prim-and-proper wife, Lucille, it all fit. Edward seemed the perfect candidate, another example of the folly of first impressions. Running for the unexpired term, he led all board candidates.

Initially, he had kept a low profile on the Board serving out the term. Then running for a full term in the following election, Edward drew opposition who was thought to be strong. He worked hard, campaigning in every corner of the county and he won big, leading all other board candidates in all of the county's thirty precincts.

That's when the trouble began. Edward liked power, and his wife warmed to being the wife of a member of the county board of education. Two examples stood out. First, her demanding the family get preferential treatment for auto service at the local dealership where county vehicles were purchased. Second, her showing up at the Forest Hill School unannounced to take her kids out of school early on a whim. Mrs. Edward Whitmore explained to the principal "those silly rules were for other students, **not** for a board member's children."

Edward started buying into his wife's ambitious delusions and started thinking for himself - independent of Red and Charles' learned guidance.

While he was in high school, Edward had a wild streak. There was the time his senior prom date wanted to charge him with rape. One of the old-line's brain trust managed to get her father a better job at a state road garage in another county, so it all went away. Given his community work, particularly with his church, everyone assumed he'd outgrown that behavior. Another peel of the onion revealed something entirely different.

As a member of the board, Edward attended meetings around the state. At one, on a small college campus in the central part of the state, he met an attractive co-ed, staffing the conference. An affair blossomed. He encouraged her to apply for a teaching position in Jordan County. And the affair continued. They were careful, never getting together in the county but always in Charleston, an adjoining county, or in an out-of-the-way spot in nearby Virginia.

But then Edward got overconfident and had her rent a cabin at the state park in a remote corner of Jordan County for a weekend when Lucille was visiting a sick aunt near Richmond. Edward and his lover selected the front porch of a deep-in-the-woods cabin for an "afternoon delight" at the same time a work crew was clearing underbrush back in the woods across from the cabin.

Acting quickly to keep the sordid scene from finding its way to Lawnsville's infamous gossip network, the park superintendent held a meeting with the crew explaining the privacy of guests was of paramount importance. He added anyone violating the policy would be fired.

Edward had dodged a bullet - for now. His entitlement approach to the school board would be the first of two "Edward" incidents that would bring the old-line unwelcomed attention.

After learning Principal Annabelle Lawrence hadn't responded quickly enough to a demand contrary to school policy from Lucille, Edward visited the school unannounced.

Interrupting Annabelle's regular weekly after-school meeting with the teachers, Edward dismissed the teachers and ordered the principal into her private office. He said the school was the worst in the county, adding, "Your job and all the staff jobs are in danger if you don't start running this school as it should be. You better make damn sure they all vote right, too."

The students were gone, but the staff was still around and since the transom over the principal's office door was open, the staff heard every word of his four letter word-laced threats.

With his last, "You'd better get this place straightened out, and quick," Edward stomped out. Realizing the staff had heard the discussion, Annabelle immediately called them into her office. "It is very important for all of us not to mention this to anyone," she cautioned.

Immediately after the stunned staff left her office, Annabelle called the superintendent to report what she considered to be the worst case of political interference she'd experienced in her decades with the Jordan County school system.

Superintendent Elwood Hugh thanked her for calling and for her admonition to her staff. Hugh knew if Edward's performance got into the newspaper, it could cause political problems in the county far beyond the school system. Make no mistake, he had his problems with Edward, but planned to handle it in a more subtle way.

The Superintendent decided to let Red know what happened. He briefly described the situation. "Keep a lid on this, we can't let the paper get wind of it. Are you sure Annabelle can keep the school staff quiet?" Red asked in a tone that left no doubt about the gravity of the situation.

"If anybody can, she can," Elwood Hugh answered in a not very confident tone.

All the precautions didn't work. Unfortunately for the old-line, the next day was Lucille Whitmore's appointment at the beauty shop, the fount of all knowledge for the city's all-knowing gossip network. "And Edward just told her to get that school in order, or she and all the rest of them would be gone. I mean cooks, teachers, bus drivers, and the janitor," Lucille triumphantly informed her hairdresser. She didn't notice the shocked glances coming from every dryer in the shop. Edward's wife's newly blonde head hadn't been out of the shop more than fifteen minutes when the *Crier* publisher's phone rang.

Before he could pick up the receiver, Rick had a hunch this would be a call he wouldn't soon forget. His eighty-five-year-old anonymous source laid it out ending with a vision, "And then she strutted out of the beauty shop like she owned the place," his octogenarian news source whizzed before she hung up.

Now Rick wasn't about to run a story based on beauty-shop gossip, but the rumor fit Edward's growing reputation.

The *Crier* publisher had a plan to track down the story, if there was one. First, call the superintendent, then the principal. As expected, neither would say much, but the superintendent said the matter was an internal personnel matter. *That's not a denial*, Rick thought as he put down the phone.

Before he started writing, Rick, called in Al Dill and said he should get the other pages laid out as soon as possible and leave a page one hole for a story that might be a little late. When he filled Al in on the story, the word of the day—"Holy Shit!"—filled the newsroom.

Chapter 9
Golden Oldies

Charles smiled as he walked through the house, refreshed after an afternoon nap, and headed to pick up the paper that just slammed against the screen door. His smile vanished as he read the *Crier*'s page one banner:

Board Member Threatens Bus Drivers, Cooks with Job Loss Says All Depends on How They Vote

He turned and almost broke into a run, but didn't because he didn't want anyone to see his panic. Charles just shook his head as he read the details that expanded on the headline. Rick Hill's story was complete.

Three Forest Hill Elementary support staff members had called Rick at home, too afraid for their jobs to come to the *Crier* office. Those off-the-record conversations confirmed in more detail the bare-bones report he received from his all-seeing eighty-five-year-old.

Their comments prompted the publisher to go to the horse's mouth. In answering the first question, Edward quietly explained the school visit was about a personal matter that had affected his family. With the next question—"Did you discuss the election with the principal?"—Edward's kind Dr. Jekyll turned into evil, boisterous Mr. Hyde. "It is election time, and they have to understand what they are supposed to do," Edward responded. Rick's next question unlocked the flood gates, "Damned right, jobs came up. I wanted Annabelle Lawrence to understand how elections work, and who's got a job and where they're placed can get rolled up together," Edward said.

"Shit!" Charles shouted to the empty house as he continued to read on.

Edward explained as he dug deeper. "As I said, it's election time." Just when Charles thought it couldn't get any worse, the next paragraph hit him right between the eyes.

"It's up to the principal to do the right thing. She's responsible for the school's operation—teachers, bus drivers, cooks, and janitor—and if the principal doesn't make them understand what's right, then things could happen," Edward added, the shovel going full-tilt.

Edward didn't seem to remember, or didn't care, that Annabelle Lawrence had run the school for twenty years and was revered throughout that end of the county.

"Do the principal's responsibilities include how people vote?" the *Crier* publisher pressed.

"Well, like I said, she's responsible for the whole operation. That's true for the whole county," the board member concluded.

Charles thought of the old saying, *when you're in a hole, stop digging.*

Normally, in such situations, Charles always returned to his tried-and-true Golden Rule of politics - money. He wasn't so sure that would work here. He picked up the phone. "Red, this has just got to stop. Have you talked to Edward since the paper came out?" Charles asked, not sure he wanted the answer.

"Yes," Red answered warily, "he was proud, like he'd done something good and the election was in the bag. I'd already read the thing and knew it was trouble. I tried to tell him to keep his mouth shut. Then he got to cussing Rick Hill and saying he was going to get with the mayor and take care of that no good SOB and his newspaper," Red told a now fully alarmed Charles.

"Can't meet now. I'm leaving for Charleston in a few minutes to tell the Humphrey folks how strong Kennedy is coming on. Hope to get another $8,000." alluding to his and Red's scheme to milk as much election money as possible from the two presidential campaigns.

Red chuckled, "I'm working the Kennedy people, but I'm trying for another $10,000."

"We need to meet just as soon as I get back tomorrow evening," Charles said as he hung up clinging to the hope the Edward situation would be washed away on Election Day by the wave of cash he and Red had assembled for precinct organizations.

Edward's tirade was being whispered among Jordan County board employees across the county. And on top of that, concern was growing among school board retirees that Edward's "way" would rule in county schools if he and the others got re-elected.

Eva Newland put down the phone after talking with Annabell Lawrence, eyes flashing, head shaking and a rare "shit" snarling from her lips. Her old friend's report was even worse than the *Crier* story.

Eva had known the principal for more than thirty-five years, ever since Annabelle had done her student teaching under Eva at Raven Rock Elementary. Over the years, Eva had been her mentor and even introduced her to the man she married. The young couple's first child was a daughter and they named her Eva.

All during her years in the county school system, Eva was known for her dedication to helping students, anything that got in the way of that upset her to no end. After her students, her second love was young teachers as they moved along in their careers. Oh, Eva was well aware of politics in the schools and understood how the game was played.

The politically savvy retired educator took great care to visit from time to time with folks in both of Jordan County's political factions. Just last week, Baxter Edwards visited Eva to chat, over tea of course, about the school system. "I sure hope you can help us in the election, Eva. Edward and his bunch are really hurting us," he pleaded. "It would mean a lot."

Eva listened closely, thanked him for coming, never tipping her hand, "Baxter, I'm tired and don't plan to get involved," she explained, patting her former student and son of a fellow retired principal on the shoulder.

She was frail and, like Red after an earlier visit, Baxter was sure Eva would not be involved in this election other than casting her ballot. Later, Baxter talked to his mother about how Eva seemed to be failing. Mary Edwards chuckled, explaining she had picked up some rumblings Eva was up to something. Baxter thought about his mother's comments and then disregarded them.

But behind Eva's white picket fence and flower garden, the wheels were churning. Eva was feeling her years—she was eight-one—but the fire had been stoked for this one. "I have to try."

Nearly every school employee, from teachers to janitors, who retired from the system in the last twenty years received a hand-written note from Eva thanking them for their service to the children of Jordan County.

The last few years, she had watched silently in disdain, as Edward and his cronies used jobs as political payoffs, purchased things from their local business supporters at inflated prices with money that was needed in the classrooms.

While others might have forgotten, the superintendent remembered Eva's ability to influence school board elections, but like Red and Baxter, thought the respected school retiree was "just too old now."

Ten years ago, a board president was thought to be unbeatable. In his second term, he had come to see the county school system as his private fiefdom. He personally decided where the county would buy its vehicles, insurance, and maintenance supplies. Eva was aware of the rumors, but it didn't affect the kids in the classroom, so those were not battles she chose.

Then the board president crossed Eva's line in the sand. He decided it was time to completely control the hiring and placement of teachers and principals. Rather than move cautiously, he rammed through two teacher transfers and a principal reassignment at a single school board meeting with no discussion. The weak-kneed superintendent at the time proposed the actions as if they were his own ideas. The board members approval in unanimous robotic fashion.

Then she had a come-to-Jesus meeting with the superintendent.

The then-superintendent listened politely, certain Eva was satisfied by the notion she had read him the riot act and would go quietly back to her school. He ignored her admonitions and even joked about her visit with the board president. She heard about that conversation.

Eva's plan was put into action quietly. On Election Day, despite having spent several thousands of dollars on advertising, the "unbeatable" school board president went from top dog the previous election to last in the next one carrying just one of Jordan County's precincts, his own. That election has long been forgotten by most.

The current superintendent, then a young high school teacher, observed and remembered that election in vivid detail. But now, he saw Eva as an old eighty-one, long-retired teacher who seldom left her house. However, she did give him one suggestion he thought had merit if he could figure a way to implement it behind the scenes.

Eva had been following Edward's obnoxious behavior closely, but silently. When she heard about Edward's threats against the school principal and the staff, she decided it was time to dust off the teapot and have the girls over for a chat. Most hadn't been involved in anything close to politics for years. Idle chatter was not what this tea party was about. The steeping would include developing a countywide political lesson plan as detailed as any of the retired teachers had prepared when in the classroom. Assignments covered everything, including identifying who needed a ride to the polls. At least two cars would be available at each precinct Election Day to get voters to the polls.

A key strategy for the Golden Caravan, as they had dubbed themselves, was to concentrate on getting people who didn't normally bother to vote.

This small group of dedicated retirees knew the odds were stacked against them, but they were motivated by a sense of caring for Jordan County students. They were ready to take on the old-line's political dynamo.

Chapter 10
People Learning to Read

Having a few minutes until the campaign committee meeting began, Red started to think about the Edward situation compared to ticklish situations in past campaigns.

One for the ages was a time when three of Joshua Benfield's girlfriends got together and filed to run against him for sheriff. "That one is still legend," Red chuckled.

He remembered the old-line candidate was seeing three girls and separately told each she was "the one."

Joshua, in one of his drunken overtures, got mixed up and called one by another's name. The first one, Louanne, bumped into Lorraine at the grocery store. Louanne thought Lorraine was her only competition for Joshua's affection. Then in a whispered conversation in front of the fresh corn, Lorraine said Joshua had done the same thing with her when he, in a bourbon-induced fog, called her by the name of yet a third girl, Lucy.

They planned revenge. They were smart, Red remembered. They decided how much it would take to get them out of the race. With careful planning, they all filed for sheriff just hours before the deadline. When Red tried to contact them separately, each said she would meet him only if the other two were present.

Ladies in church circles were clucking. Red laughed out loud, remembering his late father asking him, no, bribing him, with the promise of a new car to help make that mess go away. Red met with the three and sealed the deal.

His dad had sworn him to secrecy and not to breathe a word around his mother, Elmira – a fine Christian woman – she'd kill 'em both.

Red had to call in an IOU to get a used-car dealer in an adjoining county to handle that part of the deal. The dealer still kids Red about it.

Each of Joshua's ladies got $150 cash and a $250 car – a used car but a car nonetheless. Then there was $1,800 his dad spent on his new car. The election was a squeaker - Joshua Benfield won by fewer than fifty votes

In this election, Red would be grateful if $2,850 could make the present mess go away. Hopefully, tonight the group would bring some good news.

The first knock signaled the war council was arriving. "Hey, Charlie, looking forward to hearing what's new out your way. Norma made some iced lemonade and cookies, they're on the kitchen table, help yourself," Red said, mindful of Charlie's strict adherence to temperance.

In short order, the four others gathered around the old oak dining-room table.

"Okay, I need to know what's going on. What are you hearing?"

Old Jim Bob, from the mountain, jumped right in. "It's not good. Eddy Bill seems to be okay, but the school board is just tight. Edward is doing things that just don't sit well with folks. It could affect our whole slate. It's so bad, not sure money will do it," he said, mopping his forehead with a red bandanna.

"Course, a little walking-around money won't hurt none. And I heard Preacher Brown is upset with Edward acting like a jackass. There's that teacher he's supposed to be messing with," Jim Bob concluded.

"What are the rest of you hearing?" Red asked, sounding more confident than he felt.

Joe Brown, the most reserved one of the group, jumped in, "About like Jim Bob said, this thing with Edward is up my way, too. Not too bad. On the other hand, folks are calling, wanting to work Election Day. Don't think we'll have any trouble getting out the vote,"

Red turned to Charles Woolton, "Are you hearing much about Edward?"

"It's not too bad, but it's talked about," Charles said in a slow Virginia accent inherited from his mother's Roanoke birthplace. It's that damned newspaper. Hill is stirring things up with the *Crier*," he concluded.

Red was surprised when every head at the table nodded in agreement.

"Jimmy Ed, what're you hearing?" Red asked, continuing around the table.

Jimmy Ed was a veteran of many campaigns. He had the pulse of the retired folks in town. He and his wife went to different churches, unusual in the county, and both were active and knew how to listen.

"The retired teachers are as mad as I've ever seen 'em. Heard they were spitting nails over this Edward thing," Jimmy Ed said, shaking his head.

"Eva is not happy. She at least listens to us most times, but she won't even talk to me about it. Says we'll talk later. Don't think she'll be involved, she looked bad the last time I saw her. But might be something you want to check on. Red, you might want to visit with her," Jimmy Ed suggested.

Red, ever-outwardly-positive, was churning inside. He expected to have a little trouble with the Edward thing, but was surprised to see it so wide-spread.

As for Eva, he and Charles had discussed it and decided that at eighty-one, she would do no more than make a few phone calls, if that.

"How can we get it right?" Red asked.

"It's gonna be tough. That paper is just keeping everything stirred up with those letters to the editor and editorials. Everybody's reading it," John said as the others again nodded in agreement.

As the reports continued, Red was realizing this election was unlike any he'd had in quite some time. The biggest problem? It was the *Crier*'s coverage of local government agencies—particularly stories about the board of education. And then Edward talking to Rick Hill about his visit to Forest Hill School really was the worse thing for the old-line Red could remember.

To make matters worse, Bill Joe's promise had the potential to cost the old-line one end of the county. Money couldn't influence either family. To Red's knowledge, this was the first time either had ever asked for a favor.

It was time to turn the conversation in a different direction.

"What are Baxter and that bunch putting out?" Red asked, pressing on with apprehension.

Again it was Jim Bob jumping right in without looking at anyone for permission. "They are working overtime with this talk about Edward. Maybe Charles needs to hold a prayer meeting with Edward," he concluded.

Everyone chuckled at the use of the polite term for getting one's ass ripped by Charles as he explained the facts of life to someone who has strayed and needed the fear of God instilled in them.

"Joe?" Red asked, focusing on the careful analyst of the group. Joe Brown had inherited some money from his mother's side and worked out of his home as a sales rep for a farm equipment company. He held things close, but had traffic with a lot of different folks in about every hollow in the southern end of the county.

"This election just feels different. Folks are paying more attention and they're asking more questions. I think it's because there's more in the newspaper about what's going on.

"It could cause us to lose some houses and hurt us up and down the slate." He looked each man in the eye, using an old traditional term for election precincts. They all tolerated his normally arrogant attitude because he generally was on target.

"John?" Red had carefully chosen the order in which council members would speak. He knew John would get the others' attention with his calm, methodical analysis and fired-up presentation.

John enjoyed his position of going last, and drew his five-foot-five-inch frame to its fullest at the foot of the table opposite

Red. "There's no doubt the *Crier* is having a big influence. I hear people talk about them stories everywhere I go. Our precincts are really going to have to be organized earlier than normal. The major thing is to get the precinct captains and start going door-to-door before Election Day.

"With the commission seat and three board seats on the line, we have to have every precinct wrapped uptight," John concluded.

"Red, there's one thing that can't wait until next week." John continued, ruffled up like the bantam rooster with which he was often compared. "It's money, all the precinct folks are asking about it," he concluded slamming his hand on the table.

Red was ready to dance around the issue until he saw all heads nod in agreement again. He knew they couldn't leave the meeting in a gloomy mood.

He stood up at the end of the table, a sign that something important was about to be discussed. "Let 'em know money will not be a problem," Red emphasized, knowing the money question was on every council member's mind.

"But one thing I can tell you is we want at least three cars hauling in every precinct. Larger ones will have four," Red emphasized to drive home the point – "money is not a problem."

Red knew his conversation with Charles would include details about what this campaign committee was picking up around the county, particularly about the impact of the *Lawnsville Crier*.

Red now realized how important it was over the years to have Joseph Ballengee running the *Crier*. "Damn Joseph for selling it," Red cussed silently.

Looking around the room, Red knew they needed to hear more encouragement. "We will have more money to run precincts than I can ever remember," he added, looking each man in the eye. "There will be a $50 bonus for each precinct captain where our board candidates are in the top three." That bought an "amen" and smiles from every council member.

Chapter 11
Giving Board of Education a Real Lesson

Superintendent Elwood Hugh put together the council of PTA Presidents to keep in touch with what people in the county were saying about the schools.

The politically astute educator purposely scheduled this council meeting a month before primary Election Day and another a week before. One item on the agenda seemed routine. Council President Sammy Brownly brought it up, coincidentally while Elwood was in the restroom. Each county PTA had endorsed it seemingly without coordination – holding a Candidates Night for board candidates at every school. Approval was given to ask the Board approval before the superintendent had flushed. During the brief discussion, no one mentioned a retired school employee had suggested the event during a recent PTA meeting.

"With three board members up for election, it seems like something folks want," Sammy said.

Some cynics might believe the superintendent had planned the whole thing—who's to know? True or not, it made good fodder for political gristmills of the county.

The morning after the council vote, Sammy dropped an announcement about Candidate Night on the publisher's cluttered desk. "Thought you might be interested in this," the PTA council president said departing before Rick could read it. Interested? Rick decided immediately, "Page One!"

PTA's Request Permission for Board/ Candidates' Nights in County Schools

"An important element of the successes we have in the school system is the support and involvement of the public, particularly parents and school PTAs," the superintendent responded in Rick's telephone interview

It seemed to Rick the superintendent's statement, maybe by design, made it nearly impossible for school board members to vote against holding Candidate Nights. Such use of school buildings had to be approved by the board.

It hit the fan when the three incumbent board members facing the voters in six weeks, read the *Crier* story. Orville Browne, whose office was near the superintendent's, was at the board office in a flash, bursting unannounced into the superintendent's private office. Edward Whitmore and Kermit Yancy were having lunch at Susie's when they saw the *Crier*. They arrived at the superintendent's office while Browne was still ranting.

They were mad as hell for several reasons. The superintendent hadn't stopped the council's resolution, his statement in the story made it appear he was for Candidate Nights, and they had to read about it in the paper, not from a heads-up from the superintendent.

They demanded the superintendent ban the meetings. "You either cancel the Candidate Nights, or we'll fire you," Edward yelled.

Elwood Hugh replied meekly, "I can't do that, the request passed unanimously by the PTA Council and was sent to the board, not to me. Since the board approves such events at schools, you can stop it by voting against the request."

"You should be aware that members of each PTA in the county indicated they would like to hold a Candidate Night," the Jordan County school superintendent added.

After that gem, there wasn't a peep from any of the board members standing before him.

Truth be told, Eva mentioned the idea in a call to the superintendent. Then she made sure a retired school employee brought it up at a PTA meeting at every school.

One key element of Eva's plan was to develop several carefully-worded questions to be asked by her fellow retirees at each

Candidate Night. Like the superintendent, her fingerprints were nowhere to be found.

Currently, the old line, as the result of filling a board vacancy two months ago, had a solid 3-2 majority on most board votes. Further on many matters, Hattie Mae Cooper could be persuaded into giving them a four to one majority. Sam Keaton, the fifth board member, was solidly in the reformer camp. Neither he nor Hattie Mae was on the ballot this election.

With the adventures that resulted from his first city council meeting still fresh in his mind, Rick had no idea what to expect at his first board meeting. He was not aware three board members threatened to fire the superintendent over the county PTA council's request. However, given Edward's volatile reaction to news stories with which he disagreed, the publisher was certain the board president didn't want to take parents' pointed questions in public forums.

Before Superintendent Elwood Hugh introduced the Candidate Night item, he looked carefully around the room, nodding to Sammy Brownly, PTA council president. Looking directly at Edward, the superintendent explained, "You have before you a request from the county PTA council, which includes the presidents of every PTA in the county.

"Council unanimously approved this request to hold a Candidate Night at each school. Also, here is a letter from the Retired School Teacher and Employee Group supporting Candidate Nights," the superintendent said, never mentioning his meeting with the three afterward.

Sensing he was fighting a losing battle, but not being able to help himself, Edward Whitmore interrupted the superintendent. "These Candidates Nights are just a waste of time. Folks just don't understand the issues the board deals with, or how the school system works. This idea is just to stir up trouble. I'm against it. Where's the money coming from? With all these events being at night, how are we going to pay for the janitors to close the buildings afterward? Our budget is really tight."

Fully expecting the question, the superintendent smoothly announced, "All PTAs have stepped up and will pay for any overtime a Candidate Night causes."

Edward was not pleased his two board allies joined the other two board members voting in favor of Candidate Night.

Rick did not know where the idea for the Candidate Night came from, but he was certain there was an interesting story there. "Getting all the PTAs on board took some organizing," he said to himself as he took the board story out of his typewriter.

After the city council, county commission and board meetings out of the way, it'll be nice to have the hospital board to look forward to. Nice and quiet, Rick thought as he turned back to his typewriter.

Chapter 12
A Prayer Meeting for Breakfast

Charles had been on the road lately, organizing that end of the state for Sammy Monroe's race for governor, traveling to Charleston to get more money from statewide campaigns, and convincing the Humphrey presidential campaign more money was needed to hold the line against the surging Kennedy campaign. He and Red were overdue for a face-to-face on the details of the county election, particularly the "Edward problem."

Charles asked Red if he could stop by his house Friday evening. Red came through the door sputtering about Edward before he even said hello. "That interview Edward gave to Rick is really causing problems. Teachers all over the county are upset. And guess what came to me today? I heard he was up to the park two weekends ago with his young teacher friend and the maintenance crew saw them going at it on the front porch of their cabin, on the damned front porch, in broad daylight!"

"That's not the worst of it," Red continued. "He beat her up last week when she tried to break it off. Will had her taken over to the Greenbrier hospital. She had a broken arm, stayed in the hospital most of a week and has taken a medical leave of absence from teaching for the rest of the year."

Shaking his head in astonishment, Charles grabbed the phone dialing Edward's number from memory. After a brief exchange with the board member's ditsy wife, he asked to speak to Edward.

"Evening, Edward, sorry, it's so late, but I think it might be a good idea if we could get together tomorrow morning for breakfast up at the park," he said cordially enough but in a tone that left no room for refusal.

"Yes, yes, that'll be fine, see you about 8:00, if that's okay," Edward stammered in response.

"Let's make it 7:30," Charles replied coldly, changing the time and his tone as a stark reminder of who was in charge.

"Sure, I can make that," Edward said softly, understanding his attempt to take control of the conversation unsuccessful.

"Sounds like Edward might be going to prayer meeting a couple of days early," Red said, chuckling, a wicked smile crossing his wrinkled face. He was sorry he wouldn't be there to watch Edward's near-death experience. "Charles, you got to get him under control."

"Are we going to carry him on the slate for school board?" Red broached the subject that had been in the background.

"It's too late and he does bring in the votes," Charles said.

Red shook his head, "Dumb ass, and that wife of his can't keep her mouth shut. Lucille's almost as bad as he is."

"If he gets re-elected, we might have to get him to resign after the election for health problems," Charles added. "How are things going here?"

"There's a problem, at our meeting the other night, every single one said the *Crier* stories got folks to talking and it could cause us trouble in every race except the sheriff. And everyone mentioned Edward.

"They did settle down when I told them there would be more money per precinct than we have ever had. But there's no doubt there's talk out there," Red concluded.

"Red, I think we will be fine. We can throw a little more money into precinct organization for insurance," Charles offered.

Reluctantly they agreed they might have to cut into the cash stashed in their safety deposit box. Both had implemented plans to squeeze more money from the two presidential campaigns. Also, on his next trip to Charleston, Charles would ask for more from each of the statewide candidates for attorney general, secretary of state, treasurer and auditor they were supporting and particularly from Sammy Monroe, their candidate in the heated governor's race.

"Be sure to take care of Edward tomorrow," Red said over his shoulder as he headed for the door.

Edward arrived at the Bluestem State Resort's main restaurant at 7:00 a.m., to be sure to be there early for what he thought was a 7:30 meeting with Charles. He naively expected the old political boss to congratulate him on the way he laid out the facts of life in that *Crier* interview.

At 7:30, Charles did not walk through the door. It was 7:45. *Where was he?* Edward's mind was whirling. Didn't Charles know he was moving around the county getting votes for the whole team? He didn't have time to waste. Edward fumed. At 8:00 a.m., Charles came through the door with a scowl covering his face.

"Good morning, Charles," Edward called out, expecting a big congratulations in response.

"Not feeling so good this morning, Edward," Charles said, hesitating to take the proffered handshake at first. "Edward, that interview is the talk of the county and people are mad and threatening to vote against our whole ticket," Charles said.

"Hell, Charles, you can't talk to me that way. I'm the future. You've let things pass you by. People are coming my way," Edward said in a mocking way that was both disrespectful and boastful.

"Let me tell you, Edward, you're not running this thing and at this rate, you never will," Charles said, his face red and his eyes boring through Edward. "You're causing a lot of trouble, you and that young schoolteacher and threatening to fire the entire staff at the school. All this has got some of our precinct captains so mad they are ready to quit," Charles lectured.

Edward was shocked his secret was out and angrily replied, "Me and Sara Jane is none of your business, Charles, and it's been over for months."

"Don't you lie to me. You were with her in one of the cabins here two Saturdays ago screwing on the front porch in broad daylight," Charles said in a fierce whisper. "She's taken a leave of absence from teaching because you beat her up," Charles added through clenched teeth. "Now I'll tell you how it is. You and your family are going to take a vacation until after Election Day, to Myrtle Beach starting a week before Election Day. Don't make a call to anyone about anything political. I mean, disappear. You all can use my condo, it's right on the beach," Charles explained.

"I won't do that. I have too much to do here, what with the campaigns and all," Edward responded.

Over hearing the loud whispering, the waitress pouring coffee stopped and turned to the next table.

"You will, and that's not up for discussion. I'm not sure what else we'll have to do to get through this, but you're to stop campaigning now and have no contact with the *Crier*. You got that?" Charles said in a tone that made it clear there was no argument.

"And you better know that everyone on our side is in agreement with this," Charles said as Edward raised his hand in protest.

"Everyone is not," Edward said with as much courage as a beaten man could muster, "Some of my boys are working hard for the whole slate and you need every one of them, Charles."

"Red is meeting every one of them this evening and will explain the trouble we're in and tell them, not ask them, they will be working under his direction." "And if they say they don't want to, you will call them tomorrow and tell them that's what you want them to do," Charles instructed.

"Edward, you've put our whole operation at risk, I know there's a lot on your mind right now. It's time to take a breather." Charles had switched to a fatherly voice. A stern father, but a father nonetheless.

"Here's something to help out with your son's legal problems down in Tennessee," Charles said, putting an envelope on the table in front of him. Edward was stunned. Now he realized Charles knew about this older son's stupid involvement in drug deals in Nashville.

Using his position as a bank director, Charles had the bank president look at Edward's accounts and learned money was tight. A number of checks had been written to a lawyer in Tennessee in the past few months.

"Now, Edward there are a lot of folks who want you to resign from the board right now," Charles said, pausing for Edward to wonder where he stood on the matter.

"I don't believe that's the thing to do, at least not right now," Charles said letting Edward know if he didn't take the offer, things could get worse, a lot worse. "Tonight, you will call the head bus driver and cook at Forest Hill and apologize to them. Say you made a mistake, and their jobs are fine," Charles said.

The waitress came up and asked if they were ready to order. Charles didn't even look at Edward. He ordered two coffees and two orders of scrambled eggs and bacon with pancakes. She looked at Edward, and Charles said, "That'll be all."

Given the intensity of the conversation, the two men didn't notice the waitress lingered a bit longer than usual, writing the order very slowly.

Retaining control of the conversation, Charles smiled and leaned back comfortably in his chair, "Edward, I just told you exactly how it's going to be. You fight me on this and it'll get a lot worse. We'll fire all your precinct captains and I'll get someone to ask the teacher you beat up to file charges." He was bluffing to make a point of who really was in charge here.

Continuing that tact, Charles continued, "I'm glad to hear your sister likes her job in the sheriff's office, and your brother seems to be getting along well here at the park. And I spoke with your brother-in-law's supervisor at the state road regional office, Princeton. Everything seems to be fine." Message received Edward quickly realized how much he'd receive from Charles and how fast it could disappear.

"Let me think this over and see what I'm gonna do," Edward, said his hand trembling as he grasped the water glass.

"Edward, you're going to do exactly what I said to do. There's no discussion about that," Charles said shoving the envelope containing $1,200 over to Edward's. Hope this helps your son's situation."

Edward looked at the envelope and shook his head, knowing he had little choice and realizing he could need more help in the future.

"Just let me know when I can help," Charles said, knowing the hook was set. "Now you get out of town so I can try to fix things."

"Charles, don't make me resign. Will you carry me on the slate for the election?" Edward asked.

"We'll keep you on the slate. After that, I can't promise anything. Some people are very unhappy with you," he said. Charles took out his wallet and counted out $150. "A little something for the trip. If anyone approaches you or calls you about anything to do with the election, don't say a word and call me immediately, even from down there," Charles said.

Charles got up abruptly, dismissing Edward like a scolded schoolboy. "Enjoy your breakfast."

While Charles was certain this breakfast strategy was essential, he was mistaken to think the session would make the Edward problem go away.

Chapter 13
A little Help from My Friends

Charles and Red were sons of legendary Jordan County politicians. They'd learned at the knees of two acknowledged as the best politicians in the county's long and notorious political history. Red's father was a county commissioner for twenty years, and Charles' assessor for even longer. Both had served a term as sheriff.

The scions operated differently. Charles, quietly behind the scenes in Jordan and adjacent counties using that power to become a state political power. He slid into a state senate seat when a strong incumbent suddenly announced his retirement the day before the filing deadline. Charles was ready and filed his papers to run the following day, shutting out anyone from even considering a run.

Charles excelled on the state political scene building IOUs that established him as a leader in the rough, behind-the-scenes brand of politics.

Red preferred to operate in Jordan County, while occasionally getting involved in neighboring counties. In his home county, he was extremely effective organizing the precincts.

Using their political power, Red and Charles were always on the lookout for opportunities to fatten their personal bank accounts. An example was the "by chance" purchase of a large family farm stretching for several miles along one of the three rivers in the county. The parcel was at the end of a deserted state road.

While the two were partners in the endeavor, Red was out front and bought the useless land with the help of a Lawnsville attorney, Hugh Bird, who was managing the closing of an estate. The family selling the land thought they had hit the jackpot when the lawyer said he might be able to get $8,000 for the isolated 250 acres along the beautiful river.

After two weeks of not taking the family's calls, the lawyer called the family in and, shaking his head, said it looked as if he could only get them $6,000, emphasizing "we are lucky to get that."

He took out his handkerchief, wiped his eyes and told the family in his most solemn tone that he was sorry and would cut his normal fee by half, knowing full well Red would pass him a thank-you envelope in the next week or so.

Gathering around the lawyer's desk, the three money-grubbing heirs signed the documents, congratulating themselves, certain they were smart to take the lawyer's advice. "Everybody" knew the land was worthless, the thinking went, so an appraisal would be a waste of money for the land, Lawyer Bird explained.

Truth be told, a licensed appraiser would have shown the old road indeed was a long-forgotten state road, but still a state road. That fact alone would have increased the land's value considerably. But the lawyer convinced the family. "You don't want to waste money for someone to send you a big bill just to tell you what you already know."

No sooner had the family left his office than he was on the phone to Red. "It's done."

When he put down the phone, Red smiled, thinking about how important it was for his and Charles' candidate for governor to win the upcoming primary election. Given the overwhelming partisan registration in the state, it was a given the Democratic primary winner would be the state's next Chief Executive.

If Sammy won, right after the inauguration, Red would personally deliver the envelope of gratitude. It was just the natural and expected thing to do.

Shortly thereafter, the new governor would order the widening and paving of that deserted piece road and find the money for the public service district to extend water service to that remote area. This made this statewide primary one of the most important ever for Red and Charles personally. They stood to make a $100,000 on that initial investment of $6,000.

On the local level, things were tightening up for the old-line. The situation demanded a no-nonsense analysis.

Chapter 14
A Puppeteer Invisibly Pulls the Strings

Red and Charles were facing something different in this campaign. Old-line candidates, particularly those running for the school board, were facing tough questions. The reports all had one thing in common—The *Crier* stories.

Red locked the door, pulled the blinds, and he and Charles adjourned to the small, but comfortable office in the back.

As they passed through the small hallway, Red joked that if walls could talk about political deals made here over the decades, they'd have to burn the building down. Little did he know the analogy foretold the conversation that would follow.

Charles settled into one of the well-worn chairs that dated the office décor as Red handed him a cool can of sweet lemonade and placed one on the desk for himself. Charles took a long swallow before starting the conversation. Red followed suit.

The two men's adherence to the non-alcoholic libation was the result of being raised by two God-fearing, Bible-toting, prayerful mothers, who constantly instilled in them the evils of "demon rum." They vividly recalled their mothers' tirades when the fathers would come home reeking of alcohol after a night of campaigning.

Never far away was the memory of the loud sobbing of their mothers' praying wails when they learned of their sons partaking of beer in celebration of their team winning the state football championship some thirty-one years ago. Charles's mother brought him over to the Bell house and the two mothers sat their sons down and held forth. The two took turns praying – asking for divine intervention to make their wayward sons turn from their sinful ways. Those stern words still occasionally rang in the ears of the two Jordan County political kingpins.

To this day, that session coupled with the promise of an alcohol-free life they made as the mothers lay on their deathbeds did indeed keep the two men free from demon rum.

On the other hand, in a juxtaposition of religious principles, the two believed the thousands of dollars stolen by their political maneuverings was their "just-due." After putting the cans down, they turned to the problems of the present election campaign.

"Red, the stories in the *Crier* are hurting. Folks are talking about them, particularly the ones about Edward. Does Joseph have any idea about how we can turn Rick around?" Charles asked, hopefully.

"No, and he's really pissed off. He really thought Rick would keep things the way they were. In fact, he thinks it could get worse as we get closer to Election Day," Red related.

"Something has to be done," Charles said. His eyes moved from the ceiling to stare directly into Red's troubled eyes. "My concern is Rick has mentioned in a story or two the mayor and Edward are close politically. That ties the city's troubles like that stupid dump-truck deal to our slate of school board candidates. That can cause us real trouble," Charles continued.

Both were mindful the school board, with its jobs throughout the county, was key to holding political power. The board controlled all the bus drivers, school cooks, janitors, maintenance crews, school secretaries and where vehicles, furniture, and supplies that were purchased.

With their votes, school board employees and their families could determine who was elected to all countywide offices, including the sheriff and county commissioners.

Red leaned back in his chair, his feet on the weather-beaten desk used by his father for more than sixty years. "It's not just the things with Edward, the *Crier* is covering city council and the commission. Hope he stays away from the hospital board," Charles said.

"Did you hear Samuel threatened to burn down the paper over Rick's story and the photo on the dump-truck scheme?" Red inquired.

Charles didn't react right away, slowly savoring a pull on the cool libation. "When was that?" he asked, as a seed was planted.

Red almost whispered, "About a week ago, the day after the story and picture about Jonathon renting his truck to the city.

"Word was he was ranting and raving in the main hallway at City Hall. Yelling he was going to firebomb the paper and shut up that damned Rick Hill. Wayne pulled him into his office and Samuel continued and was pounding on the mayor's desk. He was yelling at the top of his lungs."

Charles asked, the seed taking root, "How many people know about the threat?"

Red replied, not yet grasping where the conversation was heading, "It was after quitting time, only him and the mayor. Maybe the police dispatcher and a couple of patrolmen were there. What can we do, Charles? This is the biggest problem I can ever remember," he said.

"There might be a way to solve our problems without us lifting a finger," Charles responded.

"How in the world?" Red asked, not expecting Charles' answer to fulfill the promise of that last statement.

"Samuel's rant at City Hall was before witnesses. What if he made good on the threat?" Charles continued in a sinister voice that startled Red. Both agreed if Samuel acted, their most serious election problem would literally go up in smoke. The discussion continued.

Charles stared at Red. "If the *Crier* stories continue, we could lose every race. Joseph selling the paper is making it really tough," the veteran politician said as he laid out the problem as he saw it.

"On top of that, Baxter's candidates, especially for the board of education, are getting some traction," Red observed. "That story about Edward's visit to Forest Hill School really hurt all three of our board members."

Returning to the previous subject, Red asked, "You don't think Samuel will do anything, do you?"

"We can't be connected to Samuel," Charles said in such a low whisper Red had to strain to hear. It was clear to both men something had to be done and nothing was off the table. "Since Samuel has already made the threat, he'd take the fall no matter what happens," Charles continued, thinking out loud.

"From what Avery told me, Samuel is right on the brink over this, and his brother, Jonathon, is even more upset," Red added.

Avery Stone operated a beer joint on Lawnsville's seedy side street and had a close relationship with the Lawnsville street commissioner and acquainted with most of Lawnville's petty crooks.

"I've got an idea about how we might be able to give Samuel a push in the right direction. We need to let him know we feel like he does about those *Crier* stories," Charles offered.

"That would put us right in the middle if something happened," Red's voice faded.

"No, no, no, we'd just set the fuse. We'd use others to light it," Charles said, his enthusiasm growing as his puppet show came into focus. "We have others carry the message," Charles said.

"Who would encourage him to make good on the threat?" Red asked, still not seeing how it could come together.

"You said Avery is real close to Samuel and his brother Jonathon. And the mayor and Samuel work together to steal from the city," Charles responded, as a plan was developing in his mind. "We just tell Avery and the mayor we understand and totally sympathize with how the Mayor and Samuel feel about the *Crier* stories. Adding we feel the stories were unfair and it seems like Rick has it out for him and the mayor," Charles continued.

"No doubt the Mayor and Avery will tell Samuel how we feel, so it might get him to thinking. Then he'd take it to Jonathon, who might run with it," Red said, warming to the idea.

"How often do Avery and the mayor come by the cleaners?" Charles inquired, pleased Red had swallowed the hook.

"Avery about once a week and the mayor almost every day," Red related.

Charles' thought was to fan the flames of the hatred seething in Samuel Johnson by using manipulated surrogates to set the wheels in motion. "You sure Avery would carry it?" Charles asked cautiously.

"Yes, he'd take it to Samuel. And Samuel would take it to Jonathon and the mayor," Red answered in the same careful tone.

"I'm sure the mayor would come right up to the cleaners and confirm you said what he heard." Charles laid out the plan for Red to carry out. "Tell Wayne it's as rough as we've ever seen it and we can't blame him and Samuel for being upset. Let him know we think it's just not right what the paper is doing."

Charles took a long cool drink, smacking his lips as he looked up at the old patterned tin ceiling, seemingly studying the swirling design.

"Wayne'll take that and run with it, I think. He won't do anything, but he might push Samuel. Wayne doesn't like to be made a fool of, and that story and picture did it to him big time, in front of the whole town," Charles said.

"Avery'll probably be in tomorrow morning," Red said as he shifted comfortably and the old chair squeaked in protest. "That'll give me a chance to set the hook."

"The mayor will probably be in tomorrow afternoon. I'll ask how everything is going, and that'll set him off talking about the paper."

Charles smiled widely, finishing off his first lemonade of the evening. "After you tell the mayor how unfair the paper has been to him and Samuel, be sure and tell him we want him to handle the city precincts and getting all the city employees and their families out to vote. Let him know it'll be considerably more than before. Tell him he'll get $1,000 to organize city precincts and another $100 for him.

"Do you think this is the way to go?" Charles asked, conspiracy oozing from every pore.

"I sure do. It's the only way," Red said, warming to the plan of leading from the rear. The puppeteers shook hands and called it a night.

The part of the plan the two liked was that it kept them in the shadows. Red wasn't listening too closely, not realizing he was the one chosen to put the plan in motion, leaving Charles as really the only one truly in the shadows - the real puppeteer.

The following morning, Avery walked through the door. Red was behind the counter reading about last night's Reds game in the Overton morning paper. "What's up?" Red asked, looking up from the sports page.

"This election seems to be heating up. Samuel is really upset about the paper," Avery said in his no-nonsense raspy voice.

"I can understand that. The story and picture were really unfair, almost like Rick has it out for Samuel and the mayor. Charles and I don't blame Samuel for being upset," Red said, contrived concern written all over his face.

"Is that really how you see it?" Avery asked, surprised at Red's forthright words supporting the city official whose reputation wasn't too good.

"No other way to see it. *Crier* really blasted him and Wayne. It just wasn't fair," Red repeated.

"He and Jonathon are madder than hell. Haven't ever seen 'em this way before," Avery related.

"Too bad about the stories. Everybody in town is talking about it," Red continued.

The two talked a bit about the Reds game the night before, and how bad the rain was for those raising tomatoes. Then Avery hurriedly headed for the door. Rather than going up to his beer joint, he briskly walked toward the city garage, entering the side door and going directly to Samuel's small, grimy office in the corner.

"What's new?" Samuel asked as his friend sat down in an old chair.

"Just been talking to Red and he says the stories in the paper weren't fair to you and the mayor and he understands why you all are so mad."

"You're lying. That's what he said?" Samuel asked.

Avery turned to his friend, "He did. Said it seems Rick is out for you two. Never seen Red so serious. Said he and Charles were talking about it and Charles feels the same way."

"I'll be damned," Samuel said, seeing Red's remark as full support for the hatred he had for the *Crier* and its publisher.

"Yeah, I wanted you to know," Avery said as he got up to get his hot dog chili ready for his lunch customers.

Just a few blocks away, Red was checking the cleaning that just arrived from the Overton plant, when Wayne Adkins came through the door. "How's it going, Mayor?" Red asked as he came to the counter.

"I'm on my way to City Hall and just wanted to stop and get the latest on the election," the mayor asked.

"Glad you did, wanted you to know we will have more money than normal for you to organize the city precincts, about $1,000 for that and another $100 for your help," Red related in a normal tone.

"Hell, that's great. More than we ever had before," Wayne Adkins said, already counting how much he could squeeze out of the $1000 to supplement his original take.

"What else is new?" Red inquired, careful not to be the first to bring up the *Crier* stories. "I'm still plenty pissed off at that damned paper. He really stirred things up with that story and picture of the dump truck," the Mayor fumed.

"Don't blame you and Samuel for being hot over that one. It was just unfair, almost like Rick has it in for you," Red consoled.

The mayor looked at Red, with a surprised look. "Didn't know you felt so strongly, Red."

"Well, Wayne, fair is fair and I thought that was just not fair. Charles and I were talking the other day about it and he feels the same way." Red emphasized. "Shame we can't wave a magic wand," Red said, seemingly offhanded moving quickly back to Election Day preparation.

"Are things moving along with the precincts?" Red asked.

"I'll have an update this week. I'm having some meetings in the next night or two. With this amount of money, should be able to have at least two cars in each precinct," Wayne Adkins explained.

"Sounds like you've got everything ready to go. Let me know if you hear anything from Baxter's crew," Red replied.

"They are moving about in every part of town. We should be able to get Edward and Orville and Kermit taken care of," Adkins said, confident the city would go big for his friend and the two other old-line board members.

After his conversations with Avery and the mayor, Samuel called Jonathon. Like his older brother, Jonathon took Red's comments as support for silencing the *Crier*. "I'll take it from here," Jonathon said, eyes glaring.

It came together just as Red and Charles, the master puppeteer had hoped. Indeed, the puppets seemed to dance on their strings. But that wasn't the only thing moving on this sunny spring day in Lawnsville.

Chapter 15
Tomorrow Turns into 30 Days

Another eventful trip to the post office would move coverage of the county hospital trustees' meetings up the list of *Crier* priorities. As in many small towns, businessmen liked to pick up their mail at the post office each morning, visit with townspeople along the way. Rick saw it as a good way to get a feel what people were talking about, get feedback about the previous day's *Crier* and perhaps pick up a tidbit for a good story. Today, Rick had an additional task, pick up a sheet of four cent first-class stamps so Anne could send out the monthly advertising invoices.

As Rick was coming out of the post office, Baxter Edwards was entering and stopped to introduce himself. "How are things going?"

"Can't complain," Rick responded in his friendly way, looking forward to seeing where this conversation would lead.

"How are things with you?" the publisher said, their eyes taking the measure of one another.

"I see you're increasing coverage of the council, county commission, and school board. Seems to be stirring things up a bit," Baxter offered.

Continuing the game of cat and mouse, Rick replied, "Well, the people deserve to know what's going on," Rick said, proud of the notice.

Living up to his cagey reputation, the reformer asked, seemingly as an afterthought, "Why isn't the hospital board being covered?"

Disappointed at the mention of the one exception to the *Crier*'s local news coverage, Rick said defensively, "I've thought about it, but it just didn't seem as important as the others."

"Hell, there's more going on up there than with any of them," the politico said gravely, as much to inform as to measure the publisher's reaction.

Rick bristled. "I'm not about to take the utterings of a street corner conversation as facts for a news story."

Not backing down, Baxter pushed on. "Well, will you print it if you find things going on up there?"

The publisher said simply, "Yes," and turned to walk away.

Hearing mumblings that indicated disbelief, Rick turned to notice Baxter's right eye—he'd had cancer removed—begin to twitch. *Damned if he didn't look like some one-eyed pirate*, Rick thought.

"I said I'd run it," the publisher said impatiently.

As a parting shot, Baxter said over his shoulder, "First, you have to attend the damned meetings."

Still stinging from the deliberate baiting, Rick hurried into the office and called the hospital. When the administrator's secretary said the next board meeting was next week, Rick asked for a copy of the agenda. In her most efficient voice she said, "I have to check with Mr. LeMasters." As he hung up, Rick looked at his watch and wondered how long it'd take for the phone to ring.

It was eight minutes. "How are things going, Will?" Rick asked as if he didn't have any idea the reason for the call.

After the usual pleasantries, the hospital administrator said, "I just wanted to confirm you asked for the board agenda."

"Yes, I just wanted to check the agenda for the next meeting," Rick said without elaboration, forcing the administrator to make the next move.

"Are you coming to the meeting?" LeMasters asked. "I'm don't know, time is really tight, I just wanted to see what was up for discussion," the publisher answered.

Will LeMasters, in an intimidating voice used to keep hospital board members in line, said, "I'll have it finished by Friday and have Sally get it in the mail."

"Oh, just call when it's ready, and I'll come and get it," Rick said, eliminating "it got lost in the mail" excuse.

In the next few hours, the powers that be on the hospital board burned up the telephone lines discussing how to keep stories about board meetings out of the *Crier*.

The next morning, the community news editor who tried to pick up every call on the first ring, announced to Rick a call from Marvin Wood, chairman of the hospital board. Wood said he and others were concerned about Rick's covering the hospital board meetings. Rick explained, "The hospital board is a public body, and therefore, its board meetings are open."

"I'd like to meet so I can explain. How about up at the dam, this afternoon about 2:00?" Wood said, picking an out-of-the-way location where nobody would be at that particular time of day.

"Fine, see you then," Rick said in a friendly tone the chairman mistakenly took for acquiescence.

The publisher purposefully arrived after the agreed-upon time and easily spotted Marvin Wood's blue pickup, his business name in bright letters on the side. After Rick got into the truck, Marvin got right to the point, "We're just worried someone will bring politics into our discussions if they know it'll get into the paper," Marvin explained.

Rick, chuckling to himself, just nodded, thinking, "Who in the hell are you kidding? Everything in town, including the funeral home you're laid out in, was involved in politics."

Assuming the nod meant Rick understood and success was at hand, the messenger surged forward. "Rick, we're worried about what trouble stories about the hospital board might cause," Marvin said, cocksure he'd be able to dissuade the publisher.

Rick calmly asked, as low key as possible, "How's that, Marvin?"

"Well, the board works well together now, despite the fact we have different political factions and we don't want to upset that," he said.

Hearing the "we," a curious smile came across the publisher's face as he mulled over the word.

Was "we" used because the chairman wanted Rick to know he wasn't acting on his own, or to let Rick know he was sent on this uncomfortable task rather than undertaking it on his own?

While at first seeing the Hospital Board meetings as not having much news value, Rick now pondered, "What's there."

It was becoming clear to Rick that LeMasters saw the hospital as his own little kingdom - "It is my hospital, it is my board and damned if anyone is going to mess it up."

"Well, Marvin, the hospital is the county hospital—a public agency, employing hundreds—and I'm going to cover the board meetings."

"We really hope you'll reconsider," Marvin mumbled, realizing his mission had been doomed from the start.

On the night of the board meeting, Rick arrived just before the meeting began to keep from having to decide who he'd chitchat with prior to the call to order.

From the agenda, it appeared as if the meeting would be routine. But as with other Jordan County's public bodies, Rick would learn this initial evaluation wasn't close to reality.

To open the meeting, Marvin Woods acknowledged Rick and noted he was welcome to ask questions after the meeting adjourned.

Uneventful bordering on boredom described the meeting's first three-quarters. The most significant items up to that point were the posting of three positions, bringing the hospital staff up to its full staffing level of 205 and expanding the often overcrowded parking lot.

William LeMasters proudly noted the parking lot expansion was necessary because the patient load from neighboring counties was increasing.

Rick noticed two other non-board, non-staff types were at the meeting, but their names weren't on the agenda. The two would be assisting the board treasurer in presenting the status of "non-current" accounts.

Board member Baxter Edwards who paid little attention, became fully focused when the treasurer's report began.

After a review of the hospital patient load and a comparison of the past month with last year's, the treasurer introduced the two gentlemen - William Anderson and Earl Bowman. They were with the Anderson-Bowman Business Financial Corporation of Kingston that was assisting the hospital business office "in reducing accounts receivable."

Mr. Anderson happily reported they had $75,000 in hospital accounts "under management," which was down from $125,000, the total "just" three months ago.

Mr. Anderson continued by saying the significant progress was due to the hard work and cooperation of the hospital's billing department in response to the firm's incentive program.

"Incentive." That word caught Rick's attention, but before he could write it down, Baxter commented about the improvement.

"Indeed," Mr. Anderson gushed.

A redness came to LeMaster's neck as the board member continued, "Could you explain a bit about the incentive program your company has for its clients?"

"That's really getting down in the weeds," LeMasters interrupted, as several other members, including the chairman, nodded in agreement.

"No, I think it's important for the board to know the details of this important aspect of our operation," Baxter continued.

When one board member, the immediate past board chairman, said he agreed, LeMasters reluctantly fell silent.

"Well, we provide awards based on performance to the business office staff," Mr. Anderson explained.

"You mean like dinners or discount coupons to a local store?" Baxter continued.

"Oh, no, more than that. These two hospital staff members are outstanding and they qualified for our free trips to Myrtle Beach with their husbands," Mr. Anderson said. Mr. Bowman reached to grab his arm, but was a second too late.

"Both of our employees received these trips?" Baxter asked in a smooth voice, belying the fact he knew he had inflicted a wound that would bleed for months.

"Oh, yes, a full week's vacation each," Mr. Anderson confirmed.

The board chairman and the administrator, LeMasters, were focused on Rick, who purposely stopped taking notes, seeming to show his disinterest in this discussion.

Seeing this, several board members relaxed, but LeMasters knew the publisher had not missed a word.

Almost immediately after the Anderson/Bowman presentation, the harried board president adjourned the meeting. As Rick approached, William LeMasters became visibly tense, expecting a question on the incentive trips. Sensing this, Rick asked about the timetable for hiring new employees and beginning work on the parking lot.

After answering the unexpected cream-puffs, the administrator, totally unsolicited, added, "Rick, you should know the collection program was approved by the full board."

"Thanks," the publisher said, smiling, realizing LeMasters' separating himself from the incentive program.

Driving from the meeting, Rick wasn't sure about the story. *How will folks respond to knowing two hospital staffers got a free week's vacation for turning some of them over to a collection agency?* Rick pondered.

It was 9:30 p.m., so he planned to spend about an hour at the office working on the story for tomorrow's *Crier* before heading home. Unfortunately, the events of the next five hours would make "tomorrow" about thirty days away.

Chapter 16
Fire Follows Guardian Angel Visit

The call came two weeks earlier from Jim Dowling, the only black on the Lawnsville police force. Jim related that Samuel Johnson, the volatile Lawnsville city street commissioner, was ranting at City Hall he was going to "firebomb that goddamn paper, and shut-up that son of a-bitch."

Watching their sons play on the same Little League baseball team, the publisher and the policeman had become acquainted. Unknown to the publisher, Jim, his mother, and sisters had discussed the "new" *Crier* with other members of Jordan County's black community. For the first time in its seventy-five-year history, the *Crier* was regularly covering events important to them – their churches, organizations and community accomplishments.

In that call, Jim explained to Rick Hill he'd be on night shift for the next three months and he'd be checking the paper every fifteen minutes or so. Rick was instructed to leave all the lights on in the building. The street light in the alley alongside the paper would make it easy to check the back of the building.

The cause of Samuel Johnson's wrath was Rick's story that exposed his dump-truck scheme to skim $1,200 a month from cash-strapped city coffers. And then two days later, a photo across the top of the *Crier*'s front page showing that same truck, belonging to Samuel's brother, Jonathon, a complete brake job at the city garage.

The loud crash of the flaming *Crier* roof collapsing jarred the publisher back to reality. The chiefs for each of the county volunteer fire departments came up to Rick and apologized for not being able to save the building. Rick Hill knew all of them by name. He had personally helped them with publicity for their annual fundraising events. Now with tears running down his cheeks, he thanked each one for the efforts.

"It was just too far gone when we got here," explained Joe Andrews, president of the Lawnsville volunteers.

As he finished the last handshake, Rick heard his name shouted from across the street. Huddled on the corner was a hardy band of *Crier* employees who lived within blocks of the paper. He went over and gave each of them a big hug. They all started talking at the same time, cursing whoever had done this, really upset and scared. Not one asked what caused the fire.

Rick said they'd meet later, at 8:00 in the backroom of Susie's Café where local civic clubs met. He didn't know what he'd say, just thought they should get together.

The crowd was growing despite the fact it was 4:30 a.m. People kept coming up, telling him what a shame it was and they hoped they found who did it. Like the *Crier* staff, all assumed it was arson. Rick thought the cause might have been faulty wiring, but found it ironic nearly everyone else assumed the same thing.

An old saying popped into his mind, "Timing is everything." The important primary election was only four weeks away. Rick was not aware *Crier* stories and his editorials had gotten the political pot boiling out in the county. Also, the paper's impact was a main feature of the conversations of the county's two old-line political kingpins.

And Rick had been doing research for additional stories before Election Day. Fortunately, he had taken his work home every night and had secured other sensitive information in the paper's antique but fireproof, safe. But, hell, it didn't make any difference now. His way to get the word out now lay in smoldering ruins.

Community news editor, Belinda (Billy) Amherst, had taken a camera home, so she was taking pictures of the fire and several of the crowd. He took the camera and got photos of the volunteers from every department. He also took photos of valuable evidence he discovered near the *Crier*'s backdoor.

Foster Black, one of the local store owners, came up, a look of shock and disgust on his face. "Rick, is there anything I can do?" he asked.

Rick dejectedly shook his head. "No, Foster, not sure what's next."

He looked over at the blazing fire and stopped. A light went on. "Dammit, I'm not done." He didn't know how but he'd come back, but he'd try.

Grabbing Foster's arm, Rick said, "Hell, yes. I want to rent that spare room you have upon Winter Street, starting now. Can you get it ready by noon? I need five desks and chairs, and later maybe an old couch or two."

"Wow, you're not stopping. It might take a bit longer, but I'll have it ready by late afternoon," the amazed storekeeper blurted out in a mixture of disbelief, amazement, and admiration.

Still shaking his head, not quite believing what he'd just told the store owner, Rick turned back toward the raging blaze.

He conferred with the city fire chief and they agreed a request should go to the state fire marshal's office to investigate the fire.

There was still some time until the staff meeting, so he walked down the alley running beside the smoldering building. Rick realized the guardian angel policeman probably saw what was going on and was jumped. Jim Dowling was short and wiry, so it would have taken more than one man to take him down.

They must have jumped him and when he fought back, so he was shot, thrown him into the patrol car and dumped on a desolate part of River Road. They spread gasoline around upstairs and down. Rick noticed the broken street light near the back of the building and glass on the ground. It had been on when he left the office the previous night.

His head was spinning, as he headed back up the alley toward the sidewalk in front of the paper.

He looked up as Joseph, the former publisher, came around the corner shaking his head. He walked up to the publisher with an outstretched hand. "I can't believe this. How do you think it started?" he asked, the first person not to say the fire had been set.

"I just don't know anything about that right now," Rick said as he saw his wife and two kids rounding the corner.

His young, but tough wife was in tears, as were the kids as she came up to hug him and whisper a soft "I love you." It didn't erase the pain, but it sure as hell lifted his spirits. Joseph stood by, expecting to return to their conversation, but the publisher just walked away with his family.

"Me, too," Rick whispered to his wife as a reporter from the Beckley paper and another from the Oak Hill television station came across the street. He wasn't sure he had any answers, but he wanted to send a message during the interviews. He noticed one of Red's gofers standing in the crowd, listening closely to Rick's rambling answers.

"How'd the fire start?" was the first question. While the exhausted publisher had expected it, he paused before answering.

"Not sure right now maybe the wiring or something," Rick said, not divulging his intent to request the state fire marshal for a full investigation.

"Was anything saved?" an earnest television reporter asked.

This was it, the opportunity for *the* message. Nodding toward the smoking building, he said, "Nothing was saved from there, but our spirit's intact." He pointed toward the corner where his staff was standing and waving.

"What do you mean?" came another query.

"We will find a way. I don't know how. It might take a while – months," Rick said, taking care to sound slightly defeated, wanting those who did this to think the task was accomplished.

"Do you think you'll be able to publish again before the election?" the Beckley newspaper reporter asked.

"No, that's not possible," Rick said, taking a handkerchief to his eyes.

"Do you think the fire was set because of your aggressive coverage of the local election campaign?" the newspaper reporter asked, not realizing she had hit the nail on the head.

"I don't think it was set," he said. "Folks get riled up during campaigns, but this would be crazy. I believe this is just an unfortunate accident," he said, trying to look surprised the question was raised.

"Right now, we don't have anything but a pile of ashes, but we have our spirit and strong community support, so we ask for as many prayers as we can get," he concluded.

"Do you feel the shooting of the local police officer had anything to do with the fire?" one astute reporter asked.

He felt his face tighten as he looked at the reporter who posed the most troubling question yet. "I haven't heard anything that would connect that tragic event to this. It happened several miles out of town," he said, shaking his head for emphasis. Rick was careful to use the word "heard" and not to use the word "seen" because he had found the badge.

When the reporters started repeating their questions, Rick excused himself and nodded to his jack-of-all-trades and pulled him away from the crowd. Rick asked in a firm voice, "Do you know anyone up on River Road?"

Zeroing in on the publisher's mysterious tone, Al perked up when he heard Rick's tough tone again. "Jimbo lives up that way and a couple of other old boys I know. Why?"

"That's where they found Jim Dowling. He was shot in the head and they're not sure he'll make it," Rick replied.

"Shit, do you think it's connected with the fire?" Al asked.

"No not at all, just keep your ears open," he said with an intensity that made Al Dill move back.

"I'll talk to those guys right now," Al said, nodding toward a few of his friends in the crowd.

"What are you going to do?" Al asked.

"We'll all talk at Susie's at 8:00. There's something I've got to attend to now," Rick said, seeing Orville Brown in the crowd coming toward him.

After listening to the agent ask, "How'd it start?"

Rick said, "Orville, I need a month's expenses, including payroll in my account by Friday."

The scared-rabbit insurance agent, president of the county board of education and a strong member of the old-line said, "I'll call the company first thing when I get in the office."

"I'm meeting with the staff at the Café at 8:00 and I expect your confirmation before that meeting. I want you there by 7:30 with the right answer."

After partaking of a Coke and a doughnut that some ladies brought down for the firemen, Rick ambled back down the street to look again at the smoking ash heap. Firemen were dousing the hot spots and smoke was rolling up through the hole that had been a roof. The thousand-pound giant rolls of newsprint were smoldering in the basement. When the firemen saw him, they parted reverently so he could get closer to the building and look down into the basement. The skeleton of the press stood like a charred sentry.

It was nearing 6:30 when one of the two local state police troopers motioned for him to come to the car and handed him their radio mic. "It's the governor," he said.

The publisher took it and gave the trooper a look that said, "this is private." Rick took the mic, remembering his late father worked at one of the first newspapers in heavily Democratic southern West Virginia to endorse the Republican Sean Ambrose for governor, four years ago.

After Rick provided the details, the governor excused himself, went off the line briefly and came back. "I'm sending the state fire marshal, his chief inspector and a team on my helicopter. They should be there in an hour or so. We'll have state police meet the chopper and bring them to the paper."

"Do you think, Charles had anything to do with it?" the state chief executive asked, bringing up the name of his political nemesis.

"Don't know, hate to think so," Rick responded.

"Rick, that son of a bitch would do anything, and I mean anything, to win an election," the Sean Ambrose bellowed.

While the governor was lambasting Charles, Rick remembered stories about the feud he'd heard from his father and Baxter Edwards.

Sean Ambrose won the governorship in the biggest upset in state political history. He was elected as a Republican in part because outlandish corruption of his Democratic opponent, Samuel Bowater, was uncovered by *The Bridgeburg Daily News*.

As director of the state procurement administration, Bowater, received thousands of dollars in bribes to ensure favored companies were winners in the state's supposedly sealed-bid procurement process. *The Daily News* story broke in mid-September and Bowater was never able to recover.

Sean's victory was astounding, given the Democrats' three to one statewide majority in voter registration. His campaign strategy was quiet and carefully developed. He had worked with several carefully selected Democratic leaders to overcome the huge Democratic registration margin. One of Sean's first overtures was to Lawnville's Charles Beauregard, Jr., a key Democratic leader in the southern end of the state. Charles parsed response indicate he was on board with Ambrose.

In truth, Charles played along only to get as much inside information as possible about which Democrats had agreed to support the Republican's campaign. Charles and Red had already secretly decided they'd be backing Democrat Samuel Bowater. Sean discovered Charles' masquerade when a Democratic supporter informed Ambrose of Charles's secretly working on Bowater's behalf. That discovery spawned one of the bitterest political rivalries in the colorful history of West Virginia politics. Sean wasn't on the ballot this year given a state constitution term limit for the office of governor.

"Anything else I can do?" the governor asked Rick in a concerned tone.

"Yes, Governor, they just found a city policeman who has been beaten and shot in the head. He's unconscious, and they don't believe he'll make it. I believe it's important we get him out of town, both for medical and personal safety reasons," he explained.

"Put the trooper on," the governor said.

Rick listened to the Lawnsville end of the conversation "yes, sir" and "right away, sir." The trooper handed back the mic.

Rick listened as the governor said one trooper would go to the hospital and stay with the gravely wounded policeman. A second helicopter was coming from Charleston with a brain specialist and a full medical team. The young policeman would be brought back to the State Capitol's best hospital.

The other trooper would stay at the fire scene and then go to the football field to pick up the fire marshal staff in the other chopper being dispatched.

"Anything else I can do, Rick?" the governor asked again.

"I think you've covered it all. Thanks very much," the publisher said.

"Rick, I'm so sorry this happened. Keep in touch. Watch Charles - he's a snake," the governor said as he signed off. There was no doubt in the publisher's mind the governor was inching to pin the fire on Charles.

Walking back toward his former office, he noticed the crowded had grown. It seemed like the entire town was there, *except* for Lester Brown, the town drunk, and Red.

This was strange. Red only lived two blocks away and Lester was always around.

When Rick first arrived in town, he gave Lester two dollars for breakfast once or twice a week. That was until he learned Lester was always first in line at the local liquor store those mornings. After hearing of Lester's early morning wine runs, Rick cut off the cash and opened an account at Susie's so Lester could get one good meal a day.

Lester lived in the shadows around town. There were times when he'd give the publisher a news tip about something he'd seen from the shadows overnight. Once Lester told Rick he'd seen a prominent Lawnsville citizen arrested by the city police late one night while speeding through the middle of town.

When Rick checked the arrest log the next morning, the arrest was not logged, but there was a blank space left on that page. The following week, Rick went back and checked the old log, only to find the arrest had been noted. Despite his station in life, Lester had a strong sense of right and wrong. Rick hoped Lester hadn't met the same fate as Jim Dowling.

As Rick crossed the street on his way to Susie's, the curious onlookers parted, some patting him on the back, offering condolences. The normal early morning crowd was gone.

As Rick entered Susie's, the insurance agent walked up all smiles. "Everything is taken care of, the money will be in your account Friday."

"Oh, Orville, that's great. Thanks for taking care of this for me," Rick said.

Tear-stained cheeks and swollen red eyes greeted him as he walked into the café's meeting room. Susie herself was finishing up taking breakfast orders as he sat down with this dedicated, hard-working, and scared staff. Only two had worked on a newspaper before. The others were eager to learn, worked hard, and together had become an effective team. Missed deadlines were mostly a thing of the past.

"Let's open with a prayer," he said as he closed the door to give the *Crier* staff some privacy to discuss the future. After seeking divine intervention, Rick started the conversation. While the staff worked hard, he knew they participated in the Lawnsville gossip network so he chose his words carefully. He explained neither he nor any of the firemen had any idea what caused the fire — expressing the idea this was probably just a terrible accident. Rick's intent with this approach was to give comfort to those who might have been involved, so they wouldn't leave town and disappear.

Rick did not mention an investigative team from the state fire marshal's office would be on the scene in an hour or so. Nor was there any mention of his finding Jim Dowling's badge and torn piece of uniform in the alley.

Smiles came when he relayed his conversation with the insurance agent. That news took the financial pressure off.

As for resuming publication, he didn't have any idea. He'd be in the exile office up in the makeshift location on Winter Street later in the day. "Are you going to rebuild?" was finally asked, the question everyone had.

"Yes, indeed," he said.

They finished their breakfast in quiet conversation about what would be next. He thanked them all for coming and hoped to have more information the following morning.

When he opened the door of the meeting room, he found the standing-room-only crowd had returned to Susie's main dining room. The publisher noticed Red back in the corner with another member of the old-line network.

As one, the entire crowd stood up, clapping, whistling, cheering and yelling words of encouragement, "Don't stop now, come back, we need you," and even one, "give 'em hell."

Red's face showed shock at this spontaneous display of support. The publisher looked him in the eye and gave a big thumbs-up to the crowd. When the noise died down, the publisher cleared his throat, "Thank you so much for that," adding, "I need something from you." The chorus started up again, "What? Name it. Want us to pass the hat?

"No, no, it's not that. We need five typewriters and as much typing paper as we can get. We'll be up in Dr. Mathney's old office this afternoon or tomorrow morning. We appreciate anything you can do," he told the crowd.

"You got it, hell, yeah, we can do that," was the response.

When it quieted down, one grizzled man from out in the county stood up and looked around the room, spit tobacco juice in his cup, wiped his chin and yelled, "Want us to bring a rope, too?" giving voice to what others were thinking. One could have heard a pin drop, they waited for Rick's answer.

The publisher took his time, nodding to the concerned faces ending by staring a hole through Red. "Nobody said life would be easy, just say a prayer for us," Rick responded.

Before he got out the last word, Preacher Erwin Edward Hathaway stepped forward and bellowed, "Let us pray." Every head bowed, he invoked the Lord's mercy on the community and strength for the brave staff as they worked to move forward, ending with a solemn "Amen." Which was followed by a thunderous "amen" from the crowd who had flocked back to the café after hearing the *Crier* staff was in the backroom. Now with two blessings from the good preacher, Rick felt some comfort, not certain what the future held, but ready to face it. "It's time to go to work."

Red came over to offer his condolences. "So sorry this happened, know how it started?" Red asked, avoiding the publisher's eyes.

Number two, Rick thought, recalling the former publisher's words earlier.

"Thank you, Red, I appreciate that. Might have been lightening." Rick's response sounded gracious, but sent a message deliberately ignoring the fact Jordan County hadn't had a drop of rain in a more than a month. Red recoiled slightly, but didn't probe further. That was the job for the former publisher, to fill him in about the true nature of the situation, or so he thought.

Rick did know one thing. He for damn sure wasn't going to tell the former publisher the truth about any of it. He would feed him some information, but it would be a matter of misdirection.

Rick found the fire chief, said he'd be back in a half-hour or so. He headed to the hospital to visit with the Dowling family. As he entered the hospital, he felt the eyes watching him. His doctor was in the lobby and greeted him asking, "How'd it start?" Perking up, the publisher registered this was number three who had asked the question, the former publisher, Red, and now the doctor. Interesting all were connected to the old-line.

As Rick got off the elevator on the third floor, which housed the Intensive Care Unit, he heard some crying and saw the black minister with Jim Dowling's mother and family.

Rick held back and the minister motioned for him to join the group. He shook hands all around. Then he knelt down and looked into the stricken mother's eyes.

"Thanks, so much for coming," the oldest brother said, patting him on the back. "Sorry to hear about the paper."

"That's not important," Rick said, devastated that – Jim Dowling - their son and brother might die because he had stepped forward to try and protect Rick's dream. "I spoke with the governor earlier and he's ready to send a medical helicopter with a brain specialist and a full medical team. They can take Jim to

Charleston. It might be best," the publisher said, not certain what the reaction would be.

They looked at each other with relief. "Our prayers have been answered," Eleanor Dowling said as Jim's siblings nodded in agreement.

"I apologize for interfering, but I am so very concerned," Rick continued. Jim's oldest brother, Joseph, motioned the young publisher away from the others.

"Dr. Stans was just by and was not encouraging. We have to try everything." Just then, the doctor came up and greeted the publisher, who told him the medical team was on its way.

"That's good and might be our only chance. We just can't do any more here," he said.

Turning back toward the grieving family, Rick continued, "The helicopter should be here in about an hour."

"He was doing the job he loved," Eleanor Dowling said, fighting back the tears.

"Please call as soon as you find out anything there," the publisher said.

They agreed one of the brothers would leave now with the mother so they could be in the State Capital when their wounded son and brother arrived at the Charleston medical center. A sister hoped she'd be allowed to ride with his brother in the state helicopter.

"Jane and the kids can come and stay with us if you all want," Rick said to the brother who would be driving the mother. The Dowlings's preacher stepped forward and asked them all to gather for a brief word of prayer.

"Let me know if there's anything I can do," the publisher said before turning down the hall to thank the trooper for his help and returned to the elevator.

The doors opened and Rick was standing face to face with the hospital administrator. *Number four,* flashed before the publisher's eyes. "Rick, so sorry to hear about the paper. Do you know how it started?" the two-faced hospital administrator said in smarmy greeting.

"Thanks, Will, think it was an accident," Rick replied.

"How's Jim doing?" the hospital overseer asked.

"Not well," the publisher said, adding, "Sean, is sending a medical helicopter, brain specialist, and medical team to take him to Charleston." He knew the name Sean would be instantly recognized. Not missing a beat.

"Whatever the family thinks is best," was LeMasters' response, Academy-Award winning concern oozing from every pore.

"Thanks, Will," Rick said as the elevator doors closed.

When Rick arrived outside the old storefront turned *Crier* office, Rick found four people waiting with typewriters. "Hope this helps," Jane Ellen Young, a retired Jordan County teacher said as her handyman toted an ancient relic. "I've had it since I was in college. Keep it as long as you need it." The young publisher guessed she had been out of college for at least thirty years.

He left the crowd under Al's care and headed to the post office. His arms were loaded with mail, another of "The Ladies of Lawnsville" pounced. Rick nearly stumbled - when she seemed to rise out of the floor. It was barely noon, and there she was, all decked out – hat and all - like she was going to church. "I'm Sarah Jane Lively," she said, sticking out her hand and ignoring that his arms were loaded with mail. Her tone sent a clear message 'You're supposed to recognize my name instantly.'

Of course, he had heard of THE Sarah Jane Lively, but this was the first time he'd had the pleasure of being in her presence. She lived up to her advanced billing. Sarah Jane lit into a tirade about the former publisher every *Crier* column he'd written the last thirty years. "And you're still letting him write that trash," she sputtered. Rick had no doubt she intended to give him the lowdown on everybody in town. Finally, she took a breath and he was able to extricate himself, explaining he'd love to talk longer, but he had to get back to the new *Crier* office.

The newspaper's new landlord was waiting. "I stopped by the phone office and they hope to have the phones in this afternoon with the old *Crier* number and five extensions," Foster Black said as he dusted off a desk that had seen better days, but would do the job. "I should have three more desks later today and the other tomorrow," he said apologetically, embarrassed for not having everything already in place.

"Thanks, Foster, great job," the publisher said.

The staff wouldn't be there until the next morning, so Rick renewed his efforts to find what could be the missing link to finding out who set the fire and put the police officer on the brink of an early grave.

He began a trek that would take him to every street and back alley in Lawnsville's small downtown. Under the blazing sun, he moved along, delayed by well-wishers and the inevitable questioners. Never wavering in his quest, he politely excused himself and moved on. Sweat soaked him as he came to the final corner. Nothing. A violent vision flashed before his eyes—Lester could have met the same fate, or worse, as Jim Dowling. Then the publisher remembered.

Chapter 17
From Nobody to Somebody

After a brief stop at Susie's, he headed down a steep path that led to the ancient river; Rick spotted Lester at his favorite fishing hole. The line of his worn-out fishing pole was taut from the swift current.

It was an out of the way spot, hidden by trees but just 300 hundred yards or so from the smoldering old brick building.

"Leave me alone, get the hell outta here," Lester yelled, shaking his head and waving the publisher away. Rick slipped and slid down the path and sat on a rock upstream from the recognized town drunk, now fully sober. Finally, Lester unsteadily came over to sit on the rock next to his breakfast benefactor. Shaking like a leaf, Lester's eyes darted back and forth to make sure no one had followed Rick. Not wanting to scare Lester off, Rick asked how the fishing was and whether Lester wanted the extra hamburger and coffee, he'd brought along.

Lester darting eyes stopped, focused on the bag. "That'd be great," he stammered.

"Been looking for you, thought you might have come out to see the fire," the publisher began cautiously.

"It's really rough for me right now," Lester said as he gobbled down the burger, washing it down with lukewarm coffee.

"No, don't know nothin' 'bout that, heard the sirens, but went back to sleep," Lester mumbled, his eyes on the fishing line, careful not to meet the publisher's stare.

"Lester, they shot Jim Dowling and he could die. It's really bad," Rick explained, knowing that the policeman's mother had always set a meal on her back porch at least one night a week for Lester. "The Dowling family has always treated you right, Lester."

"They flew him to Charleston and probably will operate on his brain sometime tomorrow. His mom, sisters, and brothers are down there with him. Lester, you need to tell me what you saw. It's important," the publisher probed, sensing the broken man sitting next to him had seen something that terrible night. The old drunk shook his head and looked to the heavens as if seeking divine intervention to carry him away. "Lester, I've never told anybody anything you've ever told me; you know you can trust me."

"They'll kill me sure. Wouldn't take them a minute to decide," Lester responded.

The publisher beat back the urge to grab the old codger and shake him for all he was worth, "Lester, there's a way you can help with nobody in town knowing a thing. I can set it up."

"Rick, I'm nobody, ain't never been anybody, won't ever be anybody, there's no way they wouldn't know and besides, no one would believe me."

Rick let out a breath as he skipped a rock across the river. "All you have to do is give the FBI their names, and they will break one of them, and that person will testify," the publisher said, almost pleading, knowing that Lester might well be the only chance there was to solving these crimes.

"You mean, I wouldn't have to go to court?" the old drunk said, now clearly focused. "Lester, I'll call the FBI and tell them you are willing to talk to them, I'll take you to Charleston," the publisher said softly.

"When?"

Trying not to let the exuberance he was feeling get into his tone, Rick said, "I'll call them and try to set it up tomorrow morning."

"Okay, I'll think about it, go call them, I'll be around," Lester said in a determined voice that surprised the publisher.

It took some doing, but the publisher persuaded a friend in the U.S. attorney's office to ask the FBI to talk to Lester at the home of another friend in an out-of-the-way neighborhood over-looking the state capital.

They were on the road early. Lester was shaking like a leaf for the entire two-hour trip. Dedicated alcoholic that he was, the thin-as-a-rail man didn't mention wanting a drink on the entire ride to meet the FBI investigators.

They'd stopped on the turnpike for a solid breakfast, so Lester was good until at least noon and they were scheduled to meet the agents at 9:00 a.m.

When they arrived, his buddy's wife told Rick where the coffee pot was and left. As she disappeared around the curve, the two FBI agents and an assistant U.S. attorney arrived, driving the standard agency four-door sedan.

Lawnsville's town drunk was really shaking now and said he decided he wanted to go back to Lawnsville and not to speak to the FBI. "Lester, those bastards tried to kill a policeman whose family has always been kind to you. It's time for you to do what's right," the publisher said gently but firmly.

Lester relented and entered the house. They sat in a comfortable room, paintings of Civil War battles covering the walls.

Lester had one rule: he wouldn't talk to the federal agents without the publisher present, and on that point, there was no debate. He trusted Rick and seemed to see through his alcohol-induced fog and understand it was perhaps one of the few times, if not the only chance, to be somebody. After making a call to the U.S. attorney explaining Lester's ironclad condition, the FBI relented, cautioning Rick that everything he heard was confidential and part of an ongoing federal investigation and not under any circumstances for publication. Rick readily agreed.

As the publisher guessed, Lester had seen the whole thing. The unofficial mayor of nighttime Lawnsville was sucking on his last bottle of wine for the day in the shadows of the alley that ran next to the *Crier* building. He had just rolled over into his nest under the rotting back porch of the old Brown family home. "This loud noise woke me up. They busted open the *Crier* back door with a sledgehammer," he explained.

Since they hadn't broken the alley street light yet, Lester got a good look at all four. "I know everyone by name; they rough me up every now and then when they had been drinking. Meaner than snakes, all of 'em," Lester related.

"They all had jugs. Guess it was gasoline to start the fire. Not long after the four broke into the building, Jim Dowling drove down the alley in his patrol car. He stopped when he saw the back door was smashed. Then got out of the patrol car, drew his pistol, and went inside. Then there was a commotion and two or three shots. Nobody came out of the building for a few minutes. Then two of the men came out carrying him all covered with blood and put him in the back seat of the patrol car. Two got into the patrol car and drove down the alley to where the other car was parked. "Both cars came back up the alley, leaving two inside the newspaper," Lester said he had dozed off and woke up when the two came back and re-entered the building.

Lester stopped, his face covered in sweat. He asked for a glass of water.

"You're doing fine, Lester," the publisher assured him, patting the town drunk on the shoulder.

"They'll kill me if they find out," Lester stammered. "That won't happen," one of the agents assured. After gulping the water and asking for more, Lester continued.

"The four of 'em came outside, threw bottles with lit fuses through the windows on the alley side right across from me. "The fire started everywhere, first on the first floor and then in the basement. The whole building was on fire. They ran down the alley, got in the car and drove away. When they were out of sight, I went down the alley to the railroad tracks and doubled back to my room at Mrs. Brown's out on River Street. Then I heard the fire station siren."

Surprising the publisher and the FBI agents, Lester's voice was strong, certain and steady. The agents looked at the assistant U.S. attorney.

Given Lester's well-earned reputation as the town drunk, it was clear the U.S. Attorney did not want—under any circumstance—to put him on the stand before a grand jury, and certainly not call him as a witness during a trial.

"It is not enough," the federal lawyer said, shaking his head.

"Lester, we need the names," the chief agent explained. *He can't stop now*, Rick thought as he studied Lester's beet-red, weather-beaten face.

"Can I have some more water?" Lester asked, despite the frightened look on his face. Lester straightened his back, brush a hand through his dirty, matted hair.

"They hurt one of the few who ever treated me decent," Lester said as he looked into Rick's eyes, tears running down his cheeks.

"Jonathon Johnson, Sammy Burton, Joey Brighton, and Donnie Joe Smith, they were the ones. I don't know which one shot Jim Dowling. That happened inside," Lester said as he grabbed for the water glass.

"Is there anything else you want to add?" the agent asked in his best Bureau tone.

"There's nothing else to tell. I hope this will help," Lester said, looking directly at the publisher.

Lester was well aware of the danger he could be in by talking to the FBI, but he trusted Rick, who always took the time to talk to him in a respectful manner and provide an occasional breakfast. And for the most important reason of all he wanted to do what was right – be somebody.

"Is there anything we can do for you?" one of the agents asked when the interview was over.

"Yes, I have a sister in Florida and want to visit her for as long as she'll have me. I got to get out of town. If I don't, I will end up like Jim Dowling," he whispered, his hands now trembling.

"We can make arrangements for the visit," the lead agent offered.

First, the federal investigators would determine if the information was credible. Given Lester's circumstances, they knew it was possible he just wanted some attention.

If the four turned out to be viable suspects, following face-to-face interviews, the federal investigators would select the one most likely to turn on the others.

There would be incentive to make a deal on the serious criminal charges - attempted murder, possibly soon-to-be murder of a police officer, kidnapping him, setting fire to a business engaged in interstate commerce using dynamite. Even with the identifications of the four who committed the crimes, the federal agents would soon have an uneasy feeling they were not likely the real brains behind the crimes.

Right before he and Lester started on their trip back to Lawnsville, Rick called the assistant U.S. Attorney who participated in the questioning aside. *The Crier* publisher handed the federal prosecutor a plastic bag with the badge attached to the torn piece of cloth and a picture he'd taken in the alley the night of the fire.

Chapter 18
Curtain Call for Puppets

A week or so after the fire, the smoke had finally stopped drifting from the huge rolls of newsprint, Charles and Red got together.

"Shame about the fire," Charles said in a sarcastic tone as he settled into the creaky old chair.

"Truly hurts my heart," Red replied in a mocking voice as he ceremoniously took out his red bandana and mockingly dabbed his eyes.

They had fanned the flames of hatred seething in Samuel Johnson by using manipulated surrogates to set the wheels in motion. And the prime suspect was the city street commissioner who had sworn in front of several witnesses, including police officers, he was going to "firebomb that damned newspaper."

"Heard anything?" Charles asked.

"No. Neither Avery nor the mayor has stopped by the store even once since the fire. The mayor usually comes in almost every day," Red related.

Charles had a thought. "Avery might have figured out that we used him to carry the message."

Red found it interesting there wasn't one rumor about the fire in the gossipy town. Not a word. None of his regulars had heard anything. Normally, Sheriff Eddy Bill, who had close ties with the state police, would keep Red informed. But that source was shut tight. The FBI, ATF and U.S. Attorney's office were running it all and keeping a lid on it.

Charles' extensive network throughout the state capital had turned up only one rumor, that some senior FBI and ATF officials from Washington had set up shop in Charleston to manage the investigation. He'd heard nothing that indicated the investigators had any progress.

"Charles, I did pick up rumors around town that the FBI had questioned Samuel, Jonathon, and the Mayor. It didn't seem much came of it," Red reported.

"Even if anything does, it is all on the city and Wayne's people. If something does happen, how will people find out about it?" Charles smiled, thinking about the smoldering hole just three blocks away. The two politicos were certain the puppets at the end of their strings had ensured old-line success Election Day.

Without the troublesome *Crier* stories, the spotlight on shenanigans of old-line officeholders had disappeared. Reports coming into Red indicated old-line candidates were well received as they campaigned around the county. The two veteran politicians saw no way that their golden rule theory of politics—"money, money, and more money"—wouldn't carry them again on Election Day.

After their rosy assessment of the old-line's election prospects, Charles brought the conversation back to the puppet show.

"Red, what do you think happened after your conversations with Avery and the Mayor? Did the mayor ever talk to you about Samuel's rant down at City Hall, when he said he was going to firebomb the newspaper?" Charles inquired.

"He might have said something like that would solve a lot of problems," Red replied.

"What did you say to Avery and the Mayor?" Charles asked.

"I stuck to what we planned – just told them both we thought the *Crier* stories were unfair and seemed that Rick was out to get him and Samuel," Red explained. "Did not say anything about taking action."

"Given what Samuel said in front of witnesses at City Hall, there's no doubt he's the No. one suspect as far as the FBI is concerned," Charles said and took a long cool swig of lemonade.

Red still did not understand the implications from the fact it was him, not Charles, who had raised the curtain on the puppet show. He thought both he and Charles were invisibly pulling strings, not realizing that he was also a puppet.

It was all smiles as Charles and Red turned to discussing details of the post-fire political situation in Jordan County.

"I got some more interesting news today. Joseph stopped by and said the paper won't be back for months, and maybe not ever," Red assured. "Says he might have to take it back over because of Rick's money problems. Then as luck would have it, right after Joseph left, Orville stopped by. I mentioned how much construction and renovation costs had increased the value of county buildings and it was about time for the county to increase the insurance coverage. Right after that, I told him it would be a shame if Rick's insurance check got delayed. He made the connection."

As a member of the school board, Orville did not directly bid on the school system's insurance or any other county business. However, he did enjoy a special relationship with an insurance agency in the next county that wrote all the county coverages and always made sure Orville received a gracious reward for his assistance in securing Jordan County's business.

Turning back to the upcoming Election Day, Red added, "I'm getting together with the boys tonight and will let you know what's going out in the county."

"It will be interesting to see what impact the *Crier* fire has had on the campaigns out in the county," Charles responded.

Chapter 19
Black Ink Is Gone: Sun Brighter

At the last meeting of his Election Day war council two weeks before, Red was upset and surprised by what he heard. Every member reported people were paying attention to the stories in the *Crier*, asking questions and talking to their neighbors.

For as long as Red could remember, Joseph Ballengee made sure the old line had a near-monopoly on the local news and, more importantly, kept any mention of Baxter-backed candidates to the bare minimum.

Then things changed. Under Rick Hill, all candidates for county offices and state legislature got a free write-up with a photograph right on the front page.

Under Rick Hill, the *Crier* was covering meetings of the city council, school board, county commission, and even the hospital board. It had become an increasingly troublesome situation for the old-line and getting worse. But all that changed on that Tuesday night when the flames tore through the one-story brick building on Church Street.

Tonight, he expected a much different tone. Smiles had replaced the gloom. The banter was jovial as they settled around the old oak dining room table.

"Well, you all are in a fine mood," Red remarked as he started the discussion. "That's good to see. After that last meeting, I thought I'd just been to a funeral."

Norma's iced tea was going to be popular tonight. It must have reached 95 today, so he had her make two pitchers before she left for prayer meeting.

Red was ready with great news and looked forward to listening to reports from around the county.

"What are you all hearing since our last meeting?" he asked.

Chomping at the bit, Old Jim Bob got right to it. "Folks are ready to vote and I think the mountain is as settled as I've seen it in a long time. We're gonna run good up and down the slate.

"We even had Eddy Bill come up the other night talking about the sheriff's race. He said how important it was to get folks out to vote to keep things moving along. It was the best I'd ever heard him."

Buried in his fog of euphoria, Red failed to pick up on the fact that Eddy Bill hadn't mentioned the board of education races. This was an indication of just how toxic Edward was for the old-line going into Election Day.

Jim Bob continued, "This last week, I haven't heard hardly anything about Edward and his stuff. Folks are still talking some, but nowhere near what it was before," the king of the mountain reported, not connecting the decrease in talk with the pile of ashes on Church Street. "Oh, and there's some talk about what a shame it was what happened to the paper," he added. The others all nodded in agreement. This confirmed his recent conversation with Charles about the positive impact the *Crier* fire had on the old-line Election Day fortunes.

"Joe, how is it up Long Branch?" Red asked, knowing he'd get a good overview with no drama thrown in.

"A lot like what Jim Bob said, 'cept there's still talk about Edward up my way, some saying he should just get out of it. There's a rumor, only heard if from one person at the post office. Said his daughter worked at the hospital and heard that Edward had beaten up that school teacher he was fiddlin' with. Has anybody heard that one?" Joe asked, looking around the room.

A mumbled "no" came from the others.

"Sounds like one that damned Baxter would start. He's been getting really dirty on this one," Jim Bob said, almost shouting.

If they'd been watching Red, they'd have seen visible recoil at Joe's comment. That was an issue he'd thought would disappear with the ambulance run to the Greenbrier Hospital arranged by Will LeMasters. Red relaxed when the others indicated that they had not heard such a report.

"Joe, what else have you got?" Red asked as calmly.

"Our Candidate Night at the school for the board candidates was bigger than anyone thought it would be - standing room only. Most folks just came to listen. But some of the questions got Edward riled. He didn't like being put on the spot."

A miss for Red: each of the group before him agreed about the tone and crowds at Candidate Nights.

Joe continued, "Like Jim Bob said, folks mention the fire at the paper, but I'm not hearing as much now as right when it happened," he related. "In moving around the county this week, I found that folks are ready for the election. The sheriff's race has always seemed pretty much settled. Eddy Bill has been out our way and is solid. Bill Joe seems to be running okay for the county commission, but a lot of folks are still unhappy about his vote against hiring the lifeguards at the 4-H camp," Joe concluded as every one of the other county council members nodded in agreement. Yet another important message Red missed.

"Not much talk at all about Joe Ed Green, who is Baxter's man running for the commission. He's been out our way, but not much talk," Joe noted, satisfied that his end of the county was ready to give the old-line candidate overwhelming majorities.

"John, you picking up anything?" Red asked, turning to the newest member of the group.

"There's a big family in Hopping Hill who's been mad at Eddy Bill over him not hiring the son of one of the brothers as a deputy. Haven't heard much from them in the last week or so. And Baxter and his bunch are going around trying to tie Bill Joe to Edward. That dog won't hunt," he concluded using the country phase for an idea that folks just won't believe.

"Charlie, what are you hearing from the preachers?" Red asked, casually checking out a rumor that had come to him this afternoon at the cleaners about some preachers out in the county were planning to take their despising Edward out on the entire old-line ticket.

"Not much stirring on the surface, but I understand some of 'em are really upset about Edward's messing with that young teacher, what with him being a deacon and all.

"My brother's a part-time preacher and knows most of them. He says only a few are really upset about Edward, but all of them are upset about the Catholic running for president. There was talk that several might preach a sermon on it on the Sunday before the election," the teetotaler of the bunch observed.

"He did say if we fattened up their collection plates a little, we could get all but three or four to 'get religion,'" he said, slapping his knee with a big old hee-haw that brought a chuckle from some of the others.

A smile flashed across Red's face as the last point was made, confirming Charles' golden rule of politics - money can solve any problem, and what it can't solve isn't a problem in the first place.

All eyes turned to Red as he stood up. "I know you all have been concerned about how much money there'll be for the precincts. You don't have to worry, they all will have $150 or so more than in the last election. There will be an extra $50 for your precinct captains for carrying precincts for all three of our board candidates." He paused for the delighted war council members to quiet down. "I'll lay out the exact amounts when we give out the envelopes Sunday afternoon before Election Day. Now, this is going to be tough. We have to make sure our votes get to the polls," he explained, as they were now hanging on his every word. "Tell the precinct captains to have at least three cars hauling on Election Day."

Given the tone of the meeting, Red was sure the school board races were in good shape. Eddy Bill's race for sheriff seemed locked up, and Bill Joe Ratliff seemed certain to keep the old-line majority on the Jordan County commission.

It had been a long time since he'd seen his boys so confident. His conversation with Orville Brown had only added to his confidence about the coming Election Day.

Chapter 20
Insurance That Wasn't

When Rick had examined business insurance policies for the *Crier*, he bought an expensive one that included business interruption coverage and provided for staff salaries for six months if something happened. He thought back to insurance agent, Orville Brown, telling him before that first staff meeting the check to cover operating expenses would be in his account by the Friday after the fire.

Later that same day, an hour after his emotional meeting with the staff in Susie's backroom broke up, the worm showed up at the makeshift office. Rick barely heard the knock at the door, it was so timid.

He knew from the expression on Orville's face trouble was afoot. Rick sat back and waited to hear what type of manure was about to be spread. The message was like a sucker-punch to the gut. The mealy-mouthed agent started by apologizing and then pulled the rug out from under the publisher. "Rick, I'm sorry, but they tell me that no money will be available until the final report from the state fire marshal's office is received by the company's main office and reviewed by company lawyers.

"There's a strong possibility that no money will be paid under the policy if arson is found to be the cause," the worm related.

Rick got up from the ancient chair a retired school teacher had brought by and walked toward the agent, noticing how fast the worm was backpedaling, "Orville, just remember this: I'll be around long after this election and you can bet I have a very long memory."

"Sorry all this happened; there's just nothing I can do," the worm said over his shoulder as he fled. From the smugness of the worm (a designation the agent would have forever), Rick felt there was a lot more going on. Little did he know how right he was.

Right after the worm left, Rick was still seething when he picked up the phone. It was a *Washington (D.C.) Standard* reporter wanting to expand on the national wire story about the fire. Rick mentioned that his hope for the paper's quick return just had been dashed by his insurance glitch. The veteran Washington reporter seemed to have a sixth sense about how things worked in small towns, asked, "How's the agent connected?"

Tongue fully locked in cheek, Rick, said, "Wow, I never thought of that."

To which the *Standard* reporter chuckled. "Right. Sounds like you're under a pile of bullshit."

To which Rick responded, "And it's getting deeper."

Right now, the most important thing for Rick was to hold his staff in place and hope for a miracle. Slumping back in his chair, he thought about the meeting he'd have to have with his staff the next day. There'd be no bullshit; he tell 'em right up front there's no money, and he wasn't sure when there would be.

He left the office with a heavy heart and drove home as dark of night crept over the small town. His sagging spirits brightened as he listened to the adventures of the school day from his two high-spirited children as they sat around the table enjoying one of Anne's special meals.

Once the kids were in bed, he related the latest on the insurance money to his wife. "Bastards," Anne fumed, using her favorite descriptive word, as she came into the living room with a couple of beers.

"I've got to make payments even with the paper destroyed, or we'll lose everything," he lamented. He thought about the small inheritance from his grandmother disappearing. They tried to boost each other's spirits as they climbed the stairs to bed. Tomorrow would come too soon.

Rick got up an hour early and left for the office careful not to wake Anne or the kids, wanting extra time to prepare for his loyal, hard-working staff. He knew the first step was to be honest with them.

Chapter 21
Antiques' From the Heart

When Rick arrived at the *Crier* office in exile, there were more well-wishers, and curious people along the sidewalk peering in the windows of the *Crier*'s decrepit new office. Several were lugging ancient typewriters dug out from cluttered basements, attics, and garages. Others brought along tables and chairs, most of which looked like contemporaries of the typewriters. Almost everyone asked when the paper would be out again. Once they had departed, Rick locked the front door and fled to the quietness of his cubbyhole to think before the meeting with his staff.

A loud knock at the door brought him back to reality. The staff was excited and arrived early to look over the new office space that had originally been an auto dealership, then a flower shop, and vacant for a year before becoming the new home for the *Lawnsville Crier*.

After the meeting the previous morning, they all relaxed, having been assured their paychecks would keep coming. Things were about to change. From the forlorn look on Rick's face, they could tell that all was not well. Rick turned toward the anxious faces, not knowing which words to use or how the staff would react.

They sat on sagging chairs, refugees from a junk pile.

"This is hard for all of us," the publisher said in a serious tone. "Now, I'm going to get through this little meeting; it just might take me a while. I have some bad news. Things have changed since our meeting yesterday," he said. "Afterwards, I learned that the money from the insurance policy might not be available at all and we won't know until the company reviews the final report from the state fire marshal's office," his eyes moving from one weary staff member to another.

"I expect to get into the safe in the next couple of days and the checks for this week will be ready Friday."

"What happened between our meeting and now?" Belinda "Billy" Amherst, the community news editor, asked, getting right to the point.

"I wish I knew," Rick responded, the pain clear in his somber tone.

"That son of a bitch," Al blurted out. "They've got him dragging his feet on this."

"I'm here, and he won't stop me," Rick continued. "I know your jobs are important to you and your families. I understand some of you might need to get another job just as soon as you can find one. I don't want you to hesitate for one minute to do that if you have to.

"For those of you who stay, I want you to keep track of every hour, hell, every minute. My intent is for you to be paid for every minute you put in eventually. I'm not sure when I'll be able to pay you again if you can stay on."

"Orville Browne is holding this up," the get-to-it community news editor groused. Rick knew he could count on her to wade through the bullshit and get to the heart of the problem.

"Let's just say, he's being thorough in examining the claim," the publisher said with a noticeable flash in his eyes.

"Bastard," was her only response. The local agent—his moniker, the worm, recently and for eternity bestowed by Rick.

Not wanting to dwell on that problem now, he moved on quickly. "First, the paper will be back. I just don't know when. I'd like you to talk it over with your families and let me know in the next day or two if you can stay on. My plan is to have the news staff to start tomorrow morning. Gather the news, work on the stuff you were working on, cover the meetings and games as you usually do, write the stories, date them. When we start publishing, all of them will be run. For the back shop crew, I don't have anything new. Just keep checking back. Questions?"

There were none. Then the community news editor spoke up. "I'll be here tomorrow."

"Me, too," the sports editor, the managing editor, the ad manager, and the classified ad person called out almost in unison.

"Can we get any better typewriters? These are a mess," the community news editor said in her normal, tough-love tone that had endeared her to the staff.

"I've got some sharp pencils and erasers if that'll help," he said, smiling. "See you tomorrow." He retreated to his office.

Rumpled, as usual, Al bounced through the door of the postage-stamp office of the publisher.

"I have an idea. I'd like to go visit the *Tribune* [West Virginia's largest newspaper and Al's former employer] to see if they have any surplus supplies and stuff laying around.

"I still have a few friends there," he said, looking forward to his midnight requisition to help the *Crier* rise from the ashes. The publisher chuckled at the thought of Al stalking the halls of his former employer and taking everything that wasn't nailed down.

Turning serious, he motioned Al to a weather-beaten desk in the corner. "I'm a bit worried and would like your thoughts. I'm thinking our friends in Overton are going to offer to buy the *Crier*. They haven't returned my phone calls about printing. I think they're circling like vultures," the publisher said.

"Wouldn't be surprised at anything that bunch does, they are squirrelly at times. You just need to keep moving forward," Al replied.

"One other important thing," Rick said. "Did you pick up anything from your buddies up on River Road?" he asked. Rick had told only the U. S. Attorney's office the fact he found the badge connecting the shooting to the fire.

"Not sure, but there was a commotion at about 2:00 in the morning. Folks heard a couple of cars racing up the road," Al replied. "Nobody heard any shots. "They found Jim Dowling way up Dang-it Hollow about halfway between the old Jeb Jones's farm place and Ivan Sowder's place. They're about three miles apart. They ran the police car up an old trail. They'd never have found it if Jim hadn't managed to flip on the police lights and siren.

"Heard anything from the hospital?" Al asked, worried about Jim Dowling his former Little League catcher. The publisher shook his head grimly.

"I better get on the road; I got Jo's van, so I'll have plenty of room," Al said as he left on his beg, borrow or steal mission. The publisher appreciated Al's effort. But the delay in the insurance claim was a cloud that could doom the *Crier*.

It was just about three weeks until the election: Twelve candidates for sheriff, a dogfight for the board of education with a majority of the seats up, the controlling seat for the commission, a ballbuster of a race for governor and attorney general, and a presidential primary drawing national attention. The *Crier* was losing thousands and thousands of dollars of desperately needed ad revenue - literally gone up in smoke.

The *Crier's* phones continued to ring. The fire story had gone national. Rick had done interviews with state bureaus of both national, every major national radio network and several major newspapers. He was careful not to connect the fire with Jim Dowling's shooting.

They asked again and again if the fire was the result of the paper's aggressive local news coverage. In a cautious tone, he said he would be surprised if the fire had been set.

Giving a graphic picture of the situation, he described the new *Crier* newsroom and what he had to work with. Just a devoted news staff and some old typewriters and furniture brought in by folks around town. He added, "I just can't find anyone to print the paper for us."

No more had he hung up than the phone rang again, a repeat call from the veteran *Washington Standard* reporter with some questions regarding the Democratic presidential primary between Minnesota Senator Hubert H. Humphrey and Massachusetts Senator John Kennedy. Flattered at being asked about the race with national implications, Rick made what would prove to be a bad prediction: "There is no way that the Catholic John Kennedy could win in this heavily protestant state," he said.

The *Standard* reporter then asked about the fire and what the publisher saw for the paper's future. "What's your goal?" the reporter asked.

"To get the damned paper out. It could be months," he replied, laying on more of a Southern drawl than he normally used.

The old guy on the other end gave a big "hell, yeah," from his vantage point of having been raised in the South. "How are you going to do that?"

"Hell, I don't know, I've got a smoking hole in the ground. I don't have a press, no composing equipment, I'm in a hell of a mess, but I won't give up." Rick caught himself, apologizing for his profanity-laced comments.

"Hold it right there," the veteran scribe said. "Shit, you wouldn't be a real newspaperman, if you weren't upset. Good luck, kid," he said, right before the click. When he was finished with the interviews, Rick was wrung out and it was well past normal quitting time, so he called it a day and headed home for a fitful night of sleep.

Little did the publisher know the old reporter's story would run in papers across the country. And it would include the reporter's (not Rick's) opinion that the fire had been set. Then the *Crier* publisher was compared to the pamphleteers who helped to fan the flames of the American Revolution.

Rick was up bright and early the next morning, not knowing what to expect that first day for the newspaper that couldn't print. He wasn't sure how long the staff would be able to keep their commitment to work without pay.

He unlocked the door, flipped on the light and was facing of old desks; sagging, squeaky chairs and an array of ancient typewriters.

The first to arrive was the community news editor spewing a four-letter word tirade about a confrontation at the grocery store the night before. It started when someone within her earshot said, "The damned paper got what it deserved." Billy got upset, just telling the story. But with a wicked smile said, Joe Morris, the store-owner, had to intervene. "It was not pretty," she said, chuckling at the thought of the missed opportunity to have a brawl in front of the meat counter. "Dumbass," she said as she sat down before the antique typewriters.

When the sports editor arrived, the three had a short conversation. She was to contact all the stringers in the four adjacent counties, telling them to get their news in on schedule. The sports editor would take all Little League baseball team photos as well as arrange for one of the high school's team.

Next through the door was Larry Loom, the ad manager. His was the most perilous situation: a new job, a young, stay-at-home wife and a new baby. Normally, he would be a major cog in the operation, with no paper nothing for him to do. The publisher feared he'd be offered another job. The ad manager said his parents and in-laws had called offering help. He said he'd be okay for a couple of months.

Rick had called both funeral homes and told them to keep the obituaries coming in, that eventually they'd be published. Obits were among the best-read of all the newspaper's sections and in some respects an effective free advertising tool for the funeral homes. Even if the funerals have already been held, the obits will provide a clipping for the families and inform readers who had passed.

The typewriters so generously offered were of the Stone Age, barely above hammer and chisel on stone. With pencils sticking out of the gray tightly wrapped bun perched on the top of her head she was struggling with the antique, the community news editor was muttering language used in front of the meat counter last night. Anyone walking into the office would think the sports editor was a sailor given the words pouring out his mouth as the typewriter clanked along.

He was amazed at the enthusiasm of the staff, on the phone gathering information, banging out the stories, not knowing when they would be published. It had been three days since the fire and it was about three weeks before the election.

Al burst through the door. "I need some help unloading the goodies."

Never had Rick seen a van more fully packed - new typewriters still in boxes, photo lab equipment, and five almost new desk chairs. Rick wondering how Al made it out of Charleston without being arrested for burglary asked, "Are the Charleston police far behind?"

"There was an old storage room where guys had been putting things for years. An old friend of mine unlocked the door and said, 'Take what you need.' I did, he even helped me load it up."

First in line was the community news editor, grabbing a typewriter, "Hallelujah, now we can get some work done," she yelled.

There was no doubt in Rick's mind that the worm - with strong encouragement from Red and Charles—was holding up the insurance claim. The two, no doubt based on what Joseph Ballengee passed along, believed the scheme made it certain the *Crier* would not be back before the election and could drive the publisher out of Lawnsville for good.

Al's bonanza was a bright spot in an otherwise dismal outlook for the *Crier*'s resurrection.

Chapter 22
A Bolt of Lightening

When the eccentric publisher of the Overton paper identified himself, an *Oh, shit,* crossed Rick's mind. Another thought, *He'll probably make some half-assed offer to take the pile of ashes off my hands.*

"Rick, I apologize it took me so long to get back to you. We had to make some arrangements. We are very sorry about what happened and want to print the *Crier* for as long as you need us and you can pay us when you can.

"We are in the process of rearranging our production schedule so we can start next week," the third-generation heir to the paper spit out in his well-known machine-gun, high-pitched, don't take a breath voice.

"God bless you. We'll be ready," Rick mumbled, choking with emotion. "We need to keep this very quiet. I'm still not sure what I'm dealing with here," he explained.

"Understood. I'll talk with my production manager and get it set for a week from today."

"We can begin bringing over copy and dummies on some of the older stories in the next day or two. I expect the first edition will be two or three eight-page sections. The next one could be more," Rick said, hoping congratulatory and political ads would be rolling in after the first one hit the streets.

"Fine. I'll be back to you this afternoon to confirm the date and schedule," the Overton publisher responded.

"God bless you, Reginald," Rick said again. "Glad we can help. We can't let the bastards win!"

Al, the grizzled newspaper veteran knew something was up when he saw the relaxed grin on Rick's face as he walked around the ramshackle newsroom looking over the staff's shoulders checking on the progress of their stories. Al motioned toward the cubbyhole office. "Okay, what have you gone and done now? You got that shit-eating grin."

Shutting the creaking door of the filthy almost office, Al sat down in an equally dirty chair. "Okay, let's have it," he said.

"I just got hit by a bolt of lightning. No less than Reginald Lawrence Thurmond III just called: They're going to print the paper."

"Oh, shit," the old newspaper veteran said, several octaves softer than his usual microphone voice. Rick and Al then developed a plan to keep the word from getting out. A key part was a clever cover story that would spread around town. "Make sure we tell it that we're hurting for money and the staff's about to quit," Rick said.

"Shit, old dear," Al blurted out with customary understatement as he and Rick were putting the pieces together in the cramped space.

Not a word was to leak out. They'd call the route drivers and in-town paper carriers the night before the phoenix edition and tell them there'd be an important meeting at the paper's office the next day. In the four days since the call from Reginald Lawrence Thurmond III, Rick had gathered all the catch-up stories the staff had written, made dummy page layouts, slipped out of town after dark and took them to Overton. There were all the Little League baseball team pictures, the Woman's Club news and piles of copy from the stringers spread across four counties and nearly two scores of obituaries. As the plan developed, the vision of flames licking through the windows and from the roof of the old *Crier* building flashed before Rick Hill's eyes.

Since no arrests had been made, he thought his fears about another attempt to stop the *Crier* were well-founded. No hints the investigation was making progress. Red seemed to be sending one or two of his gofers in every day to buy classified ads.

They all got the same story directly from the publisher: "Sorry, it could be months before we're able."

Rick's staff members were reporting that some of Red's cronies would stop them on the street, in the grocery store and even in church, trying to get information about the *Crier*'s return. "I just don't know if we'll be back before the end of the year," Rick would tell the many folks who'd stop him on the street, but he had his staff hard at work. The office pace was picking up; everyone was getting their regular beat stories done. Rick was staying late to finish several special election-related stories.

Thurmond had agreed he could handle a first edition of three eight-page sections, tripling the normal *Crier* page count of one. Rick increased the press run by 1,000 - thirty percent more than the normal.

Not taking any chances of a leak, Rick told the staff it could be the end of the year before the *Crier* could come back. He told them if anyone, and he meant anyone, said anything about the paper in a threatening way, he wanted to know about it as soon as possible, even if it was 2:00 in the morning. As he hoped, the staff shared his frustration with their friends and neighbors. This was all part of Rick's plan to use Lawnsville's legendary gossip network to guard the *Crier*'s secret.

Without the threat of newspaper stories getting folks stirred up and talking, Red and Charles thought prospects for the upcoming election couldn't be better. Money from their favored statewide candidates was more than they had projected. And, of course, more would be added to the thousands they'd squeezed from the two presidential campaigns. Optimism the reformers got from *Crier* stories had literally gone up in flames.

Chapter 23
Fake Left, Run Right

Rick's plan to bring the paper back was shrouded in layers of secrecy, a bit of outright deception thrown in. Nobody except Al knew the details.

An important element of the new publisher's fake left, run right strategy was his almost daily visits with Joseph Ballengee when the former publisher dropped off his column.

Now, as Rick was plotting the paper's resurrection, he decided to use Joseph to keep Charles and Red and their cronies in the dark. It could decrease Joseph's credibility with the old line when the *Crier* re-emerged. Recently, Rick told his predecessor, "That he felt the staff was ready to quit and the owners of papers in surrounding counties had turned down his requests to print the *Crier*, making it virtually certain the paper would not reappear until a building was built and a new press purchased. As he listened, Joseph shook his head in contrived sympathy. The quick drop off his column and then head—as Rick suspected—to report to Red. Rick's intent was to keep everybody else off balance so the first edition would hit 'em between the eyes.

Closeted in his cubbyhole, he finished up the main stories for page one of the *Crier*'s phoenix edition. He called the route drivers out in the county telling them to come to an important meeting the next day at noon. Rick deflected all questions, saying it was about the future of the paper. He knew several of the drivers had connections to the old line and would report the call as soon as he hung up. After overhearing Rick's conversations with the route drivers, the staff just looked at each other and shook their heads. In phone calls to all the in-town carriers, Billy, the community news editor, told them to report right after school the next day.

The staff headed home that afternoon, very sad, certain that tomorrow they would be told the effort to bring the paper back had failed and it was closing for good.

Under cover of darkness, Al and a friend with a 12-gauge shotgun would drive in a closed van over the curvy, hilly, highway to the angel's printing plant, 45 minutes away. It was a long night at the guardian angel's printing plant. The *Crier* wouldn't get to press until after the Overton paper's run was completed at 1:30 a.m. Rick, in a separate vehicle and with an armed friend riding shotgun, took off in a different direction, all part of the plan to throw off anyone watching. Both had copies of the stories in case Al and his shotgun warrior ran into trouble. Since no arrests had been made in connection with the fire and Jim Dowling's shooting, it was prudent to be prepared.

Just before dawn on phoenix day, before Lawnsville awoke, Rick and ad manager Larry Loom helped Al and his friend unload the precious cargo. The bundles were brought into the 100-year-old building through the alley loading dock and stacked in a dark back corner covered with a black tarp. His devoted staff all worked in the front office area and none noticed the tarps when they arrived at 7:30 a.m.

At 10, Rick called the staff together and suggested they all take an early lunch. He was buying. Using the same grave tone he'd used in the calls the previous night to the route drivers, he said he would have an important announcement after they'd finished lunch. With glum looks on their faces, the staff began to open the tasty bag lunches Susie, the perky café owner, had personally delivered. To make the gloomy atmosphere worse, Rick and Al went into the publisher's cramped office to eat away from the others.

At 11:00 sharp, he and Al walked out of his office. The stony silence of the staff spoke volumes: all expected Rick to announce the *Crier*'s obituary.

Anne, pulling Harriet and Charlie along, walked in the door just as he began. He stopped, went over to his children giving them big hugs and kisses and a heartfelt "I love you" to his wife.

Rick had planned to open with talk about the fire, but he couldn't hold it in. He motioned for the staff to follow him into the dark corner of the back room, threw back the tarp and yelled, "Let's get these papers put together!" There was stunned silence as the staff looked at the large bundles. A loud cheer erupted, joined by hugs and jumping up and down around the room. "Now, know that you have made me proud—let's get to work," Rick continued. "The route drivers will be here in an hour. We need to have all the sections stuffed, papers counted, bundled, and ready to go. "Don't make any calls to anyone about what's going on; it has to hit with a big splash." Wanting as many people as possible to get this phoenix issue, the publisher added 20 papers to each bundle.

A ragged sheet covered the door to the back room so that anyone walking by wouldn't see what was going on. Rick was snapping photos of his staff getting the *Crier's* phoenix edition ready. The route drivers—somber expressions on their faces—assembled in the dingy front office certain they'd be told the *Crier* was dead.

As he was with the staff, Rick had planned a gloomy opening, but his emotions took over when he looked into the faces of another group that had stuck by him. He motioned for them to follow him to the dark corner of the back room to the tarp-covered bundles. He pulled back the tarp and said, "Get these damned papers out of here; they're trashing up the place!" A wild cheer went up. Al had the camera out as the publisher helped load the cars.

In spite of the town's proud tradition of "everybody knowing everybody else's business," not one word of the impending return of the *Crier* had leaked.

As he soaked in the jubilation, Rick remembered his first experience with newspapering - when he was less than a month old his mother took him to the *Logan Banner* to visit his father the sports editor, and the back shop foreman inked his foot and pressed it to newsprint. His trip down memory lane was interrupted by the clamor of customers lined up at the counter, eager to get their copy of the phoenix issue of the *Lawnsville Crier*.

Chapter 24
Up From the Ashes

Crier Burns/ Investigators: Cause 'Difficult' To Unravel

The 72-point two-line banner screamed across the top the front page.

It was a straight news story. Splashed under the headline was a large photograph of the blazing roof caving in as flames shot into that early spring morning sky. On the inside, there was a two-page spread of photographs, including pictures of firemen from each of the county volunteer fire departments. Another section had all the Little League, junior high and high school sports stories and photos the staff had prepared since the fire. Then six pages of obits.

The Lawnsville lightning-fast gossip network was going full steam. Word spread, "the *Crier*'s back." A crowd instantly appeared on the sidewalk in front of the *Crier* office. Many cheered and clapped as the route drivers loaded the heavier than usual bundles into their cars lined up in the street in front. A financial success it wasn't. It hit the streets with no ads. To ensure that the return remained a secret, Rick decided not to tip his hand by soliciting ads. While giving a complete report on the fire and efforts to fight it, Rick took great care with the lead story to make the perpetrators think they had gotten away with it.

"This fire is a difficult one to unravel. Not much left to examine," the story quoted the state fire marshal as saying. Included was a similar statement from a U.S. Alcohol, Tobacco and Firearms headquarter spokeswoman in Washington, D.C.

A separate story on the shooting of city policeman Jim Dowling was featured under the fire story. It included a statement that "those investigating the shooting have not indicated any connection whatsoever between it and the fire."

Rick smiled as he reread that gingerly crafted sentence; the investigators hadn't said there wasn't a connection either. Rick had been in the room when Lester had given the FBI the names of those he'd seen through a drunken stupor from his nest under the Brown house's back porch. He was required to agree that nothing from that meeting would ever be published. Rick did not know the status of the investigation but got a feeling it was progressing well.

A few days ago, and with a sense of urgency, Rick had followed up and told an assistant U.S. attorney he was concerned about further violence against the staff when the paper came back, given that no arrests had been made. His own experience a few days hence, on a deserted country road would prove his concerns valid.

It was ironic and irritating to Rick that he'd been scooped by every newspaper in the country on the burning of his own paper. So, in a very inappropriate request, he had asked the U.S. attorney to announce any indictments in a morning press conference rather than the normal afternoon announcement, so the *Crier* would be the first with the story. The U.S. attorney only response, "You certainly have been through a lot."

"Amens" and shouts of "way to go" and "give 'em hell," came from the boisterous crowd as the route drivers pulled out, their horns honking, and headed for every dirt, pothole-filled road up every hollow in Jordan County and adjacent areas of four others. Once the drivers were out of sight, the crowd surged into the newspaper's office quickly. Among the first in line was one of Red's gofers who bought ten copies, scurrying off up the street as if on a top-secret mission.

One glaring omission that would raise eyebrows - not one election-related story. In an amazing coincidence, the former publisher, old-line political kingpins and the reformers would come to the same conclusion on the omission.

About two hours later, the unveiling was repeated when his young, in-town carriers got out of school. They cheered and scurried off, excited at the prospect of once again earning spending money. In a particular hurry was the carrier who delivered to the offices in the courthouse. He started out with 20 more copies than usual and soon was back for more. The extra 1,000 copies were exhausted in short order.

Rick hoped—correctly, as it turned out—that the catch-up articles and photos would make readers realize how important the paper was in their daily lives.

Rick called the staff together, "We're going to have to work a little late today because tomorrow's edition might be 32 pages, maybe more."

The grumpy Overton publisher had volunteered he would be delighted to accommodate up to 40 pages for the next day's issue. Not in his wildest dreams did Rick think the *Crier* would fill five sections.

Smiling, ad manager Larry Loom, phoenix edition in hand, began making the rounds to stores along Main Street offering advertising opportunities for tomorrow's issue. An hour later, the publisher's heart sank when the ad manager came through the door shaking his head, a frown shadowing his face. "How'd it go?" Rick anxiously asked the seemingly dismayed manager.

"You'll not going to be happy," Loom groaned, eyes on the floor. Rick's heart sank. "Well, we're going to need the whole 40 pages," the now-beaming Larry gushed. "Gotchya, didn't I?"

"You can be a real asshole," Rick responded, his heart beating again. "It was unbelievable. Everybody wants in. Some are taking congratulatory ads and others hard retail. We'll be filled tomorrow and the next day."

"Okay, we have to remake the dummies and see where we stand," Rick said, glad to be having some revenue coming in but it couldn't fill the hole created by the worm's delaying the insurance claim.

About an hour after the route drivers hit the road, Rick took a troubling call from one of them. As he was deciding what to do about the call, he spread a copy of the paper on his weather-beaten desk. After reliving the disaster, as written in his own words, and thinking about the effort it took to get this edition on the street, he strutted out into the front office bubbling over with pride. "Damn, you all did a great job. I'll be back in a few minutes. I'm going up to the courthouse."

"Give 'em hell," the community news editor groused, a wide grin on her wrinkled countenance. Whistling as he walked in the sunshine for the two blocks, Rick almost broke into a run. He would find that just about everyone in the courthouse had a copy of the *Crier*. The carrier Rick passed on the way through the courthouse's front doors had a big smile on his face and pockets full of coins.

Respectful glances from some and scornful glares from others greeted Rick as he followed his customary route to every office, beginning with the assessor's on the right, inside the front door. He casually inquired as to how everyone was doing and did they have any news for him.

Several old-line supporters just glared at the Rick and threw their *Crier* into the trash when he entered an office.

Saving the best for last, he climbed the stairs to the sheriff's office on the second floor of the Civil War-era courthouse. Eddy Bill was talking to a deputy with his back to the door when the publisher walked in, but turned when he noticed everyone looking toward the door. A crooked smile crossed the lawman's face as he shook the publisher's hand and motioned him into his inner-sanctum. "Damn, you got this place shook up," the Jordon County sheriff said. "Thought you might have a story about the election, particularly the school board," he said, more a not-so-subtle probe than a statement.

"Can't do that without talking to Edward. Heard he wasn't in town, might be down in Myrtle Beach," Rick replied, returning the ploy. "Right before he left, he came down and paid for a full-page ad endorsing you for sheriff. It has a big picture of you two at the 4-H Ox Roast," the publisher jabbed. "Shit, that's all I need—he's just a mess," the sheriff retorted before catching himself.

"Hell, I gave him the ad for half price," the publisher said, chuckling, not letting up as the sheriff shook his head, unable to hold back a laugh.

"Well, we might have a story about him and that young teacher who was taken to the hospital over in Greenbrier," Rick said, alluding to a rumor that had been circulating but he couldn't confirm. "You all investigating what happened to her?" the publisher asked, smile completely gone.

"Haven't gotten a complaint," the sheriff said avoiding the reporter's eyes as he admired his newly tiled floor.

"Did you talk to the ambulance driver? I hear he beat the hell out of her and broke her arm," Rick, turned junkyard dog, pressed.

"There's nothing I can do without a complaint," the sheriff said, almost pleading for this thread of the conversation to end.

"Sheriff, the ambulance drivers are bound to inform law enforcement if they suspect a crime has been committed."

"They haven't contacted me or the state police. I'll get the word to you if anything moves on that," he uttered.

"Thanks, I appreciate that," Rick said, allowing their chat to move along, understanding the sheriff just made a major concession. He was aware that Eddy Bill owed his present position to his close relationship with the old-line over the years. But found the sheriff had been straight with him for the most part and the concession the sheriff had just made was from a dedicated law enforcement officer.

"One more thing, Sheriff, today up on Rocky Branch, two guys wearing ski masks and waving guns tried to block one of my route drivers and threatened her if she didn't dump the papers into the ditch. Nothing else happened and they took off in an old red pickup when she waved her shotgun at them. "But if there's even the hint of another incident, there'll be big trouble. I think all my route drivers are hunters," Rick said.

"Message received. If there's anything I can do, let me know. We can add some road patrols," the sheriff said as he extended his hand.

"How's Jim Dowling coming along?" the sheriff asked with concern for the dedicated young law enforcement officer.

"Seems certain he won't be a policeman again," the publisher answered gravely.

"Damn," the sheriff said, bringing his fist down on the desk that had been his great-grandfather's when he served as sheriff 80 years ago.

"Well, I'd better get back to work, have to get next month's paper out," the publisher teased with a wave of the hand.

The sheriff was shaken by the publisher's report the city policeman might have suffered permanent injury. It was the only shooting of a police officer the sheriff had ever heard of in Jordan County.

"Oh, one more thing, Eddy Bill, just between you and me, I need the number of Charles' condo in Myrtle Beach. You know, Edward's no good, he could have killed that girl," Rick pressed.

"Sorry, can't help you. I have no idea what the number is," the sheriff said as he took his personal phone directory out of his top drawer. He opened it carefully, folded back a page, got up and said, "I'll be right back. Make yourself at home."

Dazed by the new meaning of "sorry, can't help you," Rick took down the number and returned to his chair. He was re-reading the *Crier* when the sheriff came back. "Well, I'd better get back to the paper, good visiting with you, Sheriff. Watch for that ad tomorrow," Rick said with a broad smile.

"Don't let the doorknob hit you in the ass," the sheriff retorted.

Walking back towards the paper on this gentle spring day, a troubling reality pushed aside the enjoyment of his saunter. *They* might strike again. Coming through the door, he motioned Al and the ad manager into the cubbyhole. They again reviewed the decoy plan to get the next day's stories safely to the printing plant. "Keep the CB on. Either of you run into trouble, let me know," the publisher said in a no-nonsense tone.

While the general public had not fully grasped the impact the fire could have on the election. The county political factions were well aware of it. Since the fire, the reformers had just about given up of having any election success, while the old-line's confidence grew every day.

But it was what was not in this first post-fire *Crier* edition that had both sides making the same assumption.

Chapter 25
He got the message

Half an hour after the decoy strategy session with Al for the second comeback *Crier* edition, Rick was in his office with the lead story. There was a knock on the door.

"Come in," he mumbled, without looking up.

"Congratulations. "Nobody thought you'd be back, certainly not before the election. How'd you pull this off?" Baxter continued his bad eye twitching.

"Clean living, the good Lord smiling on us, and the staff working like hell," Rick said, jumping up from behind his battered desk to accept the handshake.

"Will there be any political stories, or did they scare you off?" the political warhorse asked. "They are saying you got the message," Baxter said, hiding his own qualms behind the innocuous "they."

"You'll just have to wait until tomorrow to see," Rick said, taking no offense at the questioning.

"You asshole," Baxter said over his shoulder still not sure if the crusading publisher would return to his pre-fire aggressive, straightforward-style journalism.

Up the street and around the corner, Red had the same thought after he read the *Crier*'s first post-fire issue. He was visiting with a customer, when one his gofers busted through the door, slamming it back against the wall, shattering the glass.

"The *Crier*'s back and it's bigger than I've ever seen it," he panted throwing nine copies on the counter. "Big crowd up in front of the paper and the route drivers are off, horns honking, folks shouting amen. Seen some of the drivers had guns, like if anything happened."

Trying to hide his surprise, Red looked up said, "Well, that's something. Don't know how long it'll last. It's all over town he's 'bout out of money."

After his visitor left, Red hurried back to his office, scanning the paper as he picked up the phone.

"Charles, the paper's back, got three sections. Big story about the fire and another about Jim Dowling's shooting. Seems there's trouble with the investigations. No advertising at all.

"Rick was lying to Joseph all along, probably guessed he was feeding everything to us," Red observed.

After he and Red agreed to meet a little after the 5:00 p.m. closing, Charles went outside and looked up and down the street for his neighborhood papergirl who should be along anytime now. Red went back to his listening post by the front door. For the next thirty minutes, he carefully checked the entire 24 pages, and then double-checked. *He got the message*, Red thought.

In a perfect case not seeing what you're looking at, Red didn't notice that nearly everyone on the sidewalk was talking to a companion and pointing to the paper. Rick's plan was successful; people realized they missed the *Crier* and they were reading every word.

Red turned over the "closed" sign and headed back to his office, just as Charles arrived, calm written all over his smiling face. Red was eager to give Charles his other big news but knew it had to wait until after they discussed the *Crier*'s reappearance. "Evening, Red. What's new, or should I say what's news?" he asked.

"What are you so cheerful about?" Red asked, sensing his cohort's observations might match his own.

"Well let's just say I've got a feeling," Charles said nodding back toward Red's office, its walls covered with campaign buttons, bumper stickers and signs from decades of county elections.

After he'd set out the customary ice-cold cans of sweet lemonade, Red said, "Nothing about the election, not one word."

Savoring the first taste of the cool libation, Charles smiled, "Now that tells me that our young friend has seen the light."

"Think he'll stay away from the election stuff altogether?" Red asked, joining his friend in a non-alcoholic refreshment.

"There's not a doubt in my mind. The stories will be toned down and anything controversial will disappear. This is one of the hottest campaigns in years and he's didn't mention it in this very first edition back.

"With our precinct organization, I really don't think, even with election stuff would hurt us at this late date. The pre-fire *Crier* is gone.

"Oh, he has to run campaign ads. He needs the money, but I think that'll be about it," Charles confidently said. He'd see this was wishful thinking in 24 hours.

"What's Joseph think?" Charles asked.

"He's madder than hell Rick lied to him. But he believes Rick got the message too. This is a major change, given the heavy election coverage before the fire," Red opined.

"Folks were surprised the paper had been able to come back. Said they were glad to see it and remarked about their kids' or grandkids' pictures and all the club news."

"They better get used to it, because that's all they'll be seeing in the *Crier* from now on," Charles said, certain that they didn't have to worry about the *Crier*'s political meddling anymore.

Finally, Red was ready to announce his big news. "I got a call from Charleston this afternoon. Kennedy'll be holding a rally here Wednesday. I told Joe McCarthy that Humphrey was coming on strong since he was here three weeks ago. I asked for another $10,000 to hold the line. I added the preachers were really hitting the Catholic thing hard in nearly every sermon," he reported.

"Think you'll get it?" Charles asked, his mind running like a cash-register tape.

"He said money was really tight; one of his people is going to stop by the store before the rally," Red added.

"Kennedy will be coming from Bluecord College, so you'll need to have Humphrey signs all along 20," Red said, recalling the tactic they used three weeks when his people used the same tactic to show the Humphrey folks the intensity of the Kennedy campaign along that same stretch of highway. "I've asked for another $10,000 from the Humphrey folks myself. They're running low. But think I could get $5,000," Charles said. Folks couldn't remember an election when the two weren't on the same side. The split had nothing to do with politics - it was strictly a financial calculation.

When it became clear that John Kennedy and Hubert Humphrey would be spending a lot of money on their primary campaigns in the state, Charlie and Red decided they would split their endorsements in order to maximize the money they could get. Using this scheme, the two had already received a total of $25,000 from the two campaigns and more was on the way. Only a fraction of that money would actually show up in the precincts on Election Day. Most of the dollars were resting in their joint safety deposit box at the local bank. Both smiled as they took sips of cool lemonade.

"Something interesting happened yesterday," Charles said, leaning forward in his chair. "I got a call from our good publisher yesterday morning asking about my little talk with Edward out at the park. Interesting that he found out. He asked if I'd sent Edward out of town until after the election. He was just fishing and I handled it. Told him I'd heard Edward was campaigning all over the county. Said I hadn't seen him since I'd had some meetings in Charleston the last few days.

"Funny, his calling about that when he didn't have anything about the election in the *Crier* today. I guess he's just putting on a good face. Said he was just checking and really couldn't go with a rumor, and he even thanked me for taking the time to talk to him," Charles' smile indicated the mistaken assumption he'd hoodwinked the *Crier* publisher. The two parted in great spirits, certain that Rick Hill had gotten the message sent by the flames.

Just two blocks from Red's cleaners, Rick Hill was bent over the newly acquired typewriter, piecing together a jigsaw story that would shatter the notion "he got the message." It never ceased to amaze him how seemingly insignificant and unrelated tidbits of information, when put together, often formed a powerful story. Folks would hear something, call the paper and ask if it's important. Most of the time it wasn't - by itself. Then another snippet would come from another direction. With a little digging, a good reporter would find another piece that fit and then another. The lead story for tomorrow's paper was a prime example.

First, from the sports editor's sister-in-law, a waitress working in the dining room at the state park, told him while waiting on a nearby table, she heard Charles and Edward have an argument. A red-faced Charles slid an envelope to Edward who counted the $100 bills. Charles put more money on the table as he got up to leave. It was just two days before Edward left for the beach.

That same afternoon another piece of information. The *Crier's* always-probing—to some, downright nosy—community news editor was at the gas station near Edward's neighborhood. Her standard "what's new?" led Bernie station owner Randell Williams to open up without much encouragement to tell about Edward Whitmore's latest fill-up. "His daughter, Lucy, was in the back seat and said she got out of school so they could go to Myrtle Beach to visit Uncle Charles' place. Then Lucille yelled, 'That's a secret, Lucy.' Seemed strange, they're going to the beach right in the middle of the campaign," he concluded.

After berating Bernie about the high price of gasoline – now 22 cents a gallon – Billy headed straight to the *Crier* office and barged right into Rick's office.

Then still another tidbit. Al bumped into one of Edward's neighbors, who related, "They rushed around packing the car, all in a hurry. They didn't even ask us to watch the house like they always do. One of Edward's kids told my Donnie that they'd be gone to the beach for a whole week."

After listening to Al, Rick said. "Damn, Al somethings going on here. I got to do some checking."

In a quick visit to the courthouse to check the voting records, the publisher found that neither Edward nor his wife had filed for absentee ballots, confirming that the trip wasn't planned. The jigsaw pieces were fitting together, but all had to be confirmed for the story to see the light of day. Rick decided to jump into the lion's den and call Charles about his breakfast with Edward.

Rick timed this call just before the *Crier's* phoenix edition was to hit the streets so Charles wouldn't be on guard. The power broker had inside information from Joseph that the paper wouldn't be back for months. "As far as I know, Edward has been working the county pretty hard," Charles said.

Debating with himself on how to pose the next question, the publisher lightly asked, "So he's in town?"

"As far as I know. I've been in Charleston the last few days," Charles responded automatically—too quickly. So the publisher decided to go for broke.

"I understand that you and Edward had an argument at breakfast up at the park," Rick said, firing what he was certain would be the last question of the conversation.

"Oh, we were just catching up," Charles said, shaken a bit by the extent of Rick's eyes and ears. "When do you think you'll have the *Crier* back?" Charles inquired.

"Well, I'll tell you, Charles, we're not really sure, but it could be months," the publisher responded in a tone that purposely reeked of defeat and resignation.

"Too bad that the new teletype equipment you got was broken," Charles said, not knowing the former publisher was the only person Rick had given that specific information.

Whether this story would run or not depended on a final call made just after the route drivers left with the phoenix issue. Rick took the tiny piece of paper with ten small numbers he'd copied from the sheriff's private phone book and placed a call to Area Code 803. On the third ring, Edward's bubbly wife picked up and was shaken when the publisher identified himself and asked to speak with Edward. "Just a minute, I'll get him," Lucille said.

"That's a nice condo Charles has down there, isn't it?" Rick asked before she put the phone down.

"Oh yes, it was so nice of him to let us use it. Here's Edward," she said, not realizing she had confirmed an important fact for the story.

"What the hell do you want?" Edward said.

"Just wanted to see how you think the election is going," Rick responded.

"It's going so well, I decided to take a little vacation and hope to be back before Election Day," he said, obviously surprised by the call.

"Wanted to ask about the campaign. It seems Wayne Adkins is really working hard to get you all re-elected," Rick observed.

"Wayne is really helping us out. We've been close friends going all the way back to grade school," Edward confirmed not realizing he was tying his re-election bid to the city's problems.

"Did Charles suggest that you all take a vacation before the election, because of that incident at the Forest Hill School?" Rick asked, reporter's hat firmly in place.

"No, no, he doesn't tell me what to do. Me and Lucille just decided we needed a break. The campaign's been hard on her."

"Do you think that the school employees understand the issues of the election," the publisher asked, to see if his exile had mellowed Edward's view of things. It hadn't.

"Yes, I do. Like I told you in that interview, people working for the school board need to understand who's in charge. I believe they do now. Those who understand will be the ones who'll keep their jobs," he said, again proclaiming his my-way-or-the-highway philosophy of personnel management.

The conversation had ended. Rick did not mention the envelope because he really had no idea what that might be about.

Now that he had the final piece of the jigsaw, Rick finished the story that would be one of the *Crier*'s most-read stories leading to Election Day.

Chapter 26
Don't Mess with Granny

While the story describing Edward's sudden beach vacation would get the most attention, another much shorter one at the bottom of page one would remind people of the dark influences at work in Jordan County. It related how two masked men tried to block a *Crier* route driver on a rural road. They sped off when the gun-toting grandma waved her shotgun. The short, four-paragraph article didn't mention the driver's name or the location of the confrontation. Nor did it mention that such action was a federal crime and had been reported to the U.S. attorney's office. Rick wanted to keep the perpetrators thinking they were getting away with their crimes.

As the route drivers arrived, Rick invited Ethel Bowman, the driver who had been harassed the day before into his office to see how she was holding up. "Take more than snot-nosed kids to keep me from making my deliveries," she said, seemingly insulted that Rick would think otherwise.

"Did you see who they were, Ethel?" Rick asked, smiling at the grandma's toughness.

"Couldn't tell. The both of 'em had on them ski-mask things," she blustered. "But they turned tail when I waved my shotgun at them," she added.

"W*hat* were they driving?"

"An old red pick-up, dirty and a little banged up," Ethel related with disgust, proud of her always spotless 10-year-old truck left by her late husband. "Let 'em try it again. They'll end up over at Miller's," she said in a booming voice that carried through paper-thin walls. The whole staff was howling at her mention of the local funeral home favored by Democrats.

"Anyone riding with you today?" Rick asked, his concern evident.

"My nephew, Hubert, he's got a new deer rifle. My grandsons are waiting at Talcott to hook up with us for the rest of the route. I don't need any of 'em, just letting them come so they'll feel like they're helping out."

Rick led her out of the cubbyhole and turned to one of the other drivers. "They really liked all the pictures of the school kids and 4-H clubs," Jimmy Jameson related, confirming Rick's belief about the *Crier*'s importance to its readers. Rick noticed some drivers were reading the story on Edward's sudden trip to Myrtle Beach. They were offended reading all over again about Edward's threatening the jobs of the janitor, cooks, and bus drivers at Forest Hill School if they didn't support his re-election to the school board.

"It just isn't right. Enough is enough," proclaimed Lenwood Ellis, a retired school bus driver who delivered the *Crier* in the Middle Mountain area of the county.

"You'd better watch, or they'll burn this place down, too," the crusty, gun-toting grandma said as she took up a pinch of smokeless tobacco wedged discreetly between her cheek and gum.

Just as the route drivers were pulling out, the carrier who sold papers in the courthouse came through the door, "I need 25 more. The courthouse is all buzzing about his one," he panted.

The reactions weren't limited to the seat of county government. "That son of a bitch," blasted from the mayor's City Hall office. "Get me Samuel," he said, standing over the city clerk's desk. It was just after noon when Red caught up with Charles who'd been called to Charleston for a meeting to discuss last-minute strategy with Sammy on how to counter a late surge by one of his opponents for the gubernatorial nomination.

Of course, Charles had an answer for the would-be governor: "Money, more money, and more money." Charles was organizing the southeastern part of the state, so he was a key to the success of Sammy's campaign. He hoped to come out of the strategy session with another $8,000 to $10,000.

In the middle of a crucial part of the meeting, Charles excused himself to take what was announced as an urgent call. Without a hello, or any other greeting, Red exploded, "Charles, you aren't going to believe the paper today. It's a story on Edward's trip to Myrtle Beach. I don' know how he did it, but Rick called your condo and talked to Edward and Lucille. That dumbass told him that he was so certain about the election that he felt he could take some time off to be with his family. Rick also quoted you as saying that as far as you knew, Edward was campaigning hard all over the county. This is not good. The whole damned town is talking about it. To make matters even worse, the story mentioned Edward, Orville, and Yancey running as a team and the mayor's strong backing for all. It mentioned Edward's threats to the staff at Forest Hill School," Red sputtered.

Charles listened carefully, "I'll be back early this evening so stop by the cleaners about 6:30. Sounds like we need to talk."

"Anything wrong, Charles?" Sammy asked as Charles returned, a bit peeved by the interruption of this important meeting.

"No, no, I truly apologize for the interruption. We have a couple of new young people in the campaign that don't understand what 'important' means," he said smoothly, getting nods around the table.

Charles return trip over the winding roads from the state capital would have made the moonshine runners proud who were the foundation for NASCAR. Red handed Charles a copy of the day's *Crier* when he came through the door and they headed back to the office. While Charles sat absorbing the story, Red got a couple of lemonades out of the old refrigerator. "Have you gotten any calls on this?" Charles asked, still reading.

"Just a couple asking what we were going to do. People came in all day talking about it, asking if it was true," Red related.

"I told all of them that Rick had been after Edward's hide since he bought the paper and that this was just a hatchet job.

Edward's wife had been feeling poorly, and they just wanted to get away."

"Did that settle them down?" Charles asked. "Yes, it seemed to. Some don't like the paper much anyway," Red said.

"That's not the worst part. The mayor stopped in, really spitting nails over the story. He ranted about how he'd do everything he could to get Edward re-elected. He was cussing and banging the counter. Said something had to be done to stop the paper once and for all. As he was walking out the door, Wayne thought Rick would have learned his lesson from the fire. That he wouldn't walk away the next time," Red concluded.

"I tried to settle him down and told him this was not a big deal and it would be forgotten before Election Day. Didn't do any good. He still left upset. Charles, I think Wayne's going to do something else," Red said.

"If something else happens the FBI will camp out here until hell freezes over," Charles said. Patting a freshly pressed white handkerchief across his forehead, Charles added, "Red, we just have to hope Wayne or anybody else in that bunch doesn't do anything stupid. And if they do, remember, this whole mess is the mayor's problem. It's theirs and that's where it'll stay."

Really believing it would because they said so, Charles and Red turned to Edward's exile. "Stick with the story about his wife being ill," Charles instructed. They didn't grasp the image people would get from reading the story—a politician sunning himself on the beach, bragging that he had the election in the bag.

"What do you think will be coming from the *Crier* between now and the election, Charles?" Red asked.

"To be honest, Red, I don't believe anything Rick does between now and the election will make any difference," the tone-deaf politician concluded.

On that self-assured positive note, they shook hands and called it a night. Prudent analysis of the recent rise in the old line's political standing would show that it had occurred in the last three weeks, not because of organization and the golden rule of dollar signs. It was because the pile of ashes appeared on Church Street.

Chapter 27
'Almost Hell' On a Country Road

Gauging reaction to stories was usually difficult, if not impossible, for Rick Hill, but it wasn't a mystery how *Crier* readers felt about Edward's trip to the beach. The telephone lines into the paper were jammed.

Most liked the story, but his community news editor had taken several calls containing real threats, a couple in the same angry male voice that referred to the fire as a message for the paper to shut up. "Most are cheering us on. But some real nasty ones. Some smartasses bitching about us making things up," she groused in a tone that rivaled a chain saw at work.

"I got about three threatening ones from the same person," the sports editor reported.

Deeply concerned about the violence already directed at the paper and Jim Dowling's shooting, Rick viewed such calls as threats not just to him but to his dedicated, hard-working staff.

"Eddy Bill, some of the calls were really bad today. They talked about the fire and said next time I won't be walking around. Staff thinks the same two or three people made those calls." Sharing Rick's concern, the sheriff said he would put extra patrols out if the publisher felt it necessary. Knowing he would take the offer before they pulled out tonight, Rick said he'd think about it. He didn't want to accept the offer now because the departure time might leak to those who, for a second time, might want to try and stop the *Crier*.

It was just before 8:00 p.m. and the vans were ready to pull out. Rick's call rousted the sheriff, relaxing in his favorite chair, watching his favorite TV show. Fully focused, the sheriff said,

"I've got to call out another deputy and relocate two already out, but hell, I said call. When do you need them?'

Rick said, "We'll be on the road in 15 minutes."

"You really are an asshole. How about not pulling out for half an hour?" the sheriff barked.

"If you see something, use your CB and let the deputies know where you are," Rick instructed Al and Larry. As the armed drivers walked toward the vans, no one noticed a slight movement in a dark doorway across from the *Crier* office. They intended to walk to the vans so anyone watching wouldn't know which van had the "gold." However, to the shadow, Rick seemed to give extra attention to one particular decoy van – the one he was driving.

The three vehicles departed Lawnsville in different directions. Driving the winding road south along the lake, Rick tensed as he saw headlights fast approaching from behind. Two vehicles sped by - an older red, beat-up pickup that, for a reason he couldn't pinpoint, looked familiar. Its bed was filled with old barrels. Following closely was a black four-door sedan. Their taillights disappeared around the curve on the far side of the lake bridge that connected the sparsely populated Longwood area with the rest of Jordan County.

Riding shotgun with Rick was Al's close friend, Larry, who had volunteered and brought along his 12-gauge. As they headed up the hill and around a curve just beyond the south end of the bridge, a row of barrels filled with burning logs blocked the road. The obstruction was in a narrow part of the road, so Rick couldn't get around it. There was no one in sight as the publisher brought the van to a stop about 60 feet from the flames. Rick hit the CB button saying, "We got trouble – end of bridge." There was no response. He and Larry slowly got out of the van guns in hand.

Three men wearing ski masks and carrying long guns and lit up by the flames came around the roadblock. They ordered Rick and Larry to drop their guns.

"You just don't learn. We're gonna shut you up this time," one of the armed men shouted words used in phone calls to the paper that afternoon. "Get away from the van," he growled as his round ricocheted off the pavement and hit the van. A fourth man with a gun came out of the shadows behind the roadblock and pointed toward the van.

"Let's use the van for cover and run back down the highway and try to get into the woods," Rich whispered to Larry. The four masked men started moving around the roadblock toward the van as Rick and Larry moved toward the woods keeping the van between them and the advancing gunmen. The four got around the van and spotted Rick and Larry at the edge of the woods and began firing. Rick and Larry got off a couple of rounds sending the gunmen back crouching back behind the van. "Damn you," one of the gunmen yelled as they resumed firing.

Larry and Rick backed deeper into the woods, their eyes never leaving the masked men trying to kill them. A yell sliced through the crisp spring night as a round ricocheted off the pavement and grazed Rick's left leg. He fell against a sturdy pine. Then a bullet ripped into Larry's left arm, he dropped to his knees but got up and grabbed Rick's jacket and pulled him through a muddy ditch deeper into the woods. Despite his wound, Rick picked up this shotgun and fired two shots toward the advancing masked quartet, causing them to again retreat behind the van. With his good arm, Larry dragged the bleeding, cussing newspaperman to the cover of two towering oaks as bullets ripped through trees on all sides.

"I dropped my gun when they hit my arm," Larry whispered in desperation. "Hell, I only got six shots left," Rick responded as they watched the four moving toward the woods from behind the van.

As the bright moon came from behind a cloud combining with the flames to illuminate the woods where Rick and Larry were hiding, a screaming siren came from the direction of the bridge. The marauders stopped dead turned and ran back past the van toward the roadblock. One of them tossed a lighted flare through the windshield. Car doors slammed, and what sounded like two vehicles roared off, tires squealing, as the van's gas tank exploded. "You know 'em?" the publisher asked as he and Larry watched from the woods.

"Nope, but if I meet them again, I think I'd recognize their voices," Larry said in his slow, easy drawl.

No more were the words out of his mouth than a sheriff's department vehicle, lights flashing and siren blaring, skidded to a halt near the burning van. After he called for assistance, a young deputy, gun drawn, got out and ducked behind a fender.

"Over here," Larry yelled as he helped the wounded newspaperman out of the woods.

"Who are you?" the young deputy yelled, pointing his gun and car spotlight toward the voice. Once he could identify the two, he asked, "What happened?"

"Masked men stopped us, shot both of us, and they were coming back to finish us off when they heard your siren and ran," Rick said.

As the deputy was examining the wounds, a second siren was now coming toward them. A shaken sheriff and another deputy emerged from the second vehicle. "Holy shit!" the sheriff blurted out, looking at the publisher's leg and Larry's sagging arm both covered in blood, the destroyed van and a flaming roadblock. "You okay?" Eddy Bill asked, sweat pouring off his wrinkled brow.

"We are now. Your deputy getting here saved our lives," Rick said.

Looking over the crime scene, the sheriff instructed the first deputy to get pictures and wait for the fire department and wreckers. "Take the van and anything else you can get from the roadblock to the fire station and guard them until somebody relieves you," he ordered.

Gritting his teeth, Rick uttered a "damn, that hurts," as the other deputy swabbed the wound and applied bandages. The sheriff tended to Larry's wound. "Let's get you all to the hospital," he said.

"Can't do that," Rick said, obviously in pain, but already writing the story in his mind. He'd call Al at the Overton paper hoping to get it in tomorrow's *Crier*. "Sheriff, I need to get to the *Crier* office. It's not bad," he said, looking at the blood oozing around the bandage.

As they drove back to town, the sheriff listened intently as Rick and Larry related their near-death experience. Without saying a word, Eddy Bill groused into his microphone, "This is the sheriff, who copies? What's your 20?"

"Copy that, Sheriff 3," came the clear reply, followed by "Copy that, Sheriff 2 at courthouse."

"I need both of you to set up a roadblock at the Lawnsville side of the Greenbrier Bridge. We're looking for a beat-up, red Ford pickup and a black four-door sedan. Bring the folks in it to my office as soon as you have them. "Be careful, they're armed," the sheriff said.

"Call the emergency room and get a doctor to come to the newspaper office," the sheriff added. When they arrived at the *Crier* office, the doctor was waiting. A crowd had gathered, along with a city police cruiser with flashing lights. There were gasps as the sheriff helped Rick and Larry into the office - bloodied clothes and all—through the front door. The doctor cut off what remained of Rick's left pants leg, as the publisher dictated the story to Al. "Oh, shits" and "damns" were cascading at the other end of the phone. Larry's bloodied shirt was removed as the nurse inspected the wounds. Luckily, both were minor.

Rick looked at the next day's front page layout, "Al, put this story in place of the photo of the Brownie's visit to the firehouse" he said through clenched teeth as the doctor sewed up the wound.

"Is something wrong? You sound funny," Al asked.

"Hell, Al, read the damned story. I just got shot, Larry just got shot and the doctor is here at the office sewing me up," Rick said. "Can you get this in tomorrow's paper?'

"You know that old bastard had a typesetter stay late just in case," Al said. I think we'll be okay. But all the Brownies and their parents will be pissed at you, getting shot up like that and pushing them off the front page," Al said, and laughing at his own extremely inappropriate attempt at humor.

After the nurse and doctor left, the sheriff, apologizing, asked Rick and Larry to go over their story again. Because of the bright flames of the roadblock, Larry and Rick could describe the ski masks worn by the four men, one brown and yellow, one black and the two others blue and red.

Even at this late hour, Lawnsville's gossip network was on full alert. At 11:00 p.m., Red got a call from his cousin, a nurse at the hospital. She reported a doctor and nurse had gone to the newspaper in connection with a shooting. She had no further details.

It was 11:15 when a deputy pulled up in front of the newspaper office and rushed inside. "Sheriff, it's Joe on the radio; says it's urgent."

"You bring them to my office as fast as you can. Have Willie stay with the pickup, call the wrecker, have him bring the pickup to the fire station and put it inside, next to the burned-out van," Eddy Bill ordered. Coming back into the newspaper office, Eddy Bill said, "We got three of them. Want to come to the office with me?"

The publisher nodded and got up, using a cane the community news editor had given him as a gag gift on a landmark birthday. As they sat down in the sheriff's inner sanctum, three deputies arrived with the three handcuffed men who had been in the red pickup.

"Who do we have here?" the sheriff asked.

"Sammy Burton, Joey Brighton, and Donnie Joe Smith," the chief deputy responded.

Hearing the three names, Rick's eyes were focused. They were three of the four names Lester Brown had told the FBI were at the fire and Jim Dowling's shooting. Rick didn't react. But would call the FBI first thing the next morning.

Donnie Joe Smith, the tallest and oldest of the three, said defiantly, "We ain't got nothing to say; what's he doing here?" He threw a smartass glare at Rick, who was ready to take his cane to the one he thought might have sent the bullet ripping into his leg.

"Oh, you were just out for a Sunday drive," the sheriff said. "Mr. Hill is using a cane because somebody shot him and another man tonight. Two counts of attempted murder, I'd say," the sheriff said slowly.

The smiles vanished and Sammy Burton, the youngest, blurted, "Wasn't me, I didn't shoot nobody, I swear."

Joey Brighton lunged at Sammy, punching him across the face with handcuffed fists, opening a cut on his lip and knocking him to the floor before being thrown against the opposite wall by two burly deputies. The third man, Donnie Joe Smith, took a step forward toward Sammy, but before he could land a punch was slammed against the other wall by an even bigger deputy.

"Take the two troublemakers over to the jail," the sheriff said adding, "and make sure you tuck them in real good." The two deputies nodded in a way that told the publisher the two might have their faces rearranged during the 'tucking in.'

"Don't you say anything or I'll take care of you," Donnie Joe Smith snarled at the petrified Sammy Burton.

There was a commotion in the hallway, and one of the deputies came back. "Sheriff, those guys just tripped and fell down the stairs. What should we do?"

"They'll be all right; take 'em over to the jail, let the jailer check them out. If nothing's broken lock 'em up," Eddy Bill said. "Must be a loose board on those stairs," he said, smiling at Rick.

"Want something to drink?" the sheriff asked Sammy, bleeding from the attack.

"Water," Sammy said, confused and staring at the floor. As a deputy took Sammy to the outer office to get a cup of water, the sheriff's phone rang.

He glanced at Rick, "Evening, Red, up mighty late aren't you?" After listening carefully, the sheriff confirmed the bare bones of the incident. Rick and Larry had suffered minor gunshot wounds and he didn't expect to have anything else until the next day. The publisher noticed the sheriff hadn't told his political ally that anyone had been arrested. "News travels fast," the sheriff said after putting down the phone.

When he hung up from his brief conversation with the sheriff, Red quickly called Charles.

When the deputy returned with his young charge, the sheriff took a chair next to the trembling handcuffed prisoner. Putting a hand on his shoulder, the sheriff gently noted, "Awfully late for you boys to be out, Sammy. Let me take off those cuffs."

"We's just hanging out driving around seeing what's going on," the young man answered beginning to realize the trouble he was in.

"What was going on, son?" the sheriff asked the young thug.

"Didn't know you all were skiers. Found those ski masks behind the backseat of the truck," the sheriff said.

"I don't know nothing about that, Sheriff; never been skiing, never wore one of them things," he stammered in a voice that barely carried across the room. The sheriff reached over and picked a piece of material from a ski mask out of Sammy's hair and holding it in front of his face.

"Don't know nothin' about that either. I didn't do no shootin'," the young man stammered.

"Hard to ski and shoot. We found guns in the back seat of the truck been fired recently. What's that about?" the sheriff asked, knowing one gun found in the pick-up had not been fired.

"Maybe if we put you in a cell for the night with Joey and Donnie Joe, that'll help you remember," the sheriff said.

"Sheriff, they'll kill me sure iffen I tell you anything. Damn, I need to think."

"How many of you were out there on Bluestem Road, Sammy?" the sheriff asked.

"Out where? We was out Forest Hill way, other end of the county," Sammy said, clearly overwhelmed and trying to dance through a situation that had started out as an invitation to "have some fun and pick up 20 bucks."

The sheriff pressed on. "Who all was in the second car at the roadblock?" The prisoner fell silent and his face grew even paler, something that had seemed impossible moments before.

"You know that you all could take the fall here for attempted murder and it seems from what little I know, you all also might be guilty of some federal crimes. Now that's big-time, you could go away for a long, long time," the sheriff said, tightening the noose.

"If you tell me the whole story, Sammy, then there might be something I could do to get 'em to cut you some slack. Otherwise, there's nothing I can do to help you," the sheriff stopped suddenly, letting the silence squeeze the prisoner's brain.

Tears were rolling down the boy's face. He began to sob and shake his head, "I just can't."

The sheriff shrugged, "Okay, we'll talk tomorrow. You think about what I said."

"Please don't put me in with them," the young prisoner said, now on his knees sobbing. Eddy Bill, turning to a deputy, "Take him to the holding cell behind the courtroom and have somebody watch him all night. Make sure he gets something to eat and more water."

The line of questioning told Rick that the sheriff had no idea about the scope and results of the federal investigations into the fire and Jim Dowling's shooting.

After the deputy and prisoner had departed, Eddy Bill turned to the publisher, "I wonder if this is related to the fire and Jim Dowling's shooting?"

"Maybe so, Eddy Bill, but I'd say that you might not want to be too close to this one," Rick answered,

"Why's that?" the sheriff asked, trying unsuccessfully to keep the anxiety from his voice.

"Well, it seems to me that these boys didn't get out on that road all by themselves just for the hell of it. This thing could end up being really messy. Might be wise to turn them over to the FBI," Rick added, looking squarely into the eyes of the sheriff.

"I'll think on it," the sheriff said, realizing that the publisher seemed to be sending him a message.

Rick rose from the chair and limped toward the door. "Eddy Bill, I can't express how grateful I am that you had those patrols out tonight. It saved my life," the publisher said.

"I'd appreciate it if you didn't let anyone know that it was anything special. You know, just report it as a routine road patrol," the sheriff explained.

"Hell, we can't let anyone know you went out of your way to help me. That could cost you 500 votes," Rick shouted over his shoulder as he headed for the steps that had been so tricky for the prisoners.

"Watch those damned stairs," the sheriff replied, his well-known laugh ringing through the deserted old courthouse. "David's at the front door and will drive you home," the exhausted sheriff added. He decided to call the FBI the next day about his suspicion young Sammy might have been involved in the *Crier* fire and Dowling's shooting.

When Rick limped into the house, his worried wife gasped, then wept through a string of "bastards" when he told of his flirtation with the hereafter. They decided without debate she and the kids would leave early the following morning to stay with her parents at the other end of the state until after Election Day and perhaps until after the perpetrators were locked away.

After a short night of sleep, Anne and Rick awoke and explained to the kids they were going on a special vacation. Their embrace was emotional. He drew his wife and two kids close, not sure when he would see them again. He just couldn't bear to add the "if" to the thought.

Chapter 28
Path to White House Goes through Courthouse

Despite the throbbing leg and a strong suggestion by his doctor to take the day off, Rick arrived at his office at his usual 7:15 a.m., after his family departed.

Knowing the day would be hectic, he decided to make an early visit to the post office. Just as he was getting the mail from the box on the lower tier, he felt a presence. "That Edward ought to stay in Myrtle Beach if you ask me," Emma Crooke said, more as a growl than the genteel voice one would expect from the keeper of all things proper in Lawnsville. "He ought not be allowed within a mile of a school, let alone on the school board," she sputtered, as if listening to her comments was Rick's sole purpose in life.

"Good to see you, Mrs. Crooke," he said with as much deference as he could muster.

"He should resign from the board. It's the only decent thing to do," she continued, just getting up a good head of steam.

"Nice to see you, too. I have to get back to the paper," he managed to say between her outbursts limping for the door, cane in hand, trying to escape.

"Well, it's good to see the *Crier* back," she said, heading for her box on the other side of the post office.

As he limped his way back to the office, Rick was greeted by honking horns and thumbs-up from folks driving by. Others came out of stores to ask how his leg was. News travels fast in a small town.

Before re-reading today's *Crier*, Rick called the FBI agent in charge of the investigation into the fire and Jim Dowling's shooting. The agent was very interested when the publisher informed him that three of the men Lester named as being involved in those crimes being arrested in connection with the roadblock. With these latest crimes, the feds had even more leverage to use on the targeted weak-link of the three.

Then Rick turned to today's *Crier*. The story on the handling of county money was across the top of the front page, but it was the short story under it that shocked *Crier* readers. Reaction to the money story would come later.

The shorter one, which pushed the Brownie troop off page one, was only five paragraphs reporting that the publisher and Larry had been wounded and would have probably been murdered if the deputy sheriff hadn't come along on a routine road patrol. It included what the ambushers yelled about shutting up the *Crier*. Since it was written right after the incident, it didn't mention the arrests. That would come in tomorrow's *Crier*.

Once the paper was on the premises and the stuffing was underway, Rick called the state wire service office with the roadblock story. The bureau chief took the story in awe. "You could have been killed. What are you going to do?" he asked.

"What do you mean?" Rick asked.

"Are you going to stop publishing?" the bureau chief asked.

"Hell, no, the sons of bitches aren't going to stop us," Rick bluntly responded. "Never entered my mind."

"Amazing, that takes guts," the bureau chief said in a respectful tone. "I've got to get this on the national wire. Good luck," he concluded.

Rick took a copy of the paper into his cubbyhole and began to tremble as he read his account of his near-death experience the previous night. "That happened to me? Damn. That's was close," he uttered to himself as he relived what had been a blur then, but was sheer terror to read now.

While he loved running the *Crier*, he thought about the strain the job had put on his family and the fact his shooting caused his family to flee for their safety. "Is it worth it?" he wondered.

Rick turned to the story across the top of page one. Unlike the other two in this three-part series on the handling of county funds, this one got the readers' attention, particularly those living out in the county. It showed the county had lost $25,000 in revenue the previous year by keeping county funds in non-interest-bearing accounts at the local bank.

The story included the fact the week after the fire, the commissioners, including the one up for re-election, on a one-2 vote turned down a request from the 4-H camp director for $1,500 for summer lifeguards "because we just don't have the money." That vote meant that the 4-H camp's swimming pool would be closed to campers the entire summer. If children wanted to swim, they'd have to do so in the Greenbrier River. Insurance provisions rule prohibited swimming in the pool without a lifeguard present. Rick did not anticipate the uproar this story would cause in hundreds of homes across the county. Almost every family out in the county had at least one child in a 4-H club and nearly 100 percent of those kids attended 4-H camp in the summer.

Rick checked in with the staff about any calls they'd received about the county money and the roadblock stories.

"My calls were concerned about you being shot. They were worried about the guy's bad aim," the crusty community news editor growled. All eyes were on Rick to see how he'd react. All howled when they saw him smile as he limped back to his office

He dialed the sheriff's office. "Eddy Bill, remember what I told you last night about calling the FBI on those boys? The story of my shooting is going out on the national news wire in less than an hour. "I suggest you call the FBI before they read the story," he suggested.

"This is getting big. Damn, I guess you are looking out for me," the sheriff replied, adding, "Already have."

Then Rick turned to getting ready for tomorrow, a day that would stretch his staff to near breaking point. In less than 24 hours, John F. Kennedy was having a rally at Courthouse Park. Afterward, Rick would have a one-on-one interview with him. He wasn't the only person who would have a special day.

This was the most meaningful day in Red's 40-plus years of Jordan County politics. His presidential candidate was in

Lawnsville and Red would have a personal meeting with him in the private office of Red's close friend, the county clerk.

The rally was announced two days prior and Red was scurrying about to make sure Courthouse Park would be jammed. His war council and all the precinct captains had been working the phones. When the Kennedy campaign people called to check on the rally's final arrangements, Red told them how strong Humphrey was coming on in the county. A senior Kennedy staffer was skeptical, indicating he felt they were in good shape in every county in that part of the state. Red hung up, concerned that he might not get the requested extra $10,000.

To boost his argument, Red confirmed with Charles to make sure Humphrey campaign signs would be wall-to-wall along the route Kennedy would travel into Lawnsville. Red had made the dire prediction of certain Humphrey victory yesterday to Joe McCarthy, who was heading up the Kennedy campaign in the state. If his rally went well, there was no doubt a large portion of Charles' request to the Humphrey campaign also would be granted.

At the same time, Rick was surveying the crowd up at Courthouse Park, the Kennedy advance man's assistant, decked out in a $500 suit, was entering the cleaners. Red turned the closed sign and nodded toward his office. After carefully sitting in a rag-tag antique chair and being served a cool can of lemonade, the young Harvard graduate student shook his head and said he had bad news; he'd be able to give Red only a third of the requested $10,000.

It took more than a $500 suit to deter Red. "If you can't do what I asked for, just keep the damned money. It won't make any difference. Let me tell you something. I'm fighting a bunch of mean-as-hell, hard-shell Baptist preachers in this county and they are going all out to make sure that no Catholic wins," Red explained as if lecturing the high school kid who sweeps out the cleaners once a week.

"I'm working my ass off and you all are acting like cheapskates. I've got to get up to the courthouse. Just forget it," he said, ending his tirade. He got up, grabbed the coat to his Sunday-go-to-meetin' suit and headed for the door.

"Wait, wait. Didn't mean to upset you, but it's been tight," the campaign staffer said, sufficiently chastened and scared that he'd insulted a major campaign supporter. Stunned by the outburst from the plainspoken, savvy mountain politician, the wet-behind-the-ears Kennedy devotee believed he might have bungled his chance for a job in the White House. "I'll let Joe know how you feel when we get to the rally."

"Good. I need this money to get the type of precinct organization to match the other side on the ground. It's tough, didn't mean to hit you so hard, but I want to win this thing," Red growled, knowing he didn't need the young man's assistance. He was going to talk it over with John Kennedy himself. The two left the store, on their way to a great rally on behalf of the man who would be the next president of the United States.

Only six days until Election Day, and today, May 4, would be one of the busiest in *Crier* history. Not only did the staff have to stuff sections for a 32-page paper, but the news side, all three and a half of them, had to be at the courthouse to cover the 11:00 a.m. rally. Accompanying Kennedy would be Franklin D. Roosevelt Jr., scion of the political family whose patriarch's picture hung in a place of honor in countless West Virginia living rooms in tribute to what the depression era programs had meant to the state.

When Rick arrived at the courthouse, the crowd was electric. Contributing to the celebratory atmosphere, the high school band was playing its full repertoire of patriotic songs.

Rick's normal detached reporter's attitude was gone – this was exciting. Yesterday, he had received a call from Kennedy's press office asking if he had time to meet with the candidate for a few minutes after the rally. The interview would take place in the privacy of the sheriff's office.

Rick planned to take a picture of the candidates together, one running for the main office in the courthouse and the other a candidate for the White House.

Three weeks' prior, he had interviewed the other presidential candidate, Hubert Humphrey, after a rally in the same park. He was certain that after the general election, he would be able to say he had interviewed the next president. Since that first rally was after the fire, a story on that interview had not yet run. Tomorrow's lead story would combine the interviews and photos of both rallies.

As the two-bus caravan escorted by city police and state police cruisers pulled up, the crowd's cheers roared over Courthouse Park as the band struck up God Bless America. Noticeably absent in the caravan was a county sheriff car. Eddy Bill, knowing preachers all over the county were giving sermons against the Catholic running for president, had declined to escort the candidate to town but would meet him out of view of the public.

John Kennedy was smooth, able to fire up the crowd and had a speech tailored for the Jordan County audience. He mentioned federal policies were needed so the area could reach its full potential for tourism and the jobs that came with it. Cheers and whistles filled the air as the candidate came down off the makeshift stage, actually the back of a flatbed truck, and shook as many outstretched hands as he could while making his way toward the courthouse where he would visit every office leaving the sheriff's for last.

Red made his way to the county clerk's office.

"How's it going, Red? Great crowd. I appreciate your hard work," John Kennedy said.

"Humphrey's folks are making a real fight, Senator. This has not been easy, but we hope to have a strong presence in every precinct Election Day. But they are making a strong last-minute push," Red said.

"Do you have everything you need to make it work?" the Massachusetts senator asked. "I saw his signs coming into town. It seems they're campaigning hard."

Smiling on the inside at the great job Charles' sign crew had done, Red shook his head. "We're doing the best we can with what we have, Senator, but I won't lie to you, I don't know if we can match them coming down the stretch. You can count on us to keep fighting," Red said, noticing the candidate's nod to his top aide standing on the other side of the small office.

"I know you're working hard and know that my entire family and I really appreciate it," the candidate responded, standing to signal the end of the meeting.

"Got to get to rest of the offices. Joe here wants to talk to you," the presidential candidate said over his shoulder as he headed to the sheriff's office.

Everyone else followed the candidate out, leaving just Red and Joe McCarthy.

"Good to meet you, Red. Thank you for all you're doing," he said, taking an envelope from the inside pocket. "Hope this will help you get the job done. Thanks again." Red put the envelope in his pocket, looking forward to counting it when he got back to the privacy of his little office.

"Hell, that was so easy, I should've asked for $15,000," he chuckled to himself.

Kennedy came into the sheriff's office shaking hands all around before retiring to the sheriff's private office. As they sat down for a few questions, Kennedy first asked how Rick's leg was and added that he was sorry about the fire and glad the paper was back in business. He showed sincere concern and Rick appreciated the thoroughness of his campaign staff's briefing.

"Thank you very much. I have a great staff that works very hard," he responded. He turned quickly to his prepared questions, wanting to make the most of what he was sure would be the high point of his journalism career.

"Have you found that being a Catholic has hurt you in the campaign here in West Virginia?" Rick asked. Accustomed to answering this question, Kennedy looked the inquiring reporter in the eye and smiled, the smile that had made every woman who attended his rallies swoon.

"Not at all. I've found the people of West Virginia accept me for what I can do for the country rather than where I pray."

"What do you feel is the most pressing foreign policy issue that you would face if you are elected president?" Rick asked, surprising the candidate who had not expected such an insightful question in this rural setting.

"Without a doubt, it's the Russians' projection of their power in Cuba, just 90 miles from Florida. A solution for this situation will take strong leadership and a resolve to make the hard decisions. The first thing, if elected, I would schedule a summit with Khrushchev to have frank discussions on what we will not accept."

The *Crier* publisher pressed, drawing on his American history course his sophomore year at West Virginia University, "Would that include invoking the Monroe Doctrine?"

"Rick, that's certainly an option that I would consider invoking if Russia does not leave Cuba. It is indeed intolerable to have an outpost of the Soviet Union in this hemisphere," the presidential candidate said, not realizing the national attention his statement to me in this rural setting, would receive nationally.

Rick would make a call that would result in the candidate's statement making front-page news across the country and boost his national security credentials that had been questioned by Vice President Richard Nixon, his certain opponent in the upcoming general election.

After the questions ended, the publisher took some photographs of the presidential candidate with the sheriff.

It was a red-letter day for Lawnsville. Before this campaign, it had never received a visit from a presidential candidate. Now in the last month, two had visited. As he limped into the office, all the route drivers stopped loading their cars to ask about his condition.

Some of them were steaming about the closing of the 4-H camp pool because of what the county commissioners called a money problem. "We fought like hell to get that pool in the first place. The commission could have used some of that money they gave the bank to hire the lifeguards," one route driver said. "This just ain't right. We've had about enough of this crap," another blurted.

Rick listened closely, not certain it would be reflected in the ballots cast on Election Day.

Chapter 29
History comes a-Visitin'

No sooner had he limped around and seated himself in front of the shiny new typewriter to work on the rally story than he heard a commotion out in the main office. "Get out here, we have a visitor," the crusty community news editor yelled in Rick's direction, an uncharacteristic tremble in her voice.

When the publisher opened his squeaky door, the scene left him speechless. John F. Kennedy was shaking hands with every gaping member of the staff and stunned route drivers.

"After you told me how great they were, I wanted to meet them," the presidential candidate said to Rick. Members of the national press entourage covering Kennedy would take the *Lawnsville Crier* and its staff to living rooms and front pages across the country.

Rick quickly nodded approval for Kennedy's request to speak. "You all showed courage and are a great example for newspapers everywhere. You should be proud of what you've done; the rest of us are," the presidential candidate said, flashing his magnetic smile.

After posing with the staff for photos, he said goodbye and the press entourage boarded waiting buses back on the road that would lead to the White House.

"I guess that'll give us a story for us to tell for years," Rick said to an awestruck staff.

After things settled down and the route drivers left, he called the state wire service office to report Kennedy's statement that he would consider invoking the Monroe Doctrine in response to Russia's bases in Cuba. "Now that's interesting. The other day in a national interview, he evaded answering that question," the bureau chief observed. "I'll get this right up to New York for the national wire."

The publisher turned out the rally story in short order and spent the rest of the afternoon handling candidates who were buying ads for the weekend issues. One that surprised him was Joe Ed Green, the independent candidate for county commission rumored to be backed by the reformers. He had been nearly invisible during the campaign but had come in with two ads for each of the remaining editions. These ads hit hard at the commission's vote against providing 4-H pool lifeguards. Some of the language came from yesterday's story. The zinger was the ad's headlines: IT JUST AIN'T RIGHT. THEY'VE THROWN OUR KIDS IN THE RIVER. It was a commonsense approach that could play well in the county Rick thought, but probably too little, too late for the well-meaning but low-keyed Sunday school teacher.

Given the "word" on the street about Joe Ed not having a chance in hell Election Day, Rick was almost ashamed to take the money for the ad. ALMOST – he did have to pay the Crier's mounting printing bills.

Charles' prediction about the county funds' story was half right, it had a lot of numbers. He would soon learn the folly of the second part of the prediction – people could not understand the figures. Across Jordan County they did understand what was happening to their tax dollars and many were mad as hell.

Living in Lawnsville, Charles and Red didn't understand the role 4-H clubs have in every community in the county. About mid-afternoon, the phones started to ring. For the first time, nearly all calls were of one opinion—blasting the county commission's decision on the 4-H camp pool lifeguards. Red read the story an hour before and hadn't gotten a single call on the article confirming his and Charles' feeling that no one would understand or care about it.

All that changed once route carriers delivered the Crier out in the county. A key old-line veteran precinct captain in Forest Hill was first to blister Red's ear. "My granddaughter learned to swim in that pool and has been swimming there since it was built.

Last year, she even won a trophy in a swim meet there. Now they don't even have lifeguards for the pool. Red, what the hell's wrong with those jackasses on county commission? This just ain't right," he fumed.

"My understanding is the boys on the commission are looking for the money and should have it all taken care of by their meeting in two weeks," Red stammered in a hastily constructed lie to keep the election worker mollified. Five other calls expressed the same opinion of the commission action.

While it was the story about the county's money that could have an impact on Election Day, the shorter roadblock story caused Red to nearly swallow his beloved afternoon lemonade - can and all. It had details. Red was certain the same people were responsible that set the *Crier* fire and shooting Jim Dowling. Others read the shorter story in stunned silence, realizing the *Crier* publisher was nearly killed for providing them the truth in the *Crier*.

But Jordan County government issues would take a back seat as folks saw the stately courthouse take center stage on national television evening news. Every network mentioned Kenney's' answer about invoking the Monroe Doctrine in dealing with Russia in Cuba.

John Kennedy's visit to the exile newspaper office was on two networks and the staff was all a-twitter over their newfound celebrity status. They hadn't realized what they had accomplished until they heard John Kennedy speak in the dingy office about their bravery and courage. They'd heard Rick say the same words, but he was just Rick. This was a presidential candidate, and it was on national news.

Splitting the day's front page between the earlier Humphrey rally and Kennedy's was a hit with supporters of both candidates. Rick chuckled when he looked closely at the photos of both rallies and saw that a lot of the same people attended both, but with different signs.

On his post-rally courthouse visits to various offices looking to drum up some political advertising, let it "slip" that ad space would be limited for all the pre-election issues and he might have to leave some of the political ads out. His ploy worked.

Over the next two days, all the remaining candidates for sheriff, board of education, and county commission bought last-minute ads. He tried to handle the local candidates personally. Most would pull out a wad of cash and peel off the bills, no personal checks for them. In addition, ads came in for all the statewide candidates for governor, attorney general, secretary of state, state treasurer and auditor, along with all the candidates for state House of Delegates and Senate.

The Kennedy campaign yesterday dropped off full-page ads for Saturday, Sunday and Monday. The Humphrey campaign was placing only one, for Monday. The smartass gofers for the Kennedy campaign had bristled a bit hearing that all political ads had to be prepaid. But when told the rule was ironclad, they sheepishly pulled out a check for the full amount. The publisher's philosophy on prepaid political ads was simple, losers have bad memories.

Even the last-minute ad surge was not enough to pay all the bills that had backed-up since the fire. And the delay in the insurance claim was a dark cloud hanging over the *Crier*'s future.

While the presidential primary campaigns in the state were getting a lot of national media attention, the people in this county were paying more attention to the races for sheriff, board of education and county commission. To them, that's where the power was, particularly in control of jobs.

Nearly everyone, except Eddy Bill, thought Eddy Bill would win hands-down. However, things seemed to be shifting. Three of the original 12 candidates had dropped out of the race and an ad bought thirty minutes ago was endorsing Eddy Bill's strongest opponent.

Just as Rick was about to return to his cubbyhole, the sheriff walked in and asked for a word. He had rough drafts of a half-page ad for each of the remaining pre-election issues. When asked for advice about the ads, Rick suggested several changes and said he had better pictures in his files. "Can't have you looking as ugly as you are," Rick said, chuckling. "Hell, I'll run the one of you and Edward at the Ox Roast," the publisher said, not cracking a smile.

"Damn, you don't let up," the sheriff said with a smile.

"I believe I can get the first one in tomorrow. Let me check with the layout crew, make yourself to home," the publisher said, using the same phrase the sheriff had used when he left his phonebook open with the number for Charles' beachfront condo. He purposefully left the ad featuring the three former candidates on his desk. Coming back into his office, Rick said, "The gals say they can get it set for tomorrow," noticing the ad on his desk had been moved. "Eddy Bill, if you want to run anything else, I'll be in about 7:30 Sunday morning and then after church," Rick said.

"I'll let you know, might want to," the sheriff said.

Chapter 30
Hospital Runs a Fever Over Beach Vacations

With the excitement of the presidential candidates' rally and Kennedy's visit to the paper behind him, the publisher turned his attention to the hospital board of trustees meeting, the first-ever covered by the *Crier*, that ended almost thirty days ago. It would not only be new to *Crier* readers, but troubling as well. Over the last several days, he'd made several calls about the story but no callbacks. That was about to change.

The first was from Mr. Bowman who owned the collection agency used by the hospital. In his most condescending tone, he explained to Rick his "firm's collection incentive program shouldn't appear in the paper because it was a private contract with the hospital."

Leaning back in his rickety old chair with his feet up on the desk, Rick pointed out, "The County doesn't have any private contracts, Mr. Bowman, it's a public body."

"Well, then we'll have to consider suing you if it appears."

Rick responded, "That's fine, I'd like nothing better than to get you under oath in discovery so we can ask you anything we want about your business dealings and I don't mean just with the hospital," *Damn, that felt good,* he thought, smiling.

Barely ten minutes later, Will LeMasters, the hospital administrator called, "Rick, do you have any questions on the earlier meeting?"

The publisher was ready. "I do. I missed the date you planned to begin paving the hospital's new parking lot."

LeMasters gave a curt "next week," and then, after an uncomfortable pause, added, "Oh, and about that incentive program with Bowman-Smith, it's really an 'off-line' agreement between the hospital finance committee and the company. Not really subject to the county purchasing procedure."

Rick replied, "Will, as Mr. Bowman just told you, a county agency does not have private 'off-line' contracts. It's a public agency and the comments were made in a public meeting. It doesn't seem like a big deal to me." Rick's tongue was securely locked deep in his cheek.

"Well, we have to collect the bills, if we don't, we'd have to close the hospital," the hospital administrator warily explained.

"I agree, Will, but did you have to hire a collection company and let your employees accept those free vacations to Myrtle Beach?"

Ignoring the question, the administrator again asked whether the collective incentives would be mentioned in the story. "Will, I'm still working on it and I'm a bit behind deadline, but thanks for calling."

The lead for the hospital board story dealt with the fact that increased patient load required additional staff and expansion of the parking lot and other routine matters. A separate page one story dealt with the collection process and the week-long, free luxury Myrtle Beach vacations the hospital staff members and their husbands had been given. Details of the trips were featured including names of the hotels, provided by a relative of a hospital employee who had seen a brochure on the desk of one who won a trip. To show the value of the trips, the publisher got photographs of the plush Myrtle Beach resorts. Bringing the story full circle, it referred to the story two days before on the handling of county money. It pointed out that the hospital lost $25,000 in revenue by keeping its money in non-interest-bearing bank accounts.

Rick wasn't sure the story would resonate with the readers, especially those in poorer areas of the county. People understood. They might not understand the intricacies of county finances, but they understood free vacations earned by turning county residents over to a collection agency for hospital bills. A route carrier came into his office after she read the story, "They turned my aunt over for collection when she was still sick and got a free vacation out of it. That ain't right, it just ain't right," she said, bringing a lace hanky to her eyes.

Now Rick was beginning to understand. Could this county's homespun philosophy of "what ain't fair, ain't right" burst forth from the voting booth on Election Day? Remembering the county's election history, he thought, not a chance.

The next morning, Rick arrived bright and early thinking there might be letters to the editor on the hospital story that had come through the *Crier* office's front door mail slot overnight. There were none. And on second thought, it was not surprising given that folks didn't want to talk about having trouble paying their bills.

However, his trek to the post office kept the eventful streak going. Picking up her mail, one of the retired teachers, Abigail Sweeney, asked him if he'd seen the story about the free vacations for hospital employees. Rick chuckled thinking he'd have to use larger type for his byline next time. "It's just shameful," she said as she stomped off, muttering to one of her friends as they headed for Susie's.

A doughnut would taste good, Rick thought, as he followed the two who, in deep conversation, didn't pay attention to the town's only traffic light. They also ignored the resulting screeching brakes, honking horns and obscene gestures. They joined two fellow school retirees at a front table and continued expounding on the free vacations. Rick noticed most of the people in Susie's early-morning crowd were nodding in agreement as Miss Abigail held court in her own special tone that nobody had to strain to hear.

As Rick took in the happenings at the town's traditional morning gathering place, he thought there might be more interesting news here than in the *Crier*. But if he printed any of it, he'd be in court for years, he thought as he headed back to the office.

Neither Charles nor Red thought the story on hospital employees getting free vacations would gain any reaction. Just as they had thought the story on the deposit of county money wouldn't resonate with county residents. "Most folks out in the county can't even pronounce Myrtle Beach or find it on a map," Charles said to Red. This prediction could make the two crafty old pols 0 for 2 in predicting county residents' reaction to *Crier* stories about county finances.

Back from his doughnut experience at Susie's, Rick spent several hours with local candidates delivering last-minute ads. He worked with each one, showing no favorites. Finally, he was able to retreat to the quiet of his cubbyhole to carefully plan the Saturday, Sunday, and Monday editions. Little did he know that his calmness would be turned on its ear in thirty minutes.

Chapter 31
The Wheels of Justice

Charles called Red mid-morning on Friday before the election to report on a good news call he'd received late the previous night from Ray Rogers, his friend in Charleston.

Rodgers reported that a rumor, circulating in the federal courthouse, indicated the investigation of the fire and policeman's shooting was taking much longer than anticipated and would not go before this federal grand jury scheduled to end at noon.

Brimming with confidence, Red said he would close early that afternoon and come over to Charles' house to discuss last-minute details for Election Day. Charles relaxed a bit since it was now 12:15 p.m. If anything had changed in Charleston, he was sure he would have already received a call. Just as Red knocked on the hand-hewn oak door, a ring from his private phone interrupted Charles' gaze over the beautiful river. Charles motioned Red to one of the plush easy chairs across the room.

Charles thanked Ray for the update and proceeded to give Red the latest news. "Right before the noon adjournment, unexpectedly the federal grand jury was extended to include an afternoon session. Ray said no reason was given. But word is that a paperwork mistake by a court clerk had to be corrected. Ray left the courthouse and went back to his office. Things are going well, Red."

Confidently, the two turned to Election Day operations and how much money they would be able to split. Going over the fine details, they were interrupted again by the ringing of the private phone.

Red watched as his friend turned pale and slumped back in his chair. Slowly Charles' faced changed from one of pure optimism to a frown that resembled an aging basset hound's. "Are you sure it was him?" Charles asked as he shook his head. Red noticed the trembling of Charles' hand and the sweat forming on his forehead. He knew the other side of the conversation meant trouble. Charles thanked his friend for the information and put down the phone, very slowly this time.

"It seems that Jim Dowling might have testified before the grand jury," Charles said. "Just after the grand jury's lunch break began, security was tightened at the courthouse. Additional armed guards were at every entrance, on the roof, and put at every elevator. When Ray got the call, he rushed back to the courthouse.

"Right before the grand jury began the afternoon session, an ambulance with a police escort arrived at the rear entrance of the courthouse. Sheets were held up to keep people from seeing who was in the ambulance. One of the courthouse people told Ray that a young black man on a stretcher was wheeled in and taken up to the grand jury room. It had to be Jim Dowling. Then Ray told me next they brought before the grand jury a shorter man wearing a ski mask and surrounded by federal marshals carrying rifles. Forty-five minutes later, the grand jury was dismissed and the U.S. attorney's office announced a press conference for 8:00 tomorrow morning, a Saturday. Ray says he's never heard of a U. S. Attorney having a Saturday morning press conference."

Charles' friend had no way of knowing that the U.S. attorney had remembered the plight of the publisher and the press conference time was to accommodate the *Crier*'s deadline schedule.

About an hour after the last telephone call, Red and Charles' Election Day discussions were interrupted again, this time by the roar of a helicopter flying low over the river. The two went outside and watched it land on the high school football field. Red wondered aloud, "Wonder what all that is about?"

While they turned back to their Election Day preparations, a contingent of armed FBI agents and U.S. marshals met the helicopter that carried an assistant U.S. attorney with a briefcase full of newly written arrests warrants. At the same time, Red and

Charles were watching the helicopter land. Rick Hill got a curt call from the U.S. attorney's public information officer saying only he might want to be at City Hall immediately.

The publisher burst out of his cubbyhole, grabbed a camera and ran for the door, yelling, "Al, get a camera and come on." They nearly knocked over the former publisher coming in the front door to drop off his column. Joseph Ballengee fell in behind them. Rick looked like an Olympic walking competitor as he moved along Lawnsville's narrow sidewalks.

"What's up?" Al puffed.

"Hell, I don't know, just got a call that said I should get down to City Hall," Rick yelled over his shoulder. Joseph was almost running to keep up. Several startled shoppers also joined the procession.

As they rounded the corner, three unmarked vehicles—large black sedans, a single flashing light on each dashboard—slid to a screeching stop in front of City Hall's main entrance. Six black-clad FBI agents jumped from the cars with rifles at port arms. Three agents immediately charged into the building yelling, "FBI, FBI, nobody move." The others took positions at the other entrances of the small corner building at the edge of the town's business district.

"Holy shit," Al marveled, as he joined Rick snapping away. A car pulled up next to the publisher to watch the unfolding drama and the driver reported two vans with flashing lights were in front of the jail next to the courthouse. Al nodded to Rick as he took off and headed for county lockup, camera at the ready.

Rick positioned himself in front of City Hall's front door. With an armed agent behind and another in front, a handcuffed Samuel Johnson was led out of the building to one of the sedans. Bewildered city employees followed the visibly shaken mayor out to watch the spectacle. "You son of a bitch," the handcuffed street commissioner yelled at the publisher-turned-photographer. "We'll get you," he snarled, as the agents put him into the van.

"What's going on?" Rick innocently asked the mayor.

"I just don't know, they came busting in with guns, said they were FBI," the city's chief executive said, glaring at the publisher who he suspected was responsible for the city street commissioner's arrest.

"How'd you know what was going on?" the mayor asked.

"Oh, someone called and said something was up at City Hall," Rick said innocently. "Sure are a lot of people interested in this," he said, pointing to the growing crowd. Think they're after anyone else?" the newspaperman couldn't resist asking, trying to get a reaction from the mayor.

Taken aback by Rick's direct approach, the mayor's face changed from cocky to concern. "They didn't say anything about that, just took Samuel," he muttered.

"Well, better get back and get to work, let me know if you hear anything," Rick said to the still shaken mayor. "This might not be the end of it; you know how the FBI is," he said to add to the mayor's discomfort. It worked.

Little did the two know that Samuel, handcuffed and fuming, watched from the FBI car as his chief tormenter and the mayor were having what appeared to be a friendly conversation. Since the mayor wasn't arrested, the handcuffed street commissioner wondered if the two had collaborated against him. Given the street commissioner's state of mind, it could bode ill for the city's top official when the FBI began to ask questions.

Just as Al took off for the jail, another unmarked vehicle roared up from Lawnville's East End, coming to a screeching halt on the other side of City Hall. One of the agents got out and spoke with the agent who seemed in charge. Rick couldn't tell if a prisoner was in the vehicle until an agent opened the door. Ignoring the foul epithets, he snapped away at the handcuffed Jonathon Johnson.

That wasn't the end of the excitement. Another vehicle this one a van, siren blaring and lights flashing, came down the alley from the direction of the Jordan County jail, joining what was now a traffic jam around City Hall. As if on cue, the agents got out of the newly arrived van, leaving the door open and perfectly accommodating the publisher's desire for photos. Rick was face-to-face with the two arrested in connection with the roadblock and his wounding.

"Holy shit," Rick murmured a bit too loud given that the Baptist preacher was standing next to him.

By now, the crowd stretched nearly all the way around City Hall. Al came down the alley, panting and smiling, with juicy news for Rick.

"They got two at the jail. On the way back, just out of curiosity I stopped by Avery's. I thought the two they got at the jail might be Jonathon's drinking buddies," Al proudly announced. Rick wondered why the FBI only took two of the three arrested in connection with the roadblock. He wasn't aware that Eddy Bill had called the FBI who had taken Sammy Burton into protective custody yesterday.

"Al, those were two of the guys that shot me and burned the van," Rick blurted out.

His right-hand man, who didn't see the minister either, responded true to form, "The shit just hit the fan." The preacher merely shut his eyes as if in prayer.

With these arrests, the burning of the paper and the wounding of its publisher were connected legally.

The jarring answer to Red's question about the helicopter was about to unfold.

"Hello," Charles answered the phone as calmly as a Sunday school teacher and as if he didn't have a care in the world. His cheerful demeanor again was quickly replaced by a look of utter shock. "They what? How many?" he queried. "That is something, thanks for calling," Charles said, grabbing for the glass of lemonade then slumping back in his favorite chair.

"That was Joseph. The FBI just arrested Samuel at City Hall, Jonathon at his house, and picked up two more at the county jail. He's not sure if those two are the same two arrested the other night when Rick was shot. Joseph couldn't get any more information. Rick was in his office with the door closed. Joseph believes he was talking to the U.S. attorney's office. After Samuel's arrest, Joseph saw the mayor and "Benny" Howland in deep conversation heading into City Hall with the police chief."

Putting on their blinders of total denial, Red and Charles carefully analyzed the situation and decided the whole mess remained a problem exclusively for the mayor. "Red, if you get any calls, remind everyone this started over that fool dump-truck scheme those two cooked up," Charles said, not indicating the slightest concern for the plight of the mayor, a close political ally for decades.

Red and Charles' state of denial notwithstanding, the mayor's troubles were connected to their candidates. It was the mayor who stood up on Candidate Night at schools in Lawnsville and fervently endorsed Edward and his two allies for re-election to the school board.

Up to now, people in Lawnsville only had rumors about the crimes. Once details of the federal indictments were in the *Crier,* they would understand the earlier stories on the dump-truck rental scheme led to the *Crier* fire and shooting of a city policeman.

Once back at the office, Rick learned in an interview with the U.S. attorney that Jonathon, the two taken from the jail, and the one taken into protective custody were charged with the attempted murder of a law enforcement officer, plus federal charges of interfering with interstate commerce in connection with the *Crier* fire. Samuel was charged with being an accessory and conspiracy in those charges. State charges were expected later.

The U.S. Attorney pointed out the FBI arrests had nothing to do with Rick and Larry's wounding and the roadblock. Those crimes were still being investigated.

It was clear that the two picked up at the jail by the FBI were hard-core and unlikely to become federal witnesses.

Although Lester would never testify before the Grand Jury or at a trial, the federal authorities agreed that his identifying the four enable them to solve the cases. The testimony of one, Sammy Burton, was key to convicting the others for the fire, wounding of Jim Dowling and attempted murder of Rick and Larry.

Rick had just sat down at his desk when the phone rang. "Busy day," the frail voice squeaked.

"Sure has been, I hope you're feeling well," Rick said to let the 85-year-old know he appreciated her calls.

"Them three they had at the jail worked for Samuel out of the city a couple of months ago on a paving job," she said coughing and wheezing. "Meaner than junk dogs, the three of 'em," she added, abruptly ending the call.

"This thing keeps growing," Rick muttered to himself.

"How's everything working out for you, Eddy Bill?" Rick said when the congenial sheriff picked up the phone.

"I don't want anywhere near this case," the sheriff said. "When they picked up the other two, the U.S. marshals said they had the other one in protective custody."

"I saw the mayor down at City Hall when they arrested Samuel. He didn't look too good," Rick said, plumbing for a reaction.

"Hell, he ought to be as nervous as a whore in church. Things are dropping all around him," the sheriff said.

"Heard those three boys worked on Luther's paving crew a few months ago. Know anything about that?" Rick probed.

"How the hell did you find out about that? I just found it out a few minutes ago," the sheriff said.

"Just floated in the window," Rick replied.

"Go to hell," the sheriff said, laughing out loud as he put the phone back in the cradle on his desk.

Rick's right-hand man had knocked on the door, having interrupted the publisher twice already, pointedly noting that "we need the story so we can get the hell on the road."

Ten minutes after Al's not-very-subtle third reminder, Rick opened his door with great flourish and strutted over to Al, humming a military march as he went using his cane as a baton. The staff clapped as he handed the copy over.

The story was long and detailed. Quoting from federal indictments, it painted a detailed picture of the night of the fire and the Lawnsville policeman's shooting. It was clear someone involved, other than Jim Dowling, gave testimony. It was after 7:00 p.m. when the *Crier* vans—each with an armed driver and shotgun—pulled out from in front of the dilapidated newspaper office.

Eddy Bill had three deputy cars ready to escort the vans to the county line in different directions and had arranged for the neighboring counties' deputies to meet them. Al went to the printing plant, Rick went south again and a third one added for tonight with Larry, his ad manager, went east toward Virginia.

With the U.S. attorney's press conference not until tomorrow morning, Rick would finally be the first paper in the country to have a story about the *Crier* woes.

Outside the lake's bridge collapse on March 31, 1949, that killed five construction workers and sent the 300-ton span into the Bluestone River, this might be the biggest story the county had ever seen.

It was early Saturday morning when the staff arrived. They worked to get the route drivers on the road as soon as possible. Then they'd start on stories for tomorrow's paper that Rick hoped would be 32 pages. It turned out it would reach 40 as candidates lined up to buy ads.

Rick knew that after the U.S. attorney's 8:00 a.m. press conference, he could expect calls from both state and national media. The first call came just before 9:00 a.m. from the wire service bureau in Charleston. The first question was, "Why didn't you all call us yesterday with this?"

Rick answered with a chuckle, "Well, we were a little busy. We had about as much as we could say grace over. And besides, I wanted finally to have a scoop on a story about my own damned paper."

"Wow, this ties it all together. From what I hear, the grand jury was spellbound by Jim Dowling's testimony," the wire service reporter said.

Just as Rick was turning to working on the lead story for Sunday's paper, his phone rang again, the first of five straight calls from the national media on his wounding. He patiently answered the questions, really the same questions five times.

His work on Sunday's lead story was interrupted by the route drivers wanting details on the arrest story.

"It does seem that there could be more charges coming connected to the van burning and my wounding," Rick repeated information in the story. But by him telling them, they felt like they had an inside view.

He then thanked them for the 100 new *Crier* subscribers they had signed up in the past week, adding, "I've given each of you 25 extra papers today, give 'em out and leave them at gas stations and stores along your route."

Finally, he was able to turn his attention to the lead story for the next day's paper. This one would prove to be another election-related blockbuster.

Just as Charles was finishing getting dressed, a friend called from Charleston with a report on the U.S. attorney's press conference. It was packed with more reporters than the statehouse veteran thought were in the entire state. Also attending were the governor's press officer and chief of staff, the Speaker of the House of Delegates' chief of staff and the state chairman of both political parties.

After completing the thirty minute call, Charles called Red with an update. Because of his concern that those involved might flee the state and continue to be a danger to the newspaper's staff, the U.S. attorney explained he had given the case high priority. Charles's friend had no details but reported some folks at the State House believed the case could lead to federal officers being sent to Jordan County to monitor election-related activities, before and on Election Day.

"No telling where they'll be," Charles added not overly concern given plans B and C he and Red had ready in five key precincts.

Charles continued that the U.S. attorney explained the investigation into the roadblock and the wounding of the *Crier* publisher began only two days ago, so the press conference dealt only with the fire and the shooting of Jim Dowling.

Saving the best until last, Charles said the indictments explained that the paper's coverage of the scheme to rent the dump truck to the city was the reason the four set the fire. The shooting occurred when the policeman discovered the break-in.

"On top of that, I picked up today that the three boys indicted with Jonathon had worked earlier in the year for Samuel on a city paving job," Red added.

"Today's *Crier* story said those three picked up yesterday by the FBI agents at the jail had also been arrested for the roadblock and Rick and Larry's wounding. It's all connected to the city," Charles emphasized.

"There's something else," Red said with a combination of concern and caution. "Avery also said one his buddies, who works for the city, told him the mayor was jumpier than hell. And after he read the paper, he'd had several meetings with the chief of police," Red said.

"Great news. It keeps it away from us and the election," Charles said, rubbing his hands together as he again retreated into a cocoon of self-delusion.

Charles smiled at Red as they enjoyed sweet lemonade as they gazed out on the sunlight reflecting off the waters of the gently flowing river.

Chapter 32
You Can Fool Some of the People Some of the Time

While the arrest story had readers buzzing, Rick was busy preparing a story that would show the contempt some officeholders had for Jordan County citizens. Recognizing this was the first Sunday paper in the paper's history, the *Crier* staff, route drivers, and city paper carriers all were chomping at the bit to get it delivered. It was ready for them at 7:30 a.m. the Sunday morning before Election Day.

Candidates Give Different Answers To Same Questions at Different Schools

Screamed the headline across the *Crier's* front page.

The hard-hitting lead story on school board Candidate Night would become the most-read story in the *Crier*'s pre-election return. In what proved to be a fortuitous decision, Rick, hoping against all odds the *Crier* would return before the election, decided the staff would cover board Candidate Night at every county school. By comparing notes, the staff discovered that the old-line candidates gave different answers to the exact same question at different schools.

The questions were exactly the same because Eva Newland had developed them for her fellow retirees to ask at each Candidate Night.

Politicians are often accused of talking out of both sides of their mouths. However, very seldom is the evidence as clear as that in the story.

When setting the Sunday production schedule, Rick didn't realize folks would get this Sunday *Crier* before they left for church. That timing made the Candidate Night story a major topic of pre-church conversation as scores of congregations gathered across the county.

This story informed *Crier* readers the old-line incumbent school board candidates gave different answers to the same questions at schools in the county compared with those given at schools in the city. Answers about building improvements spotlighted the differences.

At schools in the city, Edward and his running mates called attention to renovations to schools in the city as showing an effective, concerned school board. At schools out in the county, they blamed "the lack of money as the reason we just couldn't keep up with the maintenance needs of the schools. But we promise we'll do better next year." People out in the county accepted this explanation. But this *Crier* story would change that when they realized they had been lied to.

There were other reasons the three incumbents were not well received. In several instances, Edward's responses, particularly at schools out in the county, were arrogant to those posing probing questions about the three's votes on specific issues. His answers included phrases such as "you just don't understand how the school board operates," or "that's a little too complicated to explain here." Those on the receiving end of his condescending responses sat down silently, leading Edward to mistakenly believe his slickness had carried the day.

Prominent in the story was a statement Edward had made at the school board meeting after the fire when Candidate Nights was approved. "I'd like to comment on Candidate Nights the schools have been allowed to have during this campaign. Most of the questions and comments will be negative and about things folks just don't understand. I suggest we consider eliminating such events in the future," Edward concluded.

Every Candidate Night was well attended, standing room only at most. Nearly everyone Rick and his reporters interviewed said that they appreciated the events because it gave them a chance to question board candidates face-to-face.

Another thing troubling for old-line candidates was the mayor's strong personal endorsement of old-line board candidates at schools in Lawnsville. That tied old-line board candidates to the mayor and the city's problems.

Charles and Red's "ears" at the meetings failed to pick up on the fervor of the mayor's endorsement, nor did they catch the many shaking heads during the city's chief executive's anointing of Edward and crew. The two politicos didn't realize how closely their board candidates, as well as others on the old-line slate, had been tied to the city's problems. The *Crier* story certainly enlightened them.

Before he opened the office to take last-minute political ads, Rick went to church. As was the custom at small-town churches, folks gathered out front to visit before going inside. As he walked up, Rick noticed a bigger crowd than usual in front of the towering brick and stone house of worship. Some were around Sheriff Eddy Bill and Red, others were around the worm, Orville Brown. Eddy Bill took a break from holding forth, smiled, winked, and shook his hand, whispering, "You got things stirred up this morning."

Rick responded, smiling, "and let there be light."

The worm looked up and turned away. That's all Rick needed. He headed right for Brown's group, giving him a big smile and handshake, and asking cheerfully, "Orville, how are things going?"

All the worm could manage was a stammered, "Good to see you."

Rick moved toward the church's scorched hand-hewn oak doors. These doors and the original church Bible were all that were saved when the church's former hundred-year-old building burned forty-five years ago. Rick smiled recalling that some old-timers still called this building the "new" church.

No fire and brimstone sermon today, rather a thoughtful examination of responsibilities members of the congregation had to the community. Ever so mindful of the diversity among his congregation—old-liners and reformers—the preacher noted how those who put their names on the ballot "are good people concerned about the community." Heads on both sides nodded in approval of that recognition by the ever-so-nibble Leader of the Flock. Amens ricocheted off the walls.

"God bless you, how's the leg?" the preacher bellowed, shaking the publisher's hand as Rick was leaving after the service. "Hope the leg is coming along."

"Thank you, preacher, the Good Lord was watching over me, what with giving those boys bad aim," Rick said, smiling.

About 12:30, as Rick was settling into his old office chair, preparing to work on the next day's paper when his phone rang. Rick was greeted by Baxter's gravelly voice. "That story on the Candidate Nights could turn this thing 70 ways from Sunday," Baxter said, as excited as Rick had ever heard him. "We had a different guy attend at each Candidate Night, but they didn't pick up the different answers at different schools," he added.

"How's it looking in the school board races? I haven't able to keep track of things," Rick asked, the reporter in him taking over.

"Well, it's been hard for us to get a handle on it. After today's paper, my phone started ringing off the hook. Folks are upset. It's been building since the paper came back. It seems people are reading every word. Charles and Red's people are working as hard as I've ever seen, and they've got a pile of money. Anything interesting coming in the next two papers?" Baxter asked, hoping the publisher might give a hint.

"Hell, we've run out of stuff to write about," the publisher said with a chuckle. "Thanks for calling." For Monday, the lead election story would be a wrap-up on the campaigns and the issues that had been raised.

Given the overwhelming Democratic majority in West Virginia, it was an ironclad fact those winning the nominations in the Democratic primary election at the state and local levels would be the winners in the November general election.

However, elections for the board of education were different. Since by law, elected board members were non-partisan in the primary. This board election had a rare feature Jordan County not seen at least fifty years. Because of an appointment to an unexpired term late last year, three, a majority of the five-member board would be elected this Election Day. Normally there were no more than two elected in any single election.

Just as the publisher was turning to his typewriter, there was a knock at the outside door. Outside were the three reformer candidates for the board of education, Beverly Maxwell, Ray George, and Sam Keaton. Each had a separate personal ad and one joint ad, all for Monday's paper. Rick went over the copy and the photos and wished them good luck. Each peeled off cash, fully aware of the publisher's no exceptions prepayment rule, which he applied evenly for candidates from the courthouse to the White House.

Rick settled down in his cubbyhole, wanting to get the lead story finished for tomorrow's paper before the staff came in.

Again there was a pounding on the door. Warily, the publisher came out of the cubbyhole. It was Eddy Bill with four other sheriff candidates in tow. The four were dropping out and wanted to run an ad endorsing Eddy Bill. They had a rough layout for the ad with space in the middle for a photo. The publisher carefully reviewed it and asked the sheriff if he had the picture. Eddy Bill sheepishly responded, "Thought maybe you'd have time to take one."

"You sure are a lot of damned trouble, Sheriff, and you four don't care who you have their picture taken with," the publisher barked good-naturedly as he suggested they walk up to the courthouse.

The sheriff nodded appreciatively. The photo taken and hands shaken all around, the publisher headed back to the paper.

When he arrived, the ad manager was going over the volume of last-minute ads.

"Wow! Boss, you've sold so many ads, we're going to have to add another section," Larry Loom said.

"And we've got another couple of hours before we lock it up," the publisher said, smiling over his shoulder as he shut the cubbyhole's door.

For the fourth time on this afternoon of the Day of Rest, the publisher sat down to work on stories for the last edition before Election Day.

Chapter 33
Keeper of the Flame

"Keeper of the flame" was one of Rick's favorite phrases to describe custodians of the spirit and principles of an organization or a community. He hoped the *Crier* was moving toward earning that prestigious, yet humbling, moniker from its readers. Those who understand the role of a free press in a democracy know that when government operates without this watchdog, there is no accountability. The result is closer to a dictatorship. That description is perhaps a bit harsh for Jordan County, but the situation he found, is in the same family.

In this, his first election editorial, he would urge people to look closely at the issues and pick the candidates they believe would act in the people's best interest. "As protected in the First Amendment to the U.S. Constitution, freedom of the press is not so reporters can be nosy and get into to other people's business. This precious amendment is so citizens can be informed about what their—I repeat, *their*—governments are doing. That is what we do at the *Crier*.

"The most powerful and important part of Election Day doesn't belong to the candidates. It belongs to *We, the people*. It is the vote, our vote bought and paid for by the blood of those who have served the country over its 183-year history."

This would run on page one in Monday's paper. While Rick felt his best writing was about the history of the First Amendment, his readers would be moved more by the description of the importance of voting. That one vote made everyone equal.

Rick felt good after finishing the editorial. But he just couldn't get a handle on the reaction to the paper's renaissance. He crafted the stories to help folks understand what their governments were doing and how their tax dollars were being spent. He hoped that *Crier* readers were paying attention.

Chapter 34
Trying Doesn't Mean You Win

Rick finished his editorial and was looking over wire stories on state and national races. Other staff members were working on stories on the board of education, county commission, and sheriff races.

Next, he'd tackle the historic West Virginia Democratic Presidential Primary that brought the two candidates to Jordan County's Courthouse Park just two blocks away. A paragraph would note that two of the county's political leaders, normally close allies, had different horses in that spirited and expensive race.

Indeed, the last *Crier* edition before Election Day would give voters a good overview of all the candidates on the ballot.

Rick was resigned to seeing the old-line sweep all the local races as it had done in nearly every election in the last thirty years or so. As he labored on this Sunday afternoon, six unconnected election-related activities were taking place across the county, some, just blocks away. These events would determine whether Jordan County would remain as it had for decades, or if its good citizens would say "enough" with their votes.

Behind a white picket fence and lovely flower garden up the street and around the corner, Eva Newland, Lucille Brown, and three close friends who served as captains for the county's three districts were going over last-minute details of their Golden Oldies Election Day plan. All were retired teachers. There would be tea, of course, and today it would be laced with a touch, maybe two touches, of sherry, procured by Eva's yardman. Perish the thought of her—a pillar of the Baptist Church—being seen going into the Lawnsville state liquor store.

Charles and Red heard rumblings of the effort, but scoffed at the thought of a bunch of 70- and 80-year-old retired teachers having any impact on the election. Red was outspoken. "Those old biddies will be lucky if they can even make it to polls," he told a meeting of his campaign committee that included one whose wife was a retired teacher. When Eva heard the comment, fire blazed in her eyes and she smiled and dubbed her group the OBP, Old Biddies' Party. She had to change OBP to the Golden Oldies when some of the men objected.

The Goldens knew the odds were against them. The old-line had a well-funded team in each of the county's thirty precincts, would be buying hundreds of votes and had the force of one of the strongest county political organizations in the state.

But the hardy band of retirees felt they had to try. "We just owe it to the kids," Eva said hopefully. She wasn't as optimistic as she sounded.

Their plan was low-key and put together quietly. They had no money. Over the past six weeks, Eva and her core committee called or met personally with retired teachers, school bus drivers, cooks, and janitors across the county. The committee set up teams for each task - to make phone calls, take those not registered to vote to the courthouse - only a few at a time so as not to draw attention to the effort. A third group organized the Golden Oldie Caravan that would haul voters to the polls Election Day.

Eva was cautious. She had seen many an election double-cross. Other than Eva's five-member committee, no single person knew how it all fit together. It was compartmentalized. Most only knew about their role.

Eva would have fainted dead away if she knew her approach was a kitchen table version of the CIA's need-to-know concept for running deadly covert operations around the world. One important aspect of the plan was basic politics. She asked her committee to gather names of their fellow retirees who hadn't voted in recent elections. Eva felt they probably hadn't voted because nobody had asked them. Those providing names weren't told the scope of the effort and were unaware that together they were responsible for more than 200 being added to county voter rolls.

In another layer of secrecy, Eva told each district captain only how many cars each of their precincts should have hauling voters. Only Eva knew the number of Golden Caravan cars that would be rolling into Jordan County's thirty precincts on Election Day. While discussing the overall plan, Eva cleverly talked of hope to turn out fifty voters or so, deliberately mischaracterizing the scope of the effort in case word somehow got to the Lawnsville gossip network.

Sunday afternoon, Eva's organizing committee went over the Election Day implementation plan as if it were a detailed lesson plan. The day before the election, drivers for the Golden Caravan check in with the district coordinators, get their scheduled pickup lists and call to remind folks of their pickup time.

In another, much different setting, the seeds were sown that could rewrite a chapter in Jordan County political history. Perhaps the most heartfelt voting decisions were being made in the county's relatively small black community. Normally, this vote – nearly all in two precincts - was never in doubt: solid old-line territory. Given the nature of this election, particularly the Board of Education races, its several hundred votes could affect outcomes.

The shooting of Jim Dowling had brought deeper contemplation to this tightknit community. His family was respected in nearly every black home. His mother never failed to use her meager resources to help a black family in need.

On this Sunday morning something was about to change - the small church on the hill overlooking the Court House–the primary black church in the county - became electric on this Sunday two days before Election Day. Back after a four-week absence, Jim Dowling's mother, as was her custom, entered quietly and took her seat on the back pew. When she was noticed, the congregation stood *en masse* and gave her a thunderous standing ovation, tears in every eye as she reappeared after her constant, prayerful vigil at the bedside of her wounded son. The pastor came down from the altar and escorted her to the pulpit. Clutching her Bible, she reported her son's recovery was going well, but because of the injuries would not be able to ever return to his job as a policeman and would always walk with a cane.

While every member of the congregation was aware of the shooting, they didn't know of about the permanent injuries. She spoke of how they all had shared her pride when he became the first black policeman in the little town's 100+ year history.

Many in the church wept openly as she related on how close, "James had come to going home to the Lord. I praise Jesus and I know that your prayers move God to spare my dear James," Amens and hallelujahs filled the church.

No mention was made of the election or the seemingly clear political affiliation of those who had been charged with the shooting, but it was on everybody's mind.

Doug Brown, an old-line supporter for twenty-five years, sat with his son, listening and thinking about how the young policeman had taken the time to put the fear of God in his son when the youngster faced expulsion for a fight in the high school cafeteria. No doubt, Jim Dowling's intervention with the principal prevented the expulsion. The officer's stern admonition put the young man on the right path. Brown couldn't take his eyes off the frail, brave woman standing before the congregation. He made his decision, take the old-line money and tell my people to vote the way they want to.

After Mrs. Dowling returned to her regular back row pew, the Rev. Everett Talcott grasped the pulpit. During his sermon, he was able to work in a sentence or two about the important responsibility members of the congregation had to cast their votes on Tuesday. A chorus of Amens thundered through the small church.

A few blocks away, another golden rule—that of money and politics—was front and center at a gathering, not characterized by the giving of an offering, but by the taking of an offering of sorts. It was the biggest organizational effort Charles and Red had ever put together. More people were involved in the precincts and more money was being spent to get out votes, and in about 1,000 incidents, outright buying votes. In addition, the two would have, by far, more left-over election money – estimated $50,000 - to split than they had ever pocketed. This was thanks in large measure to their contrived split over the two presidential candidates.

Red and Charles were meeting with their precinct captains, who they knew would do whatever it took to win. It had been that way in Jordan County for as long as anyone could remember. The two assumed at this late date a lot of black ink on newsprint wouldn't derail their steamroller fueled with piles of green. Among the group were the Election Day specialists, who would handle vote-buying in the seven precincts where votes were traditionally for sale.

Red called the group to order. The jovial atmosphere indicated a strong consensus—things were looking good for the old-line across the county. Calls to voters continued, cars had been confirmed and outside precinct workers had been hired.

Since no one verbally responded to two negative individual reports – they were ignored. First, the *Crier* story on the school Candidate Nights had caused a lot of negative comments about old-line candidates at churches across the county that morning. Second, information that mentioned that Baxter's crew was out more than usual, knocking on doors after dark.

Since no one else commented on either point, the two felt they were minor incidents that had taken place at just one church in the first incidence, and in one neighborhood in the other. "It'll take more than knocking on doors for them to win," Red said, dismissively unaware that many normally old-line families invited neighbors over after dark to talk with Baxter's folks.

Right after Red handed the prized envelopes to the precinct captains, it was Charles' turn. Early last week, Red had approached Charles, "I think it would mean a lot if you could give 'em a little fire and brimstone," Red suggested. This was unusual – normally Red handled all the precinct organizational task. It had been several elections since Charles had played such a role in an old-line campaign. A hard-shell Baptist preacher out in the county couldn't have done better.

"We have been together a long time and fought a lot of battles. But none of our past efforts compare to this election. It's the most important in my memory. Together we can win. But to win, we must get every one of our votes to the polls. There's no doubt we can do it," he concluded, his eyes moving around the table looking each man in the eye.

He announced an extra $50 bonus for carrying their precincts for the old line's chosen candidate for governor.

"If we don't get Sammy elected, we won't get any of those jobs he plans to add to the county state road garage and at the park," Charles said.

"All of you have relatives and friends working for the school board. If we don't get Edward, Yancy and Orville re-elected they will lose their jobs. Make your people understand that. They need to get their whole family to the polls. Now you go home, work the phones and get 'em ready to vote.

"I don't care if it rains cats and dogs on Tuesday, you get our vote out. Know that I appreciate your hard work and I'm proud to be working with you," Charles said, adding a personal touch for which he wasn't known.

The captains and the specialists for precincts where vote-buying would be going on were asked to stay. All the others filed out. Then Charles a politician known far and wide across the state with a reputation to keep unsullied left, not wanting to be present for discussion of this most illegal Election Day activity. Truth be told, he and Red had gone over every detail of that aspect of the campaign in a private meeting the day before.

After those remaining got their extra envelopes, Red stood. His normally friendly voice had disappeared. This time a no-bullshit tone that got their attention, he said, "On Tuesday, deal only with those you know personally. Not anyone else. If you notice any strangers at the polling places, call me immediately," he emphasized. Given the FBI and U.S. marshal's recent activity, he felt Jordan County could be in the U.S. attorney's crosshairs on Election Day.

"And you carry your precinct for all three of our board candidates and I'll give you an extra $50 bonus on top of the $50 for carrying it for Sammy for governor," he concluded.

"Call all your buys over the next two nights. Make sure they get to the polls. They could well hold the key to our winning. And remember if you see any strangers around your precincts call me immediately."

Red and Charles did have just one Election Day plan – they had three. Plan A was the strong precinct organizations in all thirty precincts. But he and Charles had put together Plans B and C as backups in five precincts.

To implement these schemes, Red persuaded the pliable and entrepreneurial county Republican chairman, Elmer Abernathy, to appoint cooperative poll workers at these precincts. Red managed to get the county clerk to appoint inside election officials in the five who were staunch, dependable old-line supporters. The county clerk was reluctant since it meant not hiring people who had worked those precincts for years. But she did owe her office to Red and Charles.

In the five precincts under Plan B, after the polls closed and before the ballots left for the courthouse, the votes of 50 to 100 residents who didn't make it to the polls would be quickly cast "the right way" by the lead poll worker at each precinct.

If Plan B was disrupted, Plan C was ready. Under this scheme, the cars caring the ballots from the five precincts to the courthouse would detour to the lead poll worker's house to implement tactics of Plan B at his kitchen table.

Another election planning meeting was taking place just two miles away from Charles and Red's meeting. Baxter and his small group gathered. Discussions would center around what they had learned the last three weeks at evening meetings in homes across Jordan County.

To Baxter, this was one of the most unusual political campaigns he had ever known. He couldn't get a handle on it. Initially, Baxter would keep his observations to himself, not wanting to keep the others from giving their personal observations.

First, Baxter wanted to hear from the dignified farmer from the southern part of the county. Sam Nathan was a well-known reformer, but also well respected by and had a cordial relationship with many of the old-line supporters in Brownwood district.

"I keep hearing about all the money Charles and Red are putting into this one. Just this afternoon, one of my friends told me they're giving bonuses for precinct captains who carry all their board candidates" Sam related. "But some of their people invited me to their homes at night. Just doesn't add up," he concluded.

Next, Baxter turned to a member of one of the large families concentrated in the center mountain area. "Baxter, this is just confusing as hell. Folks who wouldn't talk politics with me for years called and asked me to stop by for a chat. Like Sam said, nearly all the old-line folks wanted me to stop by at night. Most had the *Crier* out and asked questions about certain stories."

"Andy, what's going on along the river?" Baxter asked of Andy Barrett, who had a keen sense about what people were thinking. "I picked up something at the gas station yesterday. Heard a couple of old retired school employees say they were planning on working the precincts out our way on Election Day.

"When I ask them about it, they just laughed and said they would be fishing Election Day. Come to think of it, the thing about them working Election Day didn't make much sense they're near seventy-five and eighty years old."

"I heard the same thing, but haven't seen anything out in the county," Baxter interjected, as he called on Howard Livingston from the far western end of Jordan County.

"What you all said about the *Crier* stories being talked about is true out our way. I've never seen anything like it. It started the first of the year and then died down with the fire, but in the last week or so, I've seen it just about everywhere I've been," Livingston said. Livingston, like the others, reported the old-line is spreading more money around than ever before in his memory.

"What's going on in town?" Baxter asked as he turned to Randy Browner. "Not as much activity as I had expected. City employees don't seem to be too involved. Oh, they've got signs in their yards, but I haven't seen them out talking to folks like they usually do. It's just hard to understand given how the mayor is campaigning so hard for Edward in the board race."

Baxter found it interesting that everyone mentioned being asked to normal old-line supporters' homes at night. *Something's going on,* the old warhorse thought.

Baxter put his hands in front of him and gazed around the table as he prepared to give his troops what he thought would be their final marching orders for this 1960 primary election.

"Sounds like this one is really hard to read. We're as organized as we've ever been. We can't match them in money, but folks we haven't heard from in years are offering to help but are doing it quietly out of sight. Hard to tell if they'll hold Election Day.

"It boils down to kids and grandkids. If they don't get a solid education from the ground up, they don't have a chance for a decent future.

"This is one of the most important school board elections in the county for the thirty-five years I've been doing this. Edward and them have got the school board headed toward an absolute disaster. They have already started making lists of bus drivers, cooks, and even teachers to get rid of if they get a solid 4-one majority. We've got to get every one of our votes to the polls," Baxter concluded, looking around the room with hands trembling and eyes red. His team was stunned - they had never seen him like this.

One of them said, "Let's bow our heads." He invoked the Lord's name and asked for strength and divine intervention on their behalf Election Day. Baxter was not a church-goer, but he appreciated the prayer and knew nothing short of Divine Intervention would defeat the old-line.

A meeting about ten miles from Lawnsville could well bring victory to the entire old-line slate. Out on Horse Run, as the publisher was bent over his typewriter back in Lawnsville, the Marcum family gathered under the old oaks. Again the discussion focused on the plight of one of their own, who had been thrust into the political equation. The commitment Charles made yesterday during his second trek to Horse Run would determine where the family's votes would go.

To make sure that Big Ed would be at the farm, Charles called early yesterday morning and asked to come back out.

"Sure, I'll be finishing up that same field," Big Ed said, a big smile on his face at the thought of the political big shot again hopscotching through the field recently served by his entire herd. From his perch on the tractor, Big Ed saw Charles wore winter boots this time. He chuckled as he turned off the roaring engine.

"Been a long time since we had a May blizzard."

Charles took the ribbing with good humor. "Your cows have their own brand of snow."

Big Ed couldn't help but laugh out loud. Getting right to the point, Charles said, "Jean Ellen will be offered that job as soon as she graduates. Folks are looking forward to having her in the school system."

Astonished, Charles watched as Big Ed scrambled down off the big green machine to offer his hand, which in Jordan County sealed a promise. "Charles, I appreciate this more than I can tell you. It means a great deal to our family and we'll be there for you Election Day."

"I'm glad I could help," Charles said, "She'll be a fine teacher."

"Get up here, hold on tight, and I'll take you over by your car. Can't have you getting any more of that brown snow on your boots," Big Ed said, again laughing out loud.

With yesterday's commitment from Charles fresh in his mind, Big Ed stood up under the towering trees and gave a stirring, heartfelt treatise on the meaning of family. "This is the very first time that we have asked for anything from an election campaign. This is about a member of our family in need."

The decision was unanimous.

Everyone stood and clapped. All the immediate Marcum family and extended family votes would go for the entire old-line slate. All the Marcums gathered around Anna, who, through her sobs of gratitude, gave each a hug and, "God bless you."

Big Ed Marcum was proud as he watched with pride about how they had come together for the good of one of their own. Their resolve was what held them together.

Every one of the relatives would be at the polls on Tuesday. Members of the family would carry the message to scores of in-laws, who, like the Marcum's, were mostly centered in three precincts in the hills and hollows in the southern end of the county. Marcum's gave their loyalty without reservation and expected no less in return.

But the gathering of the Marcum clan wasn't the last of the Sunday meetings in Jordan County about Election Day planning. While the meeting of the old-line precinct captains included plans for criminal acts on Election Day, vote buying wasn't the only illegal activity being planned. Another was being put together at Lawnsville's City Hall just two blocks from the *Crier* office.

The mayor, his closest ally on city council Benjamin "Ben" Howland, and the police chief met at 5:00 p.m. There was the fire of revenge in the mayor's eyes as he laid out the plan. His thoughts of revenge were so strong it blinded him to the consequences of his treacherous plan. Wayne Atkins spelled out the details that would be implemented at high noon the next day in front of the *Crier* office.

Chapter 35
Ready, Set, Whoa

As the sun began its descent on this balmy spring Sunday, all the pieces of the Election Day jigsaw puzzle seemed to be firmly in place. But, as is the case with a real jigsaw puzzle, a kick of the table can send the carefully completed picture into sudden and complete disarray.

Early Sunday evening, just three hours after the Marcum family's Election Day decision had been sealed, the Marcum patriarch issued an emergency summons for early the next morning.

Out on Horse Run the day before Election Day, bleary-eyed heads of all households in the Marcum clan gathered for one of Granny Marcum's country breakfasts: homemade sausage from hogs raised and butchered on the farm, pancakes, and biscuits made with wheat grown on the farm, and eggs from hens hatched and raised on the farm.

Trust was the basis for important family decisions and often was based upon reliance on the word of another. Charles had made that promise. Standing on the family's ancestral land, he gave his hand. Sunday evening an urgent call from a nephew in the other end of the county, Big Ed Marcum learned that the family's trust had been betrayed. The revelation came from a conversation the nephew had with a friend after Sunday evening services.

It seems this friend's family, the Hammers, had been assured that a granddaughter of that family's Patriarch would get the job that Charles had assured would go to Ed and Anna's daughter, Jane Ellen - Big Ed's granddaughter. In casual after-church conversation, the distant Hammer cousin said that two of the three school board members running for re-election gave the assurance personally to Basil Hammer. Edward, the other incumbent running, gave his assurance in a call from Myrtle Beach. Big Ed's nephew listened silently, not saying a word about his family's connection to that very same job. Not wanting to be rude, Benjamin made small talk with his friend before rushing home to make the call to the Marcum patriarch. Immediately Big Ed issued the summons to the heads of Marcum households. The message was short and simple, family honor called for Sunday's decision to be reversed. When they heard Big Ed's report another unanimous decision was made.

All agreed none of their ballots would be marked for an old-line candidate, for any office. Scores of calls would go out to relatives and extended families during the day and into the night.

After everyone left, Big Ed sat on the wide porch in the old oak rocker pondering his next move. This wouldn't end with the Marcum clan merely changing its position. The family's wrath would be spread further. Charles' double-cross didn't just betray the Marcum clan. It trampled on an Appalachian code of honor that went with looking a man in the eye and giving one's hand. It was in that spirit that Big Ed made the call to make sure another Appalachian clan with that same sense of honor was made aware of the betrayal. He wasn't sure what the result would be, but he wanted to do all he could to ensure the message delivered on Election Day was as strong as possible.

When he first started running the family farm fifty years before, Ed Marcum and his counterpart in the Hammer family met at the livestock auction, became close friends and had done business together over the years. They had a falling out over livestock dealings with a third party and hadn't done any business or spoken for more than ten years.

Basil Hammer, the patriarch of the Hammer family, responded to Big Ed's question with a four-word answer, "We are with you." Basil said how much he appreciated the gracious gesture in a tone that left no doubt he too saw a commitment to be a matter of honor. When he hung up the phone, Big Ed knew he had done the right thing.

Back in Lawnsville, another by-chance conversation, this one in a produce aisle at the grocery store jumbled the election jigsaw puzzle even more.

After the final reformers' strategy meeting ended, Baxter ventured to the grocery store to pick up a cantaloupe for breakfast. Purely by chance, he saw Josephine Brammer, a retired teacher and longtime friend of his mother's. After exchanging pleasantries, and detecting that the older lady had something on her mind, Baxter asked how things were. In tears, she explained she hadn't been appointed to be an inside poll worker this Election Day. Through her sobs, Baxter learned she had worked the precinct for the last five elections and was counting on the money to supplement the family budget.

"I'm not the only one. I got calls from others, some Republicans. We've been replaced by people who haven't been inside a precinct for years. Sarah Whipkey, at the county clerk's office, said they had some complaints about us after the last election."

At first, Baxter thought it was sour grapes, but on a hunch, he carefully compared the list of poll workers in the last election with ones appointed for this one. In five precincts there were all new poll workers – Republicans and Democrats. Realizing these five precincts were out of the way and normally quiet on Election Day, Baxter knew the fix was in. He summoned five of his most trusted allies to his living/war room in thirty minutes. They worked most of the night developing a multi-faceted plan to counter this latest skullduggery. The crusty political veteran wasn't optimistic. He kept wondering, *what else have we missed?*

Chapter 36
City Hospitality

Last-minute political ads swelled the day before Election Day edition to five eight-page sections, a real moneymaker for the cash-strapped publisher. It would be a blockbuster edition, with the publisher's front-page editorial, campaign wrap-up stories and political ads for candidates from the courthouse and statehouse to the White House.

As was the norm, route drivers' cars were lined up in front of the paper's office, drivers behind the wheel and ready to take the *Crier* up every road and hollow in Jordan County.

Then the mayor's plan was implemented. The city's three police cars, lights flashing and sirens blaring, came roaring from both ends of the street, blocking the route drivers' cars. A city policeman got out with a citation book and wrote tickets to each driver for blocking a traffic lane. When the publisher asked what was going on, Chief Aubrey Wyatt—clearly embarrassed—said, "Just following orders, Rick." After writing the tickets, a patrolman told the drivers to follow the patrol cars to the fire station where all the cars and their cargo would be impounded.

Glancing up the street, the publisher saw the mayor and his close ally city councilman, Benjamin "Benny" Howland watching with broad smiles on their faces. Then the mayor motioned for the police chief to join them.

After a shouting match that ended with the mayor's finger at the police chief's chest, the chief turned and walked toward the publisher. Suspecting what was about to happen, the publisher grabbed Al, dragged him into his office and gave him three specific instructions, finishing just as the police chief knocked on Rick's office door.

"You're under arrest for obstructing a law enforcement officer," the chief said, almost in an apologetic whisper. A younger patrolman stepped forward and placed handcuffs on the publisher.

As he was led away by the chief, Al got photos for what would be the lead story in the paper's Election Day edition, or before, if Al was able to carry out all of Rick's last-minute instructions.

The publisher was not taken to the county jail, but to the mayor's city hall office. Just as the chief was placing the handcuffed publisher into a chair, the mayor and Benny barged in. The police chief was dismissed as the mayor locked the door behind him. Without warning, the mayor landed a fist to the publisher's face, causing Rick to fall to the floor. The next blow landed in his back at the same time a kick hit his ribs. "Now, you wiseass son of a bitch, you're gonna find out you should have shut up," the mayor said as he landed three quick punches to Rick's face. Blood and teeth filled the publisher's mouth. Benny cowed in the corner.

Laying on the floor, Rick heard a loud crash. Shattered pieces of the mayor's office door flew across the room, torn from its hinges by Chief Aubrey Wyatt and a patrolman. The City Hall staff saw the bloodied newspaperman sprawled on the floor. Benny Howland fled city hall in a panic. He went home, unplugged his phone and drew all the blinds. He had sided with his lifelong friend on every shady deal the mayor had come up with, but this was too much.

"He took a swing at me," the mayor said to the police chief, his athletic six-foot-two-inch frame standing over the slightly built, handcuffed bleeding publisher.

"Get me some ice and towels," the chief yelled as he picked up the chair and eased the publisher into it. The mayor ordered all members of the City Hall staff to the second-floor council chambers and told two patrolmen to lock both City Hall entrances.

"Listen to me, Wayne, I had no problem stopping those cars. I can handle even arresting him, we had possible reason, but this is just too much. We're in big trouble with this one. He was in my custody. This could be a federal offense," the chief fumed. "The

FBI is already in town for the election and will be all over us if they hear about this."

Unfazed the mayor unloaded, "You work for me and you'll do what I tell you or I'll fire your ass and take your pension. You keep those cars up at the fire station, and don't let them move."

"Mayor, I believe he has a broken nose and is coughing up blood. We've got to get him to the hospital," the chief responded.

"No, no. He'll be okay. I'm going up and talk to the staff," the mayor said in a no-nonsense tone.

Strutting into council chambers, the mayor looked at his captive audience with a cockiness that fit his reputation. "I want to explain so that you will know what really happened downstairs," Wayne Adkins said.

"Today, we had to ticket the *Crier* route drivers who blocked a traffic lane in front of the paper. We had to impound their cars and the papers inside. The cars are up at the fire station. The publisher tried to interfere and the chief had to place him under arrest and brought him here. He tried to jump me and I had to defend myself.

"That's what happened and that's what you're to tell anyone who asks you. If you don't follow my instructions, you will be fired immediately. Understand?" He misinterpreted their silence as acquiescence. All the City Hall staff members had seen the publisher with not a mark on his face when he arrived at City Hall in handcuffs. Just a few minutes later, after the chief of police busted down the mayor's office door, they saw Rick Hill lying on the floor, face bloodied and still in handcuffs. The mayor dismissed the meeting and went back to his office. The mayor called the police chief into his office. "How is he?" he asked the police chief.

"He's still coughing up blood and complaining about pain in his side. I believe he has broken ribs. He's got to get to the hospital," the chief said. "He's in bad shape. I'm afraid a broken rib could puncture a lung."

"I want to charge him with assaulting me. Take him to the emergency room and don't let him talk to anyone. Don't let him out of your sight," the mayor ordered.

A flash went off as the chief led the publisher— bloodied face, swollen eyes and face and still handcuffed—out of City Hall toward the patrol car. "Thank you," Al said to the police chief as he headed up the alley toward the *Crier* office.

Al on a hunch had the *Crier*'s community news editor take a camera to her daughter who was on duty in the hospital emergency room.

As they drove by the fire station, the publisher saw his route drivers standing near their cars under the watchful eyes of two city patrolmen.

"He's under arrest," the chief answered when the doctor asked him to leave the treatment room. "Not to worry. In his condition, he's not likely to run off," the doctor said as he motioned for the chief to leave.

The emergency room nurse gasped when she saw the publisher's face. When the doctor left the room, she used the camera her mother slipped her just before she came into the treatment room. It took twenty stitches each to close the wounds over his eye and under his chin. The ribs would heal in time on their own. Including the X-rays, the stitching and other examinations, it was nearly 5:00 p.m. before the publisher was back in the custody of the chief.

As they were headed back to City Hall, "Dispatcher to chief," came over the police radio.

"Chief, over."

"Four U.S. marshals are here saying you are to release Mr. Hill, over."

"Roger that, we'll be right in," the chief answered.

"Ah, my first instruction to Al, 'call the U.S. attorney,'" Rick said to himself.

He'd learn later that Al was able to give details of the beating to the U.S. attorney because of an anonymous call to the *Crier* from City Hall shortly after the mayor's office door was shattered. When speaking to the U.S. attorney, Al learned that four marshals were already in Jordan County to monitor Election Day.

Upon returning to City Hall, the chief ,reacting to the U.S. Marshal's order, hurriedly took the handcuffs off the publisher.

"What the hell is going on here?" the mayor yelled as he came into the chief's office and found himself face-to-face with the U.S. marshals. The chief quickly explained the situation and the mayor became quiet.

"There's one other thing, Chief," one of the marshals said as he handed another official-looking document. This one ordered the route drivers' cars and their cargo be released immediately. Without a word, the chief picked up the dispatcher's microphone and ordered the two patrolmen at the fire station to "let the cars with the papers go now!"

As the mayor turned to leave the chief's office, one of the marshals stepped forward. "We're not finished with you, Mr. Mayor. You are under arrest for the beating of Mr. Hill. You will be taken to Charleston tonight and have a hearing before a federal magistrate tomorrow morning," the marshal said as he placed handcuffs on the mayor. Two of the marshals led the mayor outside. The Lawnsville Chief Executive blinked as the community news editor took her "Photo of the Year."

Another marshal took Rick first by the fire station. Repeating Instruction 3, one Al had already given them, the publisher told the route drivers to honk as they put the papers in delivery boxes to let people know the paper had finally arrived. It would be 8:00 p.m. before all the route drivers finished their deliveries.

The marshals then took the publisher to the *Crier* office and requested a statement that took about thirty minutes. "We're in town through tomorrow night, so let us know if you need us," one of the marshals said after completing the questioning.

The publisher's hunch was right. Most of the paper's subscribers were waiting with considerable anticipation for the day-before-Election-Day *Crier*. And there would be a bonus delivered with the paper: Instruction No. 2, given to Al just before the handcuffs went on. Al was to write a story about the impoundment of the route drivers' cars and the publisher's arrest. If the drivers got their cars back, the supplement could be delivered with the *Crier*. It was important to let the readers know what happened before they went to the polls on Election Day.

The owner of the small print shop in town had gladly accepted the assignment and had the 8 ½ x 11 four-pager finished about 15 minutes before the U.S. marshal ordered the drivers' cars released from impoundment.

The supplement was a home run. Al played the grizzled old reporter to perfection having managed to write the story and include three photos, one of the publisher being led in handcuffs from the newspaper office, not a mark on his face; another taken of Rick leaving City Hall, his face bloodied; and the third of the city policemen standing guard over the route drivers' cars. Carefully written, the captions gave the timeline explaining that only 20 minutes elapsed between the two photographs of the publisher, and noting that he had been in police custody the entire time. Because of timing, there was no mention in the flyer of the mayor's arrest that would be the lead story in the Election Day edition.

"Great job, Al," the publisher said, holding up a copy of the flyer and "great picture, Billy."

"You look like hell," the community news editor replied, concern evident in her face and voice.

"At least we have one good story for the Election Day issue. Make that two," he amended through swollen lips, thinking of the mayor's arrest.

Implementing the last of the publisher's pre-arrest instructions, Al had asked the staff to stay late to tell subscribers calling about the late delivery. The paper would be there "just as soon as possible and the drivers will honk when it's in your box."

"How many calls have you received?"

"Just over a thousand," the community news editor grumpily replied, reading from her carefully kept count, "And they are really mad about us being late."

It was 8:30 p.m. before the publisher received the call confirming tat the last route driver had completed her run. Nearly all the drivers said their customers came right out to get the paper when they honked.

While Rick was being treated to the hospitality at City Hall, Al and the community news editor put together the Election Day issue. With the exception of the lead Election Day story, everything else was nearly ready to go to the printer. It all had to be redone. The mayor's arrest, including a picture of him being led from City Hall in handcuffs, would be the lead story.

Since subscribers in the city had received the previous day's edition at the normal time, their papers didn't include the additional flyer. They'd get that story and photos in the Election Day's paper.

While the *Crier* would get to the printer a little late tonight, the angel had his crew ready for a faster than normal turn-around. So, the route drivers would be on the road by 7:00 a.m. Election Day. That meant most readers would have the *Crier* before many of them went to the polls.

It was evident to the publisher that normalcy was returning. The Election Day edition was down to two sections and the following day it would be about the same depending upon election "thank you" ads that might come in, mostly from the winners, of course.

Now it was home to get a good night's sleep, or as good as he could get, given his pain and that tomorrow was Election Day. Rick's nightly call to Anne and the children would not include mention of Rick's beating. After he hung up, he spent another couple of hours going over plans for Election Day coverage then headed home.

Tomorrow he'd be in the office two hours early and on the phone checking with his stringers in the communities out in the county to get a feel for voter turnout. Then it would be a late election night at the Jordan County courthouse. Given the reports Rick got about the money the old-line faction was throwing around its precinct organization, he was certain Election Night would be a time of celebration for its candidates up and down the ballot.

Chapter 37
Can Black Ink Top Mountains of Green?

A hallowed Jordan County Election Day tradition was the campaign with the most money won.

Rick fully understood that breaking the stranglehold of an entrenched county political machine in Southern West Virginia was not something that could be achieved in ten days - the time the *Crier* had been back in business.

Oh, there had been signs that some people were upset, but it was subtle. He was certain thousands of Jordan County residents would go to the polls today and stick with what they knew and had been told for years was good for them—the old-line.

Rick was at the *Crier* by 5:30 a.m. Bleary-eyed staff members began to drift in about 6:00.

The goal was to have route drivers on the road as early as possible, certainly no later than 7:30. Young carriers in the city would have the paper out early, too, since Election Day was a school holiday. Oddly enough, the lead story in today's issue was not directly related to the election.

Mayor Charged with Beating Handcuffed Publisher
City Police Seize *Crier*, Detain Route Drivers

The headline screamed across the top of the *Crier's* front page. A photo of the mayor in handcuffs being escorted from City Hall by federal marshals was beside a picture of the publisher's bruised and battered face as he was led from City Hall by the police chief.

Rick labored with the certainty the photo of his rearranged face would be what would most disturb the readers. Wrong. Readers' attention was equally focused on the paragraphs Rick included from earlier Candidate Night story, describing the city's chief executive's strong support of the old-line's board of education candidates. Those passages and the earlier arrests of the street commissioner, his brother and three cohorts who worked part-time for the city connected the old-line with problems at City Hall, the newspaper fire, the shooting of a Lawnsville police officer and the wounding and now the beating of the publisher. The question was, would those facts cause the readers to enter the voting booth and reverse decades of Jordan County political history? Rick was not confident.

As far as Red and Charles were concerned it would take more than a last-minute surge of *Crier* black ink to overcome the green of their golden rule of county politics. Besides, "all that was a city problem." A lot of folks agreed with the two political veterans. Even many who went to the polls to vote against the old-line were resigned to seeing the corrupt faction coming out victorious.

Rick waited until the route drivers were on the road, then picked up a camera and headed up to the hundred-year-old school that housed a precinct with a reputation for vote-buying. He parked directly across the street. Former Sheriff Brown was right in front. The publisher noticed many coming out of the polling place handed the former sheriff a piece of paper and he handed them an envelope. *Great photo*, the *Crier* publisher thought as he snapped away and quickly drove away as the former sheriff headed toward him. No sooner was Rick back at the *Crier* than the phone rang. The community news editor announced, "It's old Sheriff Brown, and he's spitting nails."

"Good morning," Rick said cheerfully as if he didn't know who was on the other end. "I just wanted you to know those folks were just giving me their rent money when they came out from voting, it wasn't anything wrong going on," the former sheriff said without introduction.

"Well, Sheriff, thanks for calling, I understand now," he said, remembering his father's tales about West Virginia's electoral tradition of the chain ballot.

In some areas, chain ballots were as much a part of Election Day as campaign signs. Links in the chain were forged early Election Days when the first "for sale" voter arrived outside a precinct. A campaign worker in charge of vote-buying would give the voter a folded blank piece of paper the size of a ballot that the voter would put it in his pocket. Once in the voting room, the voter signed the poll book, got a real ballot from the election clerk, and then go into the privacy of the voting booth. Once safely behind the curtain, put the ballot in his pocket, then pull back the voting booth curtain and put the blank piece of paper in the ballot box. Once outside he'd give the unmarked ballot to the precinct's paymaster and receive a half-pint of rot-gut or $3 to $5. The first link in the chain was forged.

The precinct captain would mark that ballot and give it to the next bought voter going into the polling place. Once again, inside the voting booth, the voter would put the unmarked ballot in his pocket, take out the pre-marked one. That voter would pull back the curtain put the pre-marked ballot in the ballot box, go outside give the unmarked ballot to the precinct worker in exchange for his ill-gotten gain. And so it went until the polls closed.

Since he couldn't prove the chain ballot was going on, the publisher printed the "rent money" explanation, word for word.

But Rick wasn't the only one keeping watch over Election Day activities. Red's precinct captains knew to call in every hour or so, beginning just after the traditional early morning rush. The old sheriff called in with a glowing mid-morning report. More blacks were voting than he had ever seen at this precinct. It continued all day, and they were still coming when he called Red just before the polls closed at 7:30.

In the old sheriff's more than forty years of working this precinct, old-line candidates had never carried it by less than a two-to-one margin. Everything was routine. The chain ballot was running well, in fact, he had three chains going. The black vote was heavier than normal here and at the other precinct with a heavy black vote.

Red was delighted to hear that report. He never thought to connect the turnout to Jim Dowling's shooting.

Later on, during his Election Day treks to various precincts, Rick happened to stop for gas at the same time as Douglas Brown, the first black ever to play football at Jordan County High School. They nodded to each other and the hulking giant came toward the newspaperman with a solemn face.

"Saw your story on Jim Dowling in the paper. Have you heard anything since?" he inquired, concern written all over his face not certain Mrs. Dowling had included all the details at Sunday's church service.

"His career as a policeman is over for sure. He might not be able to use his right arm. At one time they thought he might lose it altogether," the publisher responded.

"Bastards," the former Friday Night star mumbled before going back to top off his tank.

Back at the paper, the publisher was at the front counter when a respected retired principal of the formerly all-black high school came in to place a small ad for his church's annual spring picnic. Their conversation turned to Jim Dowling's condition. "His mother is really taking this hard," the retired educator said shaking his head. "She's worked so hard bringing those children up by herself, and now this. We are all praying for her," he concluded as he headed out the door.

Putting educator's "we" together with "bastards" from the gas-pump conversation, the publisher thought, *maybe, just maybe,* and then he remembered the stories he'd heard about the old-line's hold on the county's black vote.

"Ain't gonna happen," he muttered, as he retreated to his cubbyhole. "But then again..." his heart's optimism taking over the hard facts in his brain.

In addition to missing the significance of the heavy black vote, there was another Election Day activity Red failed to recognize. By mid-morning, captains in five widely separated precincts reported there was an older driver or two continually delivering equally old voters to the polls. If Red had bothered to ask the other captains, he would have learned that the Golden Caravan was rolling in all thirty of the county's precincts. He thought that some old folks out in the county just wanted to vote against the

Catholic running for president. When the polls closed at 7:30, the Golden Caravan had hauled nearly 250 voters - surpassing Eva's stated goal of 50.

Unlike Red, Baxter *heard* what he was listening to. His was a more intuitive evaluation. Baxter put together the two unrelated Election Day activities: older drivers at every precinct, and the heavy black vote. To crafty, bad-eye Baxter, the two meant something was going on he hadn't picked up on during his frequent electioneering trips out in the county. But these Election Day reports didn't fit with his nagging doomsday premonition. On his final trip around Jordan County on the day before Election Day, Baxter felt there was a good chance his reformers might be swamped by the old-line's golden rule.

One key to Red's strategy for holding onto control of the school board was six precincts, three each in opposite ends of the county controlled by the Hammer and Marcum families. Red felt the votes of the families would ensure victories in two different districts for two of the three board members needed to retain ironclad control of the board. Also, they would bring a win for Bill Joe Ratliff, to ensure continued control of the county commission. Reports indicated strong turnouts in all of these precincts. Red smiled and thought, "All this came from just one job." He was certain the mayor's hold on the city's precincts would bring the third board seat.

He and Charles had already decided Edward would take the fall for the double job promise. Given Edward's reputation, it would be easy to pin it on the nitwit.

They knew the certain success of their scheme came from Charles' second trip to see Big Ed and the lie to the Marcum patriarch. The captains at the six precincts dominated by the two clans reported the heaviest turnouts in years. Red was so confident that just after noon, he called Charles in the capital city at Sammy's headquarters with the good news.

In keeping close tabs on their clan's voting, both patriarchs found the turnout was solid not only of blood but also for their respective extended families.

As the polls' closing time approached on this historic Election Day, the crowd to view the posting of precinct totals became standing-room-only in the courtroom. Tension was in the air of the cavernous space. Those not talking leaned in to eavesdrop on nearby conversations, straining to glean every scintilla of knowledge from each comment.

Many were nervously asking what another had heard. Hell, they hadn't heard anything based on fact. The polls hadn't closed. But asking was part of the tradition.

Red, all his candidates (except Edward), his precinct captains, well-wishers, and hangers-on were on one side of the courtroom. Celebration was in the air. They were laughing and slapping each other on the back. Throughout the day, Red got reports that turnout was high in precincts that had been old-line bastions for decades. The figures would show that in twenty-eight of the county's thirty precincts, voter turnout surpassed Red's goals. The exceptions were the two city precincts where the old-line normally overwhelmed the reformers and where most of the city employees and their families voted.

Old bad-eye Baxter heard the same reports on turnout. It added to his pessimism. However, the "it just ain't right" comments he'd heard across Jordan County the week before kept ringing in his ears.

Baxter was also puzzled by Golden Caravan that showed up at all thirty precincts. He and his folks were completely surprised not a word leaked out.

Now that took some organization, Baxter thought as he envisioned tea later this week with Eva. The brain behind the Goldens wasn't in the courtroom, but Eva's nephew and his two teenage sons were there to take turns running the results to Eva's brain trust gathered for tea and, yes, a bit of sherry, two blocks from Court House Square. She was resigned to seeing the board remain in the hands of those who didn't care about the county's children, but she knew the Old Biddie Party, despite the men's complaints she couldn't give up that name, had tried their very best.

Three deputies were in the back of the courtroom, in case another Jordan County Election Day tradition—fisticuffs—fistfights broke out as the night wore on.

Overall this would be the county's highest percentage voter turnout in at least the last fifty years. Initial credit would go to the spirited campaigning and excitement over the presidential primary and the piles of money. More thoughtful analysis might suggest increased issue-based coverage in the *Crier*, one of the smallest dailies in the country, as having an impact.

Rick walked into the courtroom just before the 7:30 poll closing and would stay until the final precinct's numbers were announced. The community news editor and the sports editor rotated taking results back to the *Crier* so the results could be called into the Associated Press state bureau.

Confident, Red walked with the strut of a bantam rooster over to the publisher. "How's it look tonight, Red?" Rick asked.

Red simply could not hide his confidence, smiled broadly, "From what I heard all day seems voting was real heavy. Could be a good night."

As usual, old Sheriff Henry Brown's precinct just a few blocks away was the first to arrive. Just after noon, he had assured Red the vote was heavy and he felt confident about old-line candidates' success.

Here, Eddy Bill won and won big, outdistancing his nearest competitor by 225 votes. It was a different story for the rest of the old-line slate. Edward ran last of the board candidates. Both Kermit Yancy and Orville Brown unexpectedly ran ahead of Edward by eight and ten votes but still not in the top three. Bill Joe Hamrick led for the county commission race by a slim two-vote margin over Baxter's candidate, Joe Ed Green. The results were a shocker. Always in the past. old-line candidates enjoyed a two-to-one margin. The old sheriff's streak was broken. The former sheriff just shook his head, "Red don't understand how the count is right, we got all our voters out." Red didn't show any outward concern but was puzzled by the results given the old sheriff's usually accurate reports.

The other four precincts located in Lawnsville arrived next. In these precincts, the old-line candidates normally got sixty percent of the vote. First were the two Lawnsville precincts that historically could be counted on to be old-line but that occasionally would go with Baxter's group by the narrowest of margins. On this Election Day, Eddy Bill carried both by a twenty percent margin over his nearest competitor.

Bill Joe Ratliff, the old-line county commission candidate, had a slim ten-vote margin from the precinct. As for the old-line board candidates, Edward ran dead last. The other two old-line board candidates ran first and second with total margins of about twenty votes – far less than the twenty percent margin Red had expected.

When clerks arrived from the two city precincts where most city employees voted, Red had a big smile. He was sure they would go overwhelmingly for his slate. The voter turnout would prove to be surprising, the lowest for any precincts in the county.

With all five of the city precincts in, Eddy Bill won them all. Edward had the fewest votes of any board candidate. That was compared to the last election when he won the five Lawnsville precincts with a 400-vote margin.

In the city, the other two board candidates, Kermit and Orville ran better than Edward and were in the top three for the board seats by the slimmest of margin only twelve and fifteen votes respectively. Bill Joe Ratliff had only a thirty-vote lead coming out of the five Lawnsville precincts.

Red glanced down at the figures noting that old-line support was down significantly but smiled knowing the five newly staffed precincts and the six Marcum and Hammer polling places would more than make up the difference.

About an hour after the polls closed, precincts from out in the county began to trickle in. Over the next two hours, vote tallies for fourteen more precincts arrived at the county clerk's office. Nineteen out of Jordan County's thirty precincts had been delivered to the courthouse. As almost everyone expected, in these Eddy Bill outdistanced the other sheriff candidates by a wide margin. Bill Joe, the old-line candidate for county commission, was snowed under by the 4-H families in the county. When the fourteen precincts' total were combined with the five Lawnsville precincts, he was just fifty votes ahead of reformer Joe Ed Green. At this point in the last election, Bill Joe enjoyed a 600 vote margin.

Some of the reformers present in the courtroom were chuckling. As Baxter observed, "He got throwed in the river," referring to the Commission's vote against hiring 4-H camp lifeguards

Despite all the controversy around Edward, after nineteen voting places reported, he was last of the board candidates, but it was possible the precincts where Red had the fix-in could bring him back. At this point the last Election Day, Edward was in front by nearly 1,000 votes.

Old-line supporters were concerned by the tallies for the commission and board races, but relaxed a bit when they saw the calm, confident look on Red's face.

Rick went over the vote tallies and while old-line candidates were behind, he knew there were still eleven precincts out that could bring the old-line back in every race. *They could still pull this off,* he thought, remembering Jordan County's sordid political past.

Even with this lower than expected totals up to now, Red was confident. He had aces up his sleeve, one supplied by the county clerk's appointment of new, dependable poll workers in five out-of-the-way precincts. Ruby Miller used her position to select new Democratic poll workers from a list Red had provided. The county clerk also appointed new Republican poll clerks in the same five precincts from a list presented by Jordan County's Republican chairman. She had a feeling these new poll workers were all part of Red's plans. But she didn't know the details and didn't want to.

Red was unaware of the warnings the reformers had given workers at his five special precincts just before the polls closed. He didn't know that the secret ace might be lost because of Baxter's by-chance conversation in the produce section.

As a result of that conversation near the cantaloupes, Baxter came up with his own plan for those same five precincts. He had instructed two reformers who voted at each of the five precincts to show up to vote right before the polls closed. As they received their poll slips, one would ask the number of votes cast thus far. When the poll clerk responded, one of the two reformers would make a big deal of looking at his watch and writing down the number in his notebook. The other would remark for all the poll clerks to hear, "Better not be too many more votes getting to the courthouse; understand federal polls watchers are all over the county."

This routine was repeated in each of the five precincts and the poll clerks' reactions were the same—worried looks were exchanged. Because voting was steady, the poll clerks in Red's five chosen precincts were not able to implement Plan B during the day as originally planned, but would do it right after the polls closed or to go to Plan C on the way to the courthouse.

Now that the reformers had the late vote count at those precincts, Red and Charles' two voter-fraud plans could be in shambles. It would mean that 400 to 600 crucial, fraudulent votes might not find their way into the count. But in the five precincts after the reformer's warning, the lead poll workers decided on their own they would stop at their houses on the way to the courthouse to implement Plan C.

Their scheme was to cast illegal ballots for those who didn't make it to vote. Those shenanigans were also doomed.

To guard against such skullduggery, the reformers sat in their cars outside each of the five precincts until the polls closed. They honked their horns and waved to the poll clerks as they came out of the precincts. Baxter's team members closely followed the car taking the ballots and polls books to the Jordan County courthouse. When the poll workers saw the Reformers outside the precincts, they immediately understood that any chance for Plan C had vanished.

Red knew something was very wrong when poll workers from the five newly staffed precincts arrived at the courthouse. The dejected looks on the precinct workers' faces told Red things had not gone as planned. Red went outside of the courtroom and listened to workers from one of the precincts report what Baxter's guys had done.

"They came in right before we closed the polls, asked about the number of votes cast up to then, and then announced that the feds would be on us if the totals we brought to the courthouse were more than what we told them. They were outside looking in the windows while we were counting, so we could not do anything.

"We decided we would go to Andy's house, which is close to the precinct and check the poll books for people who didn't and cast ballots. But that got messed up. When we came out of the voting place, they were waiting and followed us all the way here, so we didn't have a chance to do anything."

Red just shook his head. "I appreciate you all trying," he said.

Going back into the courtroom, Red still had the assured look of a winner. With the six precincts controlled by the two families still out, Red was certain those would bring victory in the two of the board races and could even pull the county commission candidate, the hapless but likable Bill Joe Ratliff, over the top.

"It's going to be fine," Red assured a worried Bill Joe.

While the voting ended at 7:30, it was nearly ten before polls workers emerged from one of the five precincts and headed for the courthouse with the final tallies. They were yelling and shoving each other; several had to be separated by cooler heads.

Just as Red sat down after his conversation in the hall, the poll workers from the one precinct came through the big courtroom doors, cussing and snarling at each other, blood coming from busted lips. Two had black eyes.

Rick began snapping pictures the moment they entered the courtroom.

It would be Thursday before Rick heard a version of what happened to derail Charles and Red's Plan B and C.

Normally, only two workers—one from each political party—transported ballot boxes and voter books to the courthouse. This time all seven had come to the courthouse. It was evident the precinct had major problems among the workers. Once these precinct's records were given to the county clerk, Red met outside with the lead inside poll worker.

It seemed the Republican polls workers did not understand they were to stand down after the polls closed and let Red's poll workers cast fraudulent ballots. "They started pushing and shoving and threatening to call the sheriff. We pushed back and then someone threw a punch. It didn't last long, but we had no chance to do anything. Once that settled down, they made us recount all the votes four times before they would sign off on the results," a veteran with the old-line lamented, going on to add that some of Baxter's people caused a stir over the number of people who had voted. "Then they followed us all the way here to the courthouse. Red, I've never seen anything like this one." He shook Red's hand and headed home.

But Red remained confident certain the six family precincts would be ironclad. The count was dragging on, and most of the old-line candidates and supporters in the courtroom followed Red's lead and waited in a celebratory mood. A few others were mouthing off to Baxter's reformers, and a heated argument took place in one corner, fists started flying, and deputies waded in to make sure a full-scale donnybrook didn't break out. The fighting stopped but the heated verbal exchanges continued.

Baxter watched it all, not sure what was happening. He'd received a report on Sunday afternoon the Marcum clan had decided to back the old-line. The same with the Hammer family in the other end of the county. Baxter knew that could be enough to give the old-line a total victory.

Poll clerks from the three Marcum precincts in the southern end of the county arrived within 15 minutes of each other. Red was focused, looking for any sign of the results. The poll clerks merely nodded as they went into a small room to turn over the precinct records to the county clerk. None of them were smiling. Red felt they were just tired.

Five minutes later, the three Hammer precincts from the northern end of the county arrived. The county clerk said that all six of the precincts would be announced together in thirty minutes.

The candidates gathered around Red, asking if he'd heard anything, seeming to believe that somehow, he had mystical power that allowed him to know the results before anyone else. He just smiled and said he felt these precincts would bring good news.

Baxter was on the other side of the room closely studying the figures released so far from the county's other twenty-four precincts. He added them up three times. Baxter was certain the Marcum family votes in three precincts and the Hammer votes in the other three would bring the old-line victories for the school board and county commission.

Disbelief was evident on Red's face when he heard the results from the three precincts in the southern end of the county, where the Marcum family was strongest. Not one old-line candidate, except Eddy Bill, had carried any of the three precincts. They were beaten and beaten badly. The incumbent member of the county commission got only thirty percent of the vote in the three precincts and the old-line school board candidates were the bottom three.

The northern precincts dominated by the Hammer clan were even worse. Big Ed Marcum's message was delivered and it would be abundantly clear to Red and Charles when they analyzed precinct-by-precinct totals.

Red was certain there had been some miscounting of votes, given the fact that Charles had made two trips to see Big Ed Marcum, and the incumbent school board candidates had personally made the commitment on the job to the Hammer patriarch.

It was a disaster for the old-line. It lost the school board and the county commission seats by large margins. Reformers won two seats on the school board and the self-styled independent candidate Baxter supported won the third. A bright spot for the old-line –Eddy Bill won handily. But the reformers had the majority on the county commission. The sheriff would have to play ball with them, they controlled his office budget.

All was not lost for the old line. If Sammy won the nomination for governor, the Jordan County old line would still have influence about who got jobs at the state road garage and have a say in some of the jobs at the state parks. The old state road to Red and Charles's newly acquired riverfront property would get immediate attention.

But all that wouldn't take away the sting of being beaten in a county the old-line had controlled for decades.

Baxter and Rick's eyes met across the raucous courtroom. A slight nod said it all. They both knew that *We, the People*, won this Election Day. The people rose up, and with their ballots said, "Enough. The government's ours and we won't take this crap anymore." Whether the results indicated a permanent shift or were just a bump on Jordan County's political road would be determined in the general election just under six months away.

The publisher took in the courtroom scene—old-liners and Reformers both stunned with a common reaction disbelief—reformers cheering in disbelief while old-liners were shaking their heads in disbelief.

For Rick, the inbred cynical nature of newspaper reporters surged to the fore. The publisher thought, *wonder how long it'll be before the reformers will step in it.*

On this particular Election Day, a tornado of change roared through Jordan County and swept down every hollow and country road. On the way out of the courthouse, Rick stuck his head into the sheriff's office. "You look like you've been rode hard and hung up wet," Rick said.

"You just never quit. This has been a rough one," the sheriff answered, almost moaning.

"Must have been that great photo in the ad with you and the four who dropped out," Rick offered, just to see what would be the response.

He chuckled at the smiling sheriff's one-finger salute, adding, "You're number one in my book, too."

Unable to keep from laughing, Rick said, "I hear the best way to cure Election Day blues is a trip to Myrtle Beach."

Eddy Bill responded with a chuckle, then turned serious. "I got a complaint from the teacher. Stop by in the morning, and I'll have details."

"It'll be a day or two, we'll be tied up with after-elections stories the rest of the week Oh, by the way, congratulations," Rick said as he turned to head back to the paper for what would be a long night. He knew that upheaval in Jordan County wouldn't end with Election Day.

The future could make Election Day seem like a Sunday school picnic. Trials were looming for those arrested for the fire and the shooting of a police officer. Next would be the trials for the same men in connection with the roadblock and his own attempted murder.

And the battering of the established political faction would continue. The mayor would face charges for the beating of the handcuffed publisher and for ordering the detention of drivers in an attempt to keep a *Crier* pre-election issue from its readers. Rick understood at least one city policeman and two city employees had been interviewed by the FBI in connection with those charges.

Mulling it all over, Rick asked himself, "How in the world could the Johnson brothers come up with that scheme on their own?"

All of that was in the future. Right now, Rick and the *Crier* staff would labor late into the night on stories that would inform the readers about this historical Election Day in Jordan County. To quote Shakespeare's *The Tempest*, a sea change had come to the body politic of Jordan County. Whether it was as permanent as the transformation 350 years ago at the bottom of the sea was another question.

Chapter 38
An Earthquake, or a Bump in the Road?

On Wednesday, May 11, the sun came up as usual, moving from east to west, but its bright, warm rays spread across a much different Jordan County than the one just 24 hours before.

Between those two beautiful spring sunrises, *We the People* sent an unmistakable message, Enough, with their trip to the polls on this Election Day.

People all over the county were trying to figure out what exactly happened to cause this county-wide repudiation of the political faction that had dominated for as long as most could remember.

Charles hadn't shown his face in town. He was spending the rest of the week at the state capital, making sure that his position of influence with the next governor was solid. He put together an outstanding organization in nine southern West Virginia counties, where Sammy got 58,270 votes, more than double his nearest competitor, in winning 63 percent of ballots cast there.

In staying close to Sammy the day following the election, Charles wanted to make sure that none of the other hangers-on maneuvered ahead of him in the goodie line. With Sammy's certain victory in November, Charles and Red would have control of all state jobs in the county, at the state road garage, the state parks and at state agencies' regional offices in Jordan and surrounding counties.

This power would permit him and Red to hold their heads high around Lawnsville despite losing every local race. That the two would be splitting nearly $50,000 in cash from leftover election money would certainly help ease the ballot-inflicted pain.

The two had visions of dollar signs just thinking about the new road and water system that would cause the value of the acreage along the river to soar. "Sweet, sweet," he kept saying to himself. The envelope of appreciation that Red would deliver to the new governor would be plump.

The morning after, Joseph Ballengee stopped to commiserate with Red about the Election Day verdict. "There is no doubt in my mind that the *Crier* stories had a real impact. The day before the election, I was visiting my sister out at Sandstone and she had four or five different editions of the paper spread out on her kitchen table. She and her family had been with us for years. We lost all of 'em this time," the former *Crier* publisher lamented.

"Is there any way to get Rick to see things our way?" Red inquired apprehensively.

"I don't believe there is. He's a hard-ass. I wouldn't be surprised if he's as hard on Baxter's bunch," Joseph continued.

"That's good to hear he'll be after them, too," Red responded, not sure the former publisher's prediction would prove accurate.

Right now, his primary post-election priority was to understand this unprecedented old-line defeat. Privately, Red and Charles in a face-to-face meeting on Friday would carefully dissect the results, precinct by precinct, and attempt to identify the "whys" for the Election Day debacle.

Even after their intense review, the two would remain clueless about some of the important causes of the old-fashioned asswhumping of the old line. Despite the prospect of being close to the next governor, Red and Charles' political reputation had suffered significantly in Jordan County because of the repudiation of the old-line candidates in every precinct.

On Wednesday night after Election Day, members of Red's campaign inner circle gathered around his late grandmother's dining room table to discuss the voter rebellion that stretched from the tree-lined streets of Lawnsville neighborhoods to the far corners of Jordan County. The results would have been easy to understand if only a few precincts had gone off the reservation.

When the brain trust was assembled, Red jumped right in. "What happened?"

"Folks had settled down a bit about two weeks before the election, and then when the paper came back, people got all stirred up again," Jim Bob, who ruled over the mountain in the middle of the county offered.

"We got nearly all of our people to the polls, but they just didn't stay with us. A lot of folks believe that Edward and the mayor are two of a kind. And all day we had those retired school people hauling in old folks who hadn't voted in years," he continued, pulling out his trusty red bandanna and wiping his brow.

"What do the rest of you think?" Red inquired, hoping against hope that someone would bring some cheerfulness into the conversation.

In his measured tone, Joe Brown offered, "The story about the Candidate Night really made folks out our way mad. Most felt Edward and his bunch lied to 'em about fixing up the schools. And that damned county commission vote against opening the 4-H pool didn't help none either."

"Jimmy Ed, how do you see it," Red asked the veteran supporter who had worked elections for the old line for thirty years.

"I agree with Jim Bob. The retired school employees were active in every one of our precincts. They put it together real quiet. And another thing, over the weekend before Election Day, folks seemed to be avoiding our precinct captains when they were out campaigning," Jimmy Ed concluded. As the campaign veteran ended his comments, Red realized that most of the things being described happened after the *Crier* reappeared.

"Anything else we need to cover?" Red warily asked, looking around at the dejected faces.

John, who was usually last to be called upon, began slowly. "It was the strangest election I've ever seen. Out our way, we got nearly every one of our normal voters to the polls. Then, we made our number for vote-buying this time around, in the one precinct.

"After all that, we didn't carry a precinct. They came out, but a lot voted the other way. Not one of our candidates except Eddy Bill carried all our precincts out our way. And like Jim Bob said, people saw Edward tied to the mayor," he reported as he sagged into his chair. "I hate to say it, but it seems that we lost a lot of our sure-fire supporters," he concluded.

"I agree this was one strange election. Hard to figure," Red said.

"There is some good news from Election Day. Sammy— our candidate for governor—won statewide. We will have some influence with the county highway garage, state parks and at some state offices in Princeton," Red continued, knowing this small number of jobs could not nearly make up for the number the old-line would lose as the result of the board and county commission election. "Charles and I appreciate very much your hard work and that of your precinct captains. If you think of anything else, please give me a call," the old pol said as he got up, signaling the end of the meeting.

After the council members left, Red called Charles relating the pall over the meeting. "The guys were pretty tired and disappointed. Nobody saw this coming," he reported.

"I'll be home late Friday afternoon. I'll come by and we can talk. Make sure you have all the precinct totals," Charles said. "I've talked to Sammy and have some good news. Reminded him about the road and waterline. He's looking forward to visiting with you after the swearing-in," Charles added.

For the next two days, a parade of folks stopped by the cleaners, all asking what Red thought about the election. He knew that many of those claiming they had stuck with the old line all the way were lying based on official precinct vote totals.

On Friday morning, in preparation for the meeting with Charles, Red walked over to the old-line bank to clear out his and Charles' joint safety deposit box that held the excess Election Day cash they had accumulated. Red was so focused on stuffing all the cash into his worn leather briefcase that he failed to notice Sally Jones, a veteran bank employee lingering longer than usual in the safe deposit box vault.

During their post-election meeting that evening, Red and Charles would count the ill-gotten gains, split it, and the following day put it into their safety deposit boxes. The two would be splitting more than the $50,000 they had estimated earlier.

Charles arrived just as Red was turning over the closed sign and turning out the lights in the front of the cleaners. Not a word was spoken as they made their way down the narrow hallway to Red's compact but comfortable office, its walls covered with campaign signs and bumper stickers from Election Days past. Red put two cans of lemonade on the desk.

"What's new in the big city?" Red asked, eager to hear about Charles' conversation with the sure-to-be next governor.

"Sammy is really pleased with the work we did down here." Charles reported, giving Red some credit for his trips into Monroe, Fayette, Wyoming, and Greenbrier counties.

They discussed another bright spot for Red, his candidate for president, John Kennedy, won the state. Many expected the young Massachusetts senator to win the party's nomination and with the strong possibility of beating the sitting vice president in the November General Election. "Hope those old boys come back to play in '64," Red added winking at Charles as he patted this cash-filled briefcase before turning to a more serious manner.

"Any word on the trials?" Red inquired.

"I had lunch with Ray Rogers. He said the word around the federal courthouse is they will be in late summer. Not sure about the mayor's trial. He's hired a Charleston lawyer and will be asking for bail on Monday. Ray believes he will be out by Tuesday. Could get some serious prison time.

"Anything new on this end?" Charles asked as he savored the cool lemonade.

"Avery told me this morning that Samuel is really upset at the mayor. Believes Wayne got in cahoots with Rick to get him and his brother arrested. Hard to figure that, given the mayor beat Rick to a pulp at City Hall. No telling what Samuel and Jonathon might do," Red said, wiping sweat from his brow.

"Figured out how this happened?" Charles asked, bringing the conversation back to the election a subject they both knew had to be addressed.

"A big part was the *Crier*'s return. Everyone—our district coordinators, Joseph, just about everyone else who has come by—has mentioned the impact of the newspaper stories.

"At the meeting Wednesday, all reported they got nearly all of our normal voters to the polls, but they went against us once inside. Now that happened even though we met our buy numbers. And all of them agreed people saw the mayor, us and Edward together this election.

"And in the Marcum and Hammer precincts, we were beaten worse than any other precincts in the county. Joe Brown mentioned the Marcums got together for a meeting Monday morning after they decided Sunday to come with us. Word is that the Hammers got together Monday too. He didn't know what happened, but he's trying to find out." Confused, the two continued to try and figure out the "whys" of this historical Jordan County Election Day.

"Look here at the two black precincts. We've never got less than 60% in those precincts in at least the last thirty years." Red said completely exasperated.

"I did pick up today that last Sunday, Jim Dowling's mother took to the pulpit up at black church and described what it was like when Jim was fighting for his life. It seems the whole church gave her a standing ovation when she finished."

Red and Charles were moving toward having to finally admit to themselves that the black ink of the *Crier* had overcome their piles of paper with green ink. It certainly was apparent the two had never heard the old journalism adage: "Never go to war with someone who buys ink by the barrel!"

Red and Charles observed these soundly defeated candidates hadn't done anything much different than those they had supported over the years. They all connived to favor supporters in nearly all decisions, made sure public contracts went to businesses whose owners supported the old-line and approved the old-line bank holding the vast majority of federal funds in non-interest-bearing accounts.

The difference was that Joseph Ballengee was no longer able to use the *Crier* to keep such facts from the public. Something that escaped the two political kingpins was the *Crier* hadn't printed anything that wasn't true. The stories just included the facts, what had happened at open public meetings and exactly what old-line office-holders had said and done.

In past elections, Charles and Red had lost a couple of offices here and there, but nothing like this. Even when those earlier losses came, they were able to manipulate most of the unexpected winners to see things their way.

But this time, nearly all of the county's thirty precincts went against the old line in every race. The analysis showed, with the exception of Edward, the other two board candidates could have pulled ahead if the two clans had voted as expected.

Despite the trouble Red and Charles were having with the Jordan County Election Day analysis, some residents were over-joyed by those results.

Behind the picket fence and lovely spring flowers, Eva's phone hadn't stopped ringing. The steering committee, the Golden Cara-van drivers, and retired school employees from across the county were basking in the upsets for the Jordan County board of educa-tion. Eva's response was simple, "We did the right thing, for the right reasons, and won. It sure does make this old lady feel good."

Most promised to stop by for a post-election visit in the next few days. *I just might have to send Jasper (her yardman) down to the state store,* she thought smiling. The Golden Oldies were not alone in their celebratory moods.

On a special congregational visit, Rev. Everett Talcott was greeted by a beaming Eleanor Dowling. "And why are you so happy?" he quietly inquired.

"Oh, preacher, I just got a call from James' doctor. He might be able to come home next week," she gushed.

"Praise the Lord, we must have a word of prayer," the elderly minister responded. After the Amens, they moved the conversa-tion to Election Day.

"Indeed, it's been two glorious days in a row," Eleanor qui-etly whispered.

"You taking the pulpit last Sunday brought our congregation together. I haven't seen anything like it in years," Rev. Talcott said.

"The good Lord has answered our prayers," Eleanor Dowling replied, knowing that tonight would be her first peaceful night's sleep in nearly a month.

Election Day cheer spread out in the county. Ten miles outside of the Jordan County seat, up on Horse Run, Big Ed Marcum came down the front porch steps to welcome Basil Hammer and his wife, Emma, who hadn't set foot on the Marcum ancestral land in ten years.

"So happy you could come by. It's been too long," the Marcum patriarch said.

Removing his battered straw hat, Basil replied, "Indeed it has, Ed. I look forward to you and Esther returning the visit real soon out to Longview Creek."

"You can be sure of that," came the heartfelt response.

"I want you to know my granddaughter is withdrawing her application for that job out at the high school. When I heard about Anna's situation, we felt it was only the right thing to do. You have all of our prayers. How is she?" Basil Hammer inquired.

"Do appreciate the prayers. We don't know yet about Anna's condition. She's going to Morgantown next week for another round of tests," Ed said, his voice breaking a bit discussing the health of his beloved daughter-in-law.

The visit continued late into the afternoon, ending after the two patriarchs spent two hours rocking in the old oak chairs, reminiscing about their once close business relationship. Over the Marcum family special coffee blend, the two wives took turns bragging on their combined twenty-five grandchildren. The two patriarchs left the porch and walked under the stately oaks to a dark corner inside the 100-year-old barn. There, despite both being church deacons, they toasted their friendship with a stomach-churning drink of the renowned Marcum Mountain Elixir.

Back in Lawnsville, the person many Jordan County residents were giving credit for the Election Day results was humbled by the turn of events. Rick Hill was amazed the *Crier* was back.

Right after the fire, the young publisher was determined to fight but not very optimistic of success.

Given Anne's bitterness toward some his detractors in Jordan County, Rick even thought briefly about just giving up. But his sense of what's right held firm. Then there was the post-election call from Anne. During their time apart, she had prayed and thought about his devotion to the *Crier*. "I'm all in. I might still think you're crazy sometimes, but I'm all in. I'm lucky to have you and so is the county" she said through tears. "We'll be home tomorrow."

Rick got up from his desk and as he emerged from the cubbyhole and was struck by the scene of his hardworking staff before him, all of whom had decided to stick by him, not knowing if they would be paid.

After his third reading of the post-election *Crier*, Rick decided it would be the perfect time to visit the post office. Still limping from his wounded leg, Rick gingerly climbed the steps of the post office and was almost knocked over as Baxter burst through the door, smiling, an event Rick had never before witnessed.

"I've been doing this for more than thirty years and never had majorities on the board of education and county commission. Now, I've got to figure out what do," Baxter said.

"What happened?" Rick inquired as he took the offered hand, curious what the response would bring.

"You told the people what was going on and they said, 'enough.' It's really not that complicated," Baxter replied.

"Whoa, I think you are giving me way too much credit," Rick said, taken aback by the unexpected tribute.

"I'm not so sure. I didn't tell you before, but when we went to houses all over the county, folks were talking about the *Crier* stories," Baxter continued, wanting the publisher to know what the newspaper meant to the county.

"Baxter, that's what a newspaper is supposed to do. You do understand that we'll be watching the school board and county commission just as closely as we did when that bunch was in charge," Rick explained.

"I'd be disappointed if you didn't," Baxter responded, fully understanding the challenges the new office-holders would face from such scrutiny.

"Feel free to stop by for a chat when you have time. I'd like to know more about what happened on the ground at precincts out in the county," Rick said.

They shook hands again as Rick continued into the post office. As he came out, the worm was going in. Immediately a vision of his devoted, hardworking staff came to mind. It was time for action. Rick knew his staff's families were near the end of their rope financially.

Rick had had enough. While the money from political advertising allowed him to pay the staff some of what was due them, the bills for printing were casting a dark shadow. Rick had a gut feeling the insurance agent was dragging his feet on his claim. On Friday, the long-awaited information the publisher had requested from the state fire marshal's office arrived.

It was time to turn on the worm.

"Why, Rick, I've been trying to call you. Can't seem to catch you. Wanted to give you an update," the worm smiled.

Ignoring the kiss-ass tone, the publisher bellowed, "Where's the check, Orville?"

"That's what I wanted to talk to you about. Still having trouble with the state fire marshal's office," he said as if butter wouldn't melt in his mouth.

"Orville, just so you know, that final report has been available from the state fire marshal's office for weeks. I have a copy of it. Also on Friday, I got a copy of the receipt you signed when it was delivered to your office two weeks ago. "Now, you either get that check in here, or I'll file a complaint against you and the company with the state insurance commissioner. This seems like a newsworthy event to me, so there will be a front-page story.

"Further, when you are found guilty of breaking state insurance laws, I'll sue you personally for all the paper's lost revenue plus several million dollars. Any questions?"

The agent stammered that he'd have to check with his secretary who had been out with a sick child for the last week and things were backed up.

"The only call I want from you is one telling me that you will deliver it to my office within the week," the young publisher said, feeling much better as headed back up the street, whistling and limping as he went.

No more had he sat down than the phone rang. The ring seemed different, livelier, less harsh. It was the worm. "I'm bringing the check right down. Seems it got misplaced under some old mail and with Joanne out, we just lost track of it. I apologize, Rick," he said.

"Orville, I'll believe it when you walk in the door," the publisher barked.

Two minutes almost to the second, there was a timid knock on his cubbyhole door. "Come in," the publisher growled.

Lo and behold, it was the worm - grinning from ear to ear, he took the envelope out of his inside coat pocket and with a visibly shaking hand gave it to Rick. "Again, I'm so sorry for the hold-up."

"Orville, hold on a minute while I see if everything is included that was in the business interruption claim," Rick said as he ripped open the envelope. To his surprise, Rick found the amount was a bit more than he had expected. "Now I want to be clear. I expect the claims for the building handled without any delay. Are we clear?" the publisher explained in a sharp, no-nonsense tone.

"Of course, I'll work the company headquarters to make sure this doesn't happen again," the agent said.

"Stop the bullshit. This check is dated nearly three weeks ago. It's clear the only thing that went wrong was in your office," Rick said, now standing nearly nose-to-nose with the agent who was backing toward the door of the publisher's small office.

Rick escorted the agent to the *Crier*'s front door. When he turned, he saw that every staff member was looking at him in anticipation. From the pessimism on their faces, it was clear they were certain the worm had delivered another message of delay.

Rick held the check behind his back and put on a grave expression, which had them all shaking their heads. Waving the envelope, he gleefully announced, "We'll be having a special payday on Friday." The wary, hardworking, devoted, and talented staff jumped for joy, gathering around Rick as if he were a conquering warrior.

"I cannot thank you enough for the loyalty and dedication you have given me. I'll never be able to repay you," he said, not trying to hide his tears.

"Just keep it. We like working for nothing," the crusty community news editor said, a loving twinkle in her eye. Retreating into his cubbyhole, Rick turned to rereading the election coverage in the day-after paper. Again he was astounded at the Election Day vote tallies. Amazing, just amazing. He was proud but humbled by the outcome. It deepened his abiding appreciation of the responsibility a newspaper has to its community.

He knew he would be watched to see if he was as hard on reformer officer holders as he had been on the former incumbents. People must see that the paper was consistent in its reporting. Then he smiled at the thought of a line from a *Chicago Times'* editorial that ran in 1861:

"It's a newspaper's duty to print the news and raise hell."

Acknowledgments

Enough is the result of an effort that stretches at least 20 years. There were long periods where it gathered dust on a shelf. Then in 2009 upon retirement, I moved to hills of West Virginia in a log cabin between Cooper's Rock and Bruceton Mills in Preston County and writers' block vanished.

Many people helped along the way with encouragement, suggestions, advice, and patient responses to endless questions.

First, I acknowledge the love and guidance of my late parents, Harriet Lee and Charlie Hylton, who both worked at the *Logan Banner*. They introduced me to journalism and what its proper practice can mean to a community.

Next to my parents the greatest influence on my journalism career was Paul Atkins, the late Journalism professor at the West Virginia University P.I. Reed School of Journalism (now P. I. Reed School of Media). He taught me the importance of accuracy and fairness.

Cathy Teets -President of Headline Press introduced me the world of book publishing. I could not have a better mentor.

Marshal Jarrett - Director of the Executive Office for United States Attorneys (retired), U. S. Department of Justice, Washington, DC. Who patiently answered my seemingly endless questions about legal aspects of *Enough*.

Mark Brazaitis - Creative Writing Professor West Virginia University English Department, author of seven books. Director, West Virginia Writers' Workshop. Who provided thoughtful suggestions on what is required to be a professional author.

Bill Kawecki, Mayor of Morgantown, West Virginia who gave important suggestions which without a doubt, made the book better.

Others who have given counsel, answered questions and at times talked me off the cliff - Ralph Baldwin, classmate at Logan High School; Gene Davis, Hinton, WV; the late Claude Ellis, a towering figure in Logan County politics; Jake Glance, WV Secretary of State's Office; Lesta Sue Hardee, Chafin Library, Myrtle Beach, SC; Jane Metters LaBarbara of the West Virginia University Library, West Virginia Collection; Barton Lohr, retired banker, Morgantown, WV; Mary Beth Merritt, County Clerk, Summers County, WV; Jasmine Reed, U.S. Alcohol, Tobacco and Firearms, Washington, DC.